The Throw Away Child

By Susanne Robertson

PublishAmerica
Baltimore

© 2003 by Susanne Robertson.
All rights reserved. No part of this book may be reproduced, stored in a retrieval system, or transmitted in any form or by any means without the prior written permission of the publishers, except by a reviewer who may quote brief passages in a review to be printed in a newspaper, magazine, or journal.

First printing

ISBN: 1-4137-0094-2
PUBLISHED BY PUBLISHAMERICA, LLLP
www.publishamerica.com
Baltimore

Printed in the United States of America

The Throwaway Child

*A small child wanders
Past Heaven's open gate
He does not go near
But knows not where to wait.*

*What if God sees' him
And turns him away
He kneels at the entrance
And then starts to pray.*

*Dear Lord, I beg you
Let me rest here awhile
Can't you please find a place
For a throwaway child.*

*I ask your forgiveness
At the end of this life
For any youthful transgressions
That may come to light.*

*I'm society's burden
No ones to tend
I ask a quiet restful place
For my long journey's end.*

Published January 1997
By Susanne Robertson

Someone once said that all the world is a stage. As I stand upon it before you, know this I have taken no artistic license. Every word here written is steeped in truth, so help me God.

Prologue

"Happy birthday to you. Happy birthday to you. Happy birthday, dear George. Happy birthday to you."

Amidst clapping and smiles everywhere, George blows out his candles. There is a tender and precious moment of excitement electrifying the air. Forks start tapping clumsily on the table.

"Party, party, party," they chant.

Six strangers are sharing a moment of triumph and a happy birthday. Chocolate cake; with chocolate ice cream; and chocolate milk, these three simple requests strike such a painful cord deep within me. I feel the tears spring instantly to my eyes. All the partiers stare at me with their mouths open. I am their caregiver and this is a party so, why am I crying. I quickly wipe away the tears and replace my smile. I serve the cake and ice cream then pour six glasses of chocolate milk. All of their faces are like bright sunshine reflecting and bouncing from one client to the other, finally settling on the birthday boy. I withdraw quietly to the living room. The words chocolate cake, chocolate ice cream, chocolate milk all echo in my mind.

I am drawn back within myself to 1957.

PART ONE

CHAPTER 1

Welcome to Hell

My two sisters, Grace and June and my older brother, Willie had been spending the summer with my grandparents at the lake. Their house is very spacious to small children and everything seems so simple. Days are spent splashing in the lake or fishing with Grandma in the boat. Sometimes, on days like today, I lay flat on my stomach on the wooden dock with the sun sitting in the noon position and the water below becoming alive. I peer through the cracks in the wood of the dock and the water is a lime green. All kinds of wonderful creatures swim through the sunlight filtered water. The quiet, lazy afternoon slides by without a care. By four o'clock, PM, the sun moves away and once again the water becomes a dark emerald color and the hidden life in the lake conceals itself. I pull my sister June along the dock trying to convince her that it is time to pick vegetables for dinner. As we get closer to the house, June breaks into a full run with her arms outstretched. Standing at the end of the driveway is Momma. June is no longer interested in picking vegetables and neither am I.

"Momma, Momma," we both scream.

Momma suddenly brings her finger up to her lips "SHHH, SHHH, she says this is a surprise visit.

As Momma gathers us up in her arms, she slowly bends down and whispers in our ears, "This is a secret, you mustn't let Grandma see, I am here to take you home."

June and I are very quiet as Momma quickly puts us into the back seat of the car. We ask about Grace and Willie and Momma says that we will get them tomorrow. Momma backed out of the driveway and sped away.

She drove home nervously and she kept looking in the rear view mirror all the way home. When we walked into the house everything was different. This is the first time I ever remember seeing our house clean. There were no piles of dirty dishes in the kitchen sink. There were no dirty diapers, clothes, or toys on the floor. I could even see the floor. Momma locked all the doors and pulled the drapes. She said we were playing hide and seek.

"From whom," I asked.

"Everybody," she replied.

It was dinner time and June and I were hungry. Momma went into the kitchen and opened a can of green beans and then she got crackers from the cupboard. We spread a tablecloth on the floor in the living room. Momma took candles from the kitchen and we had a lovely picnic right on the floor.

"Bedtime," Momma said, so June and I took off our clothes and climbed into bed in our underwear.

To this day, the smell of those freshly laundered sheets and blankets never fail to evoke the last sense of happiness I ever knew as a child.

June and I quickly feel asleep not knowing that after tonight we would never spend another night at home with Momma. We woke several hours later and although it was still dark outside, there were plenty of lights on in our house. Momma was screaming and Daddy was holding her down on the floor. Grandma was talking in the living room and in the front doorway stood a policeman.

Grandma looked up and said, "Girls put your clothes on were going back to the lake."

"Momma's crying," I said. "Daddy, please let her go. We were having a picnic. Please, Daddy, please."

Grandma reached down and scooped up June. "Put your clothes on," she said, "the policeman can see your underwear."

I retreated quickly to the bedroom and put on my clothes. Driving back to the lake was a somber time as June and I silently sobbed into our hands.

Momma was very sick and she needed to be in the hospital. June and I thought she was all better. We were too young to understand the kind of sickness that she had. I knew how it felt to be physically sick, but mental illness was not something I had ever heard of before. Momma looked alright to us, we were kids, what did we know?

Grandma just kept repeating: "You shouldn't have gone with her girls, you shouldn't have gone."

June and I did not understand why we should not have gone with Momma. All the adults were really angry with us, but still no one explained anything to us about what was going on. Momma was Momma. Why was it wrong to go anywhere with her?

The next day at noon time, Daddy came out to the lake house. Grandma cried and Daddy cussed. June and I were still in trouble and we knew it. Daddy finally came out on the porch and he had a funny look on his face. I had never seen a look like it before, nor have I ever seen one since. Willie and Grace came outside and Daddy lined us up.

"Kids," he said, "I have a surprise for you. Go kiss your Grandma, you are all going to a birthday party. There will be chocolate cake, chocolate ice cream, and chocolate milk, hurry, hurry!"

We all scrambled into the house to kiss grandma. There were tears shining in her eyes as she kissed and hugged each of us and smoothed our clothes and hair.

"Susie, take care of June. She's your little sister. It's your job remember," she said quietly.

"Alright grandma, I'll be good and I'll remember" I replied.

We all went out and got into Daddy's car. Grandma was hugging her arms close to her sides, crying and waving goodbye.

"We'll pick extra vegetables tonight when we get home," I shouted out the window.

The car ride seemed to take forever. Finally, Daddy's car pulled up to a building even bigger than our school. It was made of brick and had a giant statue of Jesus with a little girl and boy standing by his knee.

"This is some place, isn't it kids," my father said.

"Looks like a funny place for a party," I said, "there are fences around the thing."

Daddy got out of the car and just walked up the steps. We all followed him like little lambs to the slaughter. The big door was opened by a catholic nun who smiled broadly welcoming us inside. Daddy stepped slowly aside as we went in single file. The marble entry floor shone so brightly that we could see our reflections. Daddy did not come in and the nun closed the door. We could see him through the window. He walked back to his car, got in and never looked back.

We looked at the nun and I said, "We're the Maloney kids and we're here for the birthday party."

The smile had disappeared and in its place was a stern look.

"Come with me," she said. We followed her quietly and soon entered a large playground. There were about two hundred kids all running around.

She opened the gate and said, "Go play, *now!*"

We pretty much stayed together for about the first five minutes. A different nun came over and took my brother Willie by the hand. They went to the other side of the playground and for the first time I saw that there was an imaginary line down the center of the playground.

"Boys and girls do not *ever* play together here," she said.

We were never allowed to play with my brother Willie again. The sun was hot and the whole play area was blacktop. There were some swings and a sliding board but nowhere to sit. There were places on the blacktop so hot that the tar would bubble up and stick to your shoes. We all played outside for hours but still no party.

The sudden sounding of bells brought a strange quiet to the playground. All the children marched like little wooden soldiers into two distinct straight lines, girls on the left, boys on the right. Someone pulled us from behind into the line. The bells kept on ringing and I could see mouths moving in silent prayer.

A pinch to the back of my arm brought tears to my eyes and a hiss behind me said, "Say the Angeles."

I was Catholic but I had never heard of this prayer. Finally, the ringing stopped but June was crying loudly now. All the other kids were staring at her in disbelief.

"SHHH, SHHHH, SHHH," the other kids tried to warn. "Too late, here she comes."

Careening like a bowling ball between the two lines, came Sister Regina bearing down on my sister like an angry bull.

"Shut up," she ordered.

June wailed louder. "I want my momma!"

Sister Regina's hand slapped my little sister's poor sweet tear stained face faster than a lightening strike. I stepped up behind Sister Regina and tugged on the back of her veil.

"Hey," I said, "don't hit my little sister."

I did not know that her veil was held on with only common pins. As I jumped back, when she wheeled around me, her veil came off in my hand. I stood there speechless. Laughter was ringing everywhere. Regina was bald and the other kids were hysterical with laughter. I was pretty sure that the red glowing eyes that she fixed on me were not heaven sent and equally sure that I was in some kind of major trouble. I tried to explain to her I only wanted her not to hurt my little sister, who I was responsible for.

"I never meant to pull off your veil," I managed to croak in the stare of those glaring red eyes.

Before the words could make their sounds, Regina's hand sliced through the air striking me so hard that my body spun around and I fell to the blacktop. I had been in my fair share of neighborhood fights, but nothing had prepared me for my first real beating. Before I could blink, I saw Regina's pointed black shoe headed for my stomach. The first kick made me vomit. I could hear

June screaming and other kids telling her to be quiet. I lay curled in the fetal position waiting for the pain to stop. What I did not know at the time, was that I would need this position countless times in the years to come.

Finally when I could no longer breathe, I passed out. Welcome to what would be my world for the next eight years.

The next thing I remember is half crawling, half being dragged up three flights of wide brown metal stairs. The pain in my side when I tried to breathe made me vomit again. I would soon learn to recognize the pain of broken ribs.

"You disgusting little troublemaker," Regina said. "Not so smart now are you?"

I was dragged down a long hallway deeper into the bowels of the monstrous place. Hands are pulling off my clothes and the shower comes on with cold water; cold, cold, so very cold.

I do not remember how I got to bed that first night. Most of my energy was spent just trying to breathe. A small bell sounding in the distance startles me awake. It is pitch black outside. I was very confused about where I am. The horrible memories of yesterday came rolling back in waves of fear. I was so hoping that it was a nightmare, but the pain in my side told me otherwise. I looked slowly around the huge room and suddenly I realize I had lost June. She was nowhere in sight. Oh God, I promised Grandma.

"June," I yell. "June where are you?"

From a good distance away I hear a small voice, "Sissy, Sissy, I can't see you. Sissy, please, find me."

I scramble around the small brown iron bed and run into the middle of the dormitory trying to find her. The ringing is louder now and I make out the black and white shape coming towards me. It was another nun. She is calling out that it is five o'clock AM.

"Get up and get dressed girls. Make your beds. Hurry up or you'll be late for mass."

A girl walks up beside me and introduces herself to me as Linda.

"Hurry up and get dressed," she says, "or you'll get into more trouble like yesterday."

"My sister, where is she I can't find her" I said with a note of panic.

"She's in the little kids section. The dorms are separated into sections according to your school grade. You must be in the second grade and so am I. Your sister is in kindergarten. She's way up in the front. Make your bed and move it! You'll make us all late to mass," she instructed.

I made my bed and quickly got dressed. In fifteen minutes we were all marching single file down to the chapel. I followed this ritual for the next eight years of my life.

Our family is Irish Catholic so Sunday morning mass was not a new experience to me, however, daily mass at St. Colman's Orphanage was certainly different. The school room class system is also in place in the chapel. Everyone slotted in a specific area. I strain my eyes and duck out of line to try and find my sister.

I never saw it coming. The hand that knocked me in the back of the head sent me flying flat on my face on the floor and making my nose bleed. I was too startled to cry and too scared to move. Hitting the floor made my ribs hurt again and that is when the real problems started.

I have always been independent and kind of stubborn. I sat up on the floor outside of the chapel and was suddenly so angry that I started to scream. Time actually stood still as I looked at the frozen faces of disbelief on the other girls in line.

From the back of the line I heard my sister Grace saying, "Susan GET UP, SHUT UP. SHUT UP."

I did not want to hear it at this point. I was almost hysterical with anger and fear. The black and white robust penguin figure was barreling down on me again. I was picked up by my hair and dragged down two flights of stairs bleeding, kicking and screaming. Sister Loretta actually picked me up by my head shaking me back and forth like a rag doll. I could not see through the blood and tears and I could not stop screaming. This struggle between the two of us went on for ten minutes until I was finally exhausted. Rough hands wipe a wet cloth across my face and a metal pitcher of cold water was poured over my head. Sputtering and crying, I sat on the floor with my hands around my knees rocking back and forth crying for my Daddy.

Sister Loretta left me sitting huddled on the floor covered in blood and urine. She locked the door behind me and this is where I spent my first full day at the orphanage. I got nothing to eat all day and by the time someone came to let me out it was dark outside. A strange girl came and got me out of the room. She was high school age. She led me up three flights of stairs and back to the shower room.

The only thing she said to me was "You don't learn to fast do you?"

At least this night's shower is warm. This girl is not unkind to me but she definitely knew how to follow the rules.

"Learn your place kid, do what they tell you, and don't be stupid," she advised.

"My little sister I said, I have to take care of her," I pleaded.

"Not anymore kid," she said.

"You don't understand," I said. "I promised Grandma. When Grandma finds out what those nuns did she's gonna be real mad. I'm pretty sure she'll kill them."

"Sorry to tell you this kid but once you get in here nobody cares what happens to you ever again," she said coldly.

"But my dad," I said, "he'll come back for us today," I stated emphatically.

"No," she said, "he won't. Once you get in here, you're here until you're all grown up and then you have to become a nun."

She gave me my pajamas and said go to bed and tomorrow to try not to be so stupid.

The second day started exactly like the first and this time I stood absolutely still in the line outside the chapel.

I moved slowly up in the line until it was my turn at the holy water fountain. I blessed myself and followed Linda into the chapel. It was such a beautiful place. The stained glass windows were marvelous and the statues of Mary, Jesus and Joseph looked real.

In the pews at the front were several rows of nuns. I could feel the blood draining from my face. Oh my God. Look how many there are. They could each take turns beating me for a day and not run out for a month.

"I am done for," I thought, "way out numbered. Now what am I going to do?"

I did a little knee bend and crossed myself and slid into the pew. Pretty soon mass started and the singing from the front sounded so sweet. I could swear that I had been transported to heaven. How could someone so evil sing so sweetly to God?

I thought I was doing all right in church until I got tired of kneeling on the hard wooden pews. I remained on my knees but kind of sat my butt on the edge of the seat.

Even in chapel, the almighty slap to the back of my head and the sharp "stay on your knees," came from behind.

My mind was still fuzzy from all of the physical abuse I had suffered in the last two days but still the anger boiled up in me and I almost hit back. Linda was kneeling next to me and reached over and grabbed my hand. Mass was nearing the end and I shut my eyes tight and prayed.

One by one, aisle by aisle the chapel started to empty. All the kids walked in a line to the cafeteria. Tables that seated four were scattered about separated by an aisle in the middle. It was immediately apparent that the sexes were separated in this room also. I saw June and started to walk to her table. Linda pulled me back again.

"No," she said, "remember only with kids in your own class."

I looked into June's face and she dropped her eyes. She had such a blank stare that I was scared for her, and for myself.

"If you really want to help her, stay where you are," Linda said.

I nodded and followed her to a table further back in the cafeteria.

Since I had not eaten anything the day before, I was ravenously hungry. The older girls were walking from table to table ladling out hot porridge from large pots. Other girls were pouring hot cocoa from pitchers. My first look into my bowl made me cringe. This was not like any oatmeal I had ever seen before. It was congealed in the bowl and when you stuck your spoon in it, the spoon stood on end by itself. I sat there looking at it hoping this was a bad dream. No such luck however, and the rest of the girls at the table started to eat.

I watched and a girl named Cathy asked if I was going to eat mine. As I pushed it away, she hurriedly changed bowls with me and began consuming mine.

"Yuck," I said, "there's no sugar or milk in it and it's all stuck together. How can you possibly eat that stuff?"

"You get used to it," she said.

I must honestly say I never did and when I grew up it was years before I could even look at oatmeal, let alone eat it.

"Oh well," I thought, "cocoa will do fine."

My first sip made me gag. It tasted like water and sawdust. I spit it back in the cup.

"What is this" I asked.

"Powered milk and chocolate," Linda said.

"This is awful," I replied.

"You spit in it," said Cathy disapprovingly, "I don't want it now."

Breakfast was at an end and my education was about to begin. As kids began to file out a very large nun walked over to me and said, "You, you're the new troublemaker right?"

I shrugged my shoulder and she said, "stay."

Linda raised her eyebrows and filed out. When the cafeteria was empty a nun turned around and instructed, "Watch me."

She began stacking chairs on top of each other, three to a pile. When they were all in the back, bus pans were brought out and I was shown how to clean the tables and take the loads out to the kitchen. A chair had been pulled over in front of two huge stainless steel sinks. They were as large as any bathtub I had ever been in.

"Start," Sister Annunciata ordered, "wash in one, rinse in the other."

I was washing and four girls were drying. By the time I was done it was lunch time. We went into the cafeteria for lunch and once again my olfactory senses were brutalized. The same girls were serving. This time one had a large pot with an ice cream scoop and the other had a pot and a ladle. The ice cream scoop slammed down on my plate and deposited a half round ball of government surplus rice followed by the second gal with her ladle full of, to this day I think, Gravy Train. It was brown uniform chunks of meat in a brown congealed gravy substance.

All the children had to wait until the entire table was served before anyone could pick up their forks to eat.

Splat! It landed on my plate with a thud and everyone else started to eat. I watched carefully to see if anybody but me wanted to throw up, but they all seemed okay. I tentatively took a bite and my suspicions were confirmed. Gravy Train, pure and simple! Nobody seemed to be touching the glutinous balls of rice.

Almost as if on cue the girls at my table all reached over and stuck the balls of rice in their dress pockets. I just stared at them and they smirked in unison.

"Later,' Linda said in response to my quizzical look.

After lunch, I followed the same routine as after breakfast. First stack the chairs then clear the tables, then wash the dishes. My punishment for being persona-non-grate was non-stop KP duty for eight years.

We got done with lunch dishes and setting the tables for dinner by 3:30 and had one and a half hours until dinner so I said, "What now?"

"Playground," the other girls screamed.

They all raced down the halls with me following into the bright sunshine. I burst through the doors feeling freedom on my face for the first time in two days; glorious sunshine and the playground. I did not realize two days ago that this area could feel so sweet.

I wandered around the yard and made my way to the back. The girls from my dinning room table were doing something that I had not seen two days before. They were playing catch ball. I walked over to them and Linda smiled.

"Want to play?" she asked.

"Sure," I said and she threw me the ball.

I looked at what she had thrown to me and stood there with my mouth hanging open. My hand contained a very dirty small ball of government surplus rice. This is what the girls were doing with those rice balls from lunch. They were so stuck together that the girls would roll them into the dirt next to the chain link fence. They would roll them around in the palm of their hands and, viola – a new round ball to play with.

At a quarter to five as if by magic, everybody started lining up again into the now familiar lines. They all marched in time down to the dining room for dinner. Never having been a Jell-O eater, I was very sorry to see a large square of lime green Jell-O with shredded carrots and raisins in it. Beside this dish was a bowl of watery chicken broth with large wooden, overgrown, aged, sliced carrots and celery leaves.

I would have given my soul for a peanut butter sandwich. Once again, my friend Cathy saved my stomach from a dietary disaster. This was standard fare for most of my time there except for the period of time when the government so generously donated what I thought must have been the biggest surplus rice haul in the history of mankind.

We ate the same things everyday for months on end. Just when I thought the food could never get any worse, it changed.

Just the words *Spanish Rice* invoke such an involuntary spasm in my stomach that it is still painful to me. My first encounter with this culinary delight made me vomit outright. Sister Annunciata became so incensed at my lack of gratitude for this wonderful meal that she scooped the vomit back into the bowl and held me down and poured the regurgitated rice back into my mouth holding my mouth shut with one hand and pinching my nose closed with the other.

She repeated this process every time I threw up until it was either saturated into my clothes or she was no longer able to scrape it off the table or the floor. I took some small measure of comfort in the fact that I was not the only child to receive this exact same treatment. Nothing but nothing made the nuns madder than to show dislike for what they called *good food*. Many times we were reminded of how lucky we were to be cared for by decent people, considering our own families dumped us here and did not want us.

I was so very confused. I could not think of anything that we had done to be placed in this children's prison. For the longest time, I thought it was because June and I had gotten into the car with Momma. But if that was why, then why were Grace and Willie in jail too. They did not go with Momma, so that could not be the reason.

Sister Regina told me over and over that my parents did not want us. She said we were dumped on the nuns as punishment for being bad. She also reminded us on a daily basis that we were both stupid and ugly. '***Society's Garbage***,' is the specific phrase she used for me.

Sister Regina would put soap in your mouth and give you a beating if she thought you were telling a lie. I did not understand. She was telling lies about me when she said I was stupid. Who would be the one to put soap in her mouth and beat her with the stick or a belt.

If I had a dime for every time Sister Regina told me I was garbage and how disgusting we kids really were, I am sure that I would be a very rich woman today.

CHAPTER 2

The Rise and Fall of My Learning Spirit

The days of summer were waning fast and soon fall was upon us. I was going into the third grade and thought school would be a welcome respite from KP duty. After one month in school, I was absolutely sure that our teacher, as well as being down right cruel was moronically stupid.

My Aunt Grace used to tell me that I was smart. When my older sister Grace used to come home from school, Momma would sit with her and read her homework questions out loud. Grace always struggled with this. I would feel so bad for her that I would give her the answer. Finally, Momma banished me from the dinning room because I was always right.

My birthday is in October and my mother sent me to St. Joseph's school when I was only four. I could already read and it made Grace mad. I never could understand why she was angry with me for reading her books.

I gathered a group from my classroom and marched down to the Reverend Mothers' office. I announced that since we could all read that we would be taking over our own class and teaching ourselves. This, in retrospect, was a bad move on my part.

The retribution was horrendous. After we had all been required to pull our underpants down to our knees and pull our skirts up over our shoulders, we each in turn had to bend over and grab our ankles. A brown brush was used to paddle our bare rear ends until there was not a patch of skin left that was not covered in welts. Since it was determined that I was the ringleader I was also put back into the kindergarten class because I was obviously retarded to think I could teach anybody.

Christmas this year was a strange event and probably the saddest holiday I ever knew. That high school girl had lied to me. Some kids' parents came and took them home for the Christmas holiday, but not the Maloney kids. There had been, however, a large party in the middle of December given by the Behr-Manning Company for the orphans. Almost everybody went except for the few considered too bad to be allowed out in public, and of course, I was included in this group.

I had never been to a Behr-Manning party so I had no idea what I was missing. I remember that all the kids came back smiling and happy. Each one had a large Christmas stocking stuffed with candy, gingerbread men, and an orange.

I turned my head and shut my eyes not wanting anyone to see the hunger or the anger in my face. Some of the younger kids were crying openly about the loss of their presents. This just confused me because I did not see anybody with presents, not one person at all.

On Christmas morning the body count of kids was down to twenty-five and still the clanging of the morning bell and the daily rising ritual started at its usual five a.m. Except for the sudden decline of children present in the chapel and the wonderful manger scene in the front of the altar, you would never have known it was Christmas morning.

Mass droned on as usual and when it was over we all traipsed down to the dinning room. My heart nearly leapt out of my chest as we entered. Sitting on each chair was a single gift.

Sister Mary Claire said, "Sit anywhere you want. Sit with a family member if you have any."

Grace, Willie, June, and I, for the first time in months, sat at the same table and shared a meal together. After breakfast we opened the gift on our chair. I got a Candy Land game. I was ecstatic. Willie, however, got a doll which he exchanged with June for her Chinese checkers game. Grace got a play jewelry set.

What we did not know was that the gifts were only on loan. After an uneventful Christmas Day, when we went to bed that night we were instructed to place our new gifts at the end of our beds. In the morning all of the new toys had disappeared.

I stayed in the kindergarten class until after Christmas. In January, I was allowed to return to the third grade. Of course, having missed October, November and December, I was now behind in everything. To make matters worse, there was now a new teacher, the dreaded Sister Loretta.

I was afraid to open my mouth, and I never raised my hand. All of the other kids knew what they were doing and I was completely lost. I knew my luck would not last forever. The time came when it was my turn to go up to the blackboard and solve the math problem. Math was new to me, and I had no idea how to do it.

Sister Loretta glared at me and called my name again. I rose slowly and trudged to the board. There were two additions and two subtraction sets on the blackboard. I stood there stupidly staring. My mind was blank and getting worse by the minute. The hairs on the back of my neck stood on end and I knew Loretta was directly behind me.

"Move aside," she said ferociously giving me a shove.

Everybody sat stone still at their desks. I was holding my breath not even daring to breathe. Sister Loretta whirled on me and came within two inches of my face. Her eyes were bulging and her breath smelled extremely foul.

"What is your answer?" she screamed.

"I don't know sister."

"What, what did you say?"

"Sister, I only came back to this class today. I haven't been here when they were teaching this," I pleaded.

"Oh I remember," she said, "little-miss-know-it-all; so smart she's going to teach herself as well as the rest of the class."

She was glaring at me and I could see the veins popping in her temples. With her hands she reached down and grabbed both sides of my hair. She began smashing my face and my head into the blackboard. She did not stop until she saw blood gushing from my nose.

She then pulled my face up to within two inches in front of her face and started spitting at me and screaming, "Now do you know the answer? Now do you know it?"

By this time I could not think at all, never mind come up with the answer. For some reason, the teaching technique of giving your student a bloody nose, and concussion did not work. I stood at the board all day long with blood seeping out of my nose and clumps of my hair lying on the floor. It would be years before I could do simple math. Every time I tried to learn, there she was, ridiculing, taunting, hitting, spitting, and demoralizing me.

I was not, however, the only person in the class with an apparent learning problem. There was another girl by the name of Louise. She was shy and withdrawn and you never really knew she was there. She had one very large flaw that Sister Loretta simply could not bear. She was left-handed.

Funny, I never heard anyone else say being left-handed made you the *Devil's Child*. Every time this girl picked up a pencil, Sister Loretta was down on her like a hawk. (If this girl is not crippled for life by the cruel treatment she received in this class, it truly should be classified as a medical miracle.)

Every time she picked up her pencil in her left hand Sister Loretta would summon her to the front of the room. We were all required to stop what we were doing and watch as Louise had to grab the edge of the desk. Sister Loretta then turned the wooden ruler on its side so that the metal strip smashed down on this girls' knuckles never less than twenty five whacks and never before her knuckles bled. Louise then had to go back to her desk and use her right hand to write. The other catch was, of course, she had to write legibly with her right hand and keep up with the rest of the class.

When she could not keep up at the end of the day, she was required to go up to the desk and again put her right hand, this time, on the edge of the desk for the ruler with metal side down and receive five whacks. This was to remind her that people who were left-handed were the *Devil's Children* and truly evil people.

CHAPTER 3

The Reappearance of Daddy

I believed with every fiber of my being that I had somehow been dropped into hell and that there would *never* be a way out.

Winter melted into spring and not too soon for me. Every day after school we were given coats, hats, and mittens and sent to play outside where we stayed until quarter to five. The winters in Upstate New York boasted temperature in the low teens and sometimes below zero. It never mattered how cold it was. We were forced to spend from three until quarter to five at night in the freezing cold.

It did not matter if you were sick or so cold that you could no longer feel your limbs. You absolutely had to stay there until it was time for dinner. A nun stood guard at the doorway to the bathroom and you were allowed to go one time only just to make sure that there was not the slightest chance that you could sneak in there just to get warm.

Winter weekends were torturous. We stayed outside all day long. We came in for lunch and dinner. This is the only time I can ever remember being grateful for all my years of KP duty.

To this day, I hate snow. I often look at Currier & Ives Snow scenes and think how pretty. Then the thought is spoiled immediately when I think of the cold.

Every once in a while we played in the courtyard playground. We liked it better there in the winter time. It was a square concrete area surrounded by the brick building on three sides.

The laundry room was in the basement and the great big air vent to the dryer came out in this yard. We would congregate in that area all trying to stand under that vent. It was about 2 feet across and we would rub our hands together and stamp our feet trying to get warm.

Of course, whenever sister saw us under the warm air, she immediately made us leave. We would cry and tell her that we were freezing and she would say, "Too bad, go run around it will make you warm." A backward glance always revealed sister standing under the vent rubbing her hands together to keep her warm.

I sometimes caught a glimpse of June across the playground. It was like watching a beautiful flower wilt. Her laughter and sparkle were gone and her eyes carried a hollowed and guarded look. June was so withdrawn, I am surprised she did not physically grow a turtle shell on her back so she could crouch inside and hide.

I waved everyday across the play ground at my brother Willie and if no one was looking, he would wave back. Whenever I passed my sister Grace in the halls or the dinning room she glared at me. Apparently, my lack of compliance with the orphan lifestyle embarrassed her. She could never understand why I could not just roll over and submit to the insanity.

There was definitely a special group of children at the orphanage that the rest of us called *God's Chosen Few*. Grace was one of them never questioning, never thinking for herself, never once admitting that what was going on was vicious and outrageous.

I was beginning to forget what my parents faces looked like. I tried so hard to hold onto the memories of my previous life. Classes ended in June and the following Sunday brought a shock so big I nearly fainted. Sunday afternoons were visiting days at the orphanage. Since no one had come to see us for almost a year, when a nun came down to collect the Maloney children for a visitor, I was almost afraid to find out who it was.

We were all rushed upstairs, quickly washed and were given clothes that actually fit us and taken to the Visitation Room. As the four of us walked in, there stood my father. He was grinning like a Cheshire cat, like he had seen us just yesterday. I felt a surge of anger at him that both surprised and shocked me. I wanted to slap his face. I wanted to scream at him. I wanted to hit and kick and punch and spit at him just like the nuns did to me. I wanted him to suffer as I had.

My face must have showed my rage because my father took a step back. The nun grabbed my hand and said excuse us for a moment. She pulled me into a nearby classroom and spoke to me through clenched teeth.

"If you dare cause one ounce of problems, if you don't behave like a perfect little daughter, I guarantee that your father will leave and you will never see him again. If you say one thing to cause trouble you will be sorry you were ever born," she threatened. I do not think she realized that I was already sorry that I was ever born. I wiped away my tears and went back to the room with my two sisters and brother who were so grateful that daddy was finally here to visit us that they forgave him immediately.

I stared at him with hostile eyes and felt my first glimmer of pure hate. The nuns were monsters, but a parent who abandoned you as far as I was concerned was much worse the lowest form of life that there was. With everything that had happened to me in the past year, forgiving my father was the last thing on my mind and the furthest thing from something I was capable of.

My father spent approximately one hour with us. He then disappeared as quickly as he did the first time, only this time, he had the good graces to at least say good bye.

After that first visit, Daddy thought it was pretty safe to show up once a month on a Sunday afternoon and play the loving father. The Visitor's Room was a long, narrow window lined room following the road. I always thought that it was too bad it did not face any other area that showed the locked gates and fences. Never once did my father tour the facility that he left his children to rot in.

The visiting room was bright and sunny and a nun was always present in the room whenever anyone came to visit. The children were carefully watched and painfully aware that everything you said or did was scrutinized. Disapproving looks were doled out at the slightest hint that you might be less than happy with your living arrangements. I was warned more than once about telling tales out of school. The discipline methods used were private and not to be discussed with anyone.

"Can you imagine how badly embarrassed your father would be if he knew how many times that we have to punish you?"

This was a direct quote from Sister Regina trying to coerce me into being silent. She was absolutely correct. As long as I did not make any waves, my father was perfectly content with the ways his children were being raised

I felt the loss of my father's love and it was nearly unbearable but I had no one else to blame except me. Every time we saw each other I absolutely could not conceal the smoldering, murderous rage in my eyes or my heart. After every unsuccessful visit with my father, my soul became more jaded and my hatred deepened.

These Sunday visiting days were also the only days where the children looked presentable. We were given special clothes for each visit, then we were returned to our normal daily attire.

I do not remember when it began to really bother me about how I looked. The wonderful school grade system for lumping kids of like size together was even part of how our clothing was distributed. We had an army barracks like room that had a locker system much like the military. Starting with rows for kindergarten and ending with rows for high school. We never actually owned a piece of clothing, not even our own underwear.

Everything went down together in large canvas laundry baskets on wheels. Clothing was doled out by putting a skirt, blouse, slip, undershirt and underpants over a locker. No care was even taken to match colors or patterns or different sizes of kids.

Because I would rather starve to death than eat most of the food served to us, I was very tiny. When I was eight years old, I was three feet tall and weighed thirty-two pounds. I was usually given two large safety pins to be gathered at my waist to keep my clothes from falling off my body. I looked foolish most of the time and like an orphan in the truest sense of the word.

Since most of my summer was spent doing KP duty again, July and August seemed to stretch on forever. The single most valuable thing I learned this year was the act of invisibility.

Quite by accident, I found the library one day while leaving kitchen duty late. Someone had accidentally burned the morning oatmeal onto the bottom of the large one-hundred gallon pot. I was so small that bending over with a paring knife in my hand, I could not reach the bottom of the pot. Sister Annunciata picked me up and set my whole body inside the pot and I bent over with a paring knife and spent two solid hours scrapping the burnt gunk off the bottom. The other girls on KP duty were long gone by the time I was finished and I was walking back to the playground by myself. I passed this door everyday at least five times a day and this was the first time I ever saw it open.

What a marvelous place. Walls lined with books cover every space. I had never seen anything like it. I sat on the cold black and white tiled floor. As I opened my first Nancy Drew Mystery book, my existence changed forever.

In these books parental love, family structure and the real world came into focus. This was a place for me to escape the pain and anguish in my own world. The dark spot, however, came along with a might roar.

"What do you think you are doing in here?"

Out of the corner of my eye, Sister Regina appeared looming larger as she walked across the room.

"I'm sorry sister," I said, "I've never been in here before, look at all these books!"

"Do you really think that we sisters would ever want to share our personal enjoyment with the likes of you? Get out of this room right now and don't ever let me catch you in here again," she yelled.

I scrambled hurriedly to my feet and made a mad dash for the door narrowly missing the pointed black shoe aimed at my backside. What neither of us realized was that volume one was still clutched in my hands. As I raced down the hall with my stolen booty in my hand, the exhilarating feeling in my heart was pure gold.

No one was watching or expecting me so I made a run for the stairs up to the dorm. No one was ever supposed to be in here during the day. I went directly to my bed and immediately crawled under it with the stolen book still in my hand. I became so taken in by the story and before I knew it the dinner bell was ringing. I hid the book under my mattress and went down to the dinning room.

After dinner, I had my usual KP duty. Naturally, by the time I was done it was time for showers and bed. I lay awake for a long time that night thinking about the book.

The next day after lunch KP, I raced up to the dorm hid under my bed and stole more of an imaginary life. I spent the rest of that summer immersed in other worlds. I made sure that I was never again caught in the library by anyone. I had become a master at being an invisible person pilfering books and living vicariously through Nancy Drew, the Hardy Boys, and Cherry Ames.

The more I read, the more resentment I felt about the way I was being treated. Sister Regina never missed an opportunity for the slightest transgression to become a major infraction worthy of a beating from hell. I learned a great deal from that library. My vocabulary became extensive and I even learned some things about human nature. I did not know that this ability would help me later in life.

In the fourth grade I had learned to shrink and hide and stay out of the mainstream. When I was not working in the kitchen, I was reading my beloved books. If I saw trouble coming my way, physically hiding became a useful tool.

One beautiful sunshiny day I found an undeniable place of absolute comfort. I sat by myself in the back of the chapel. Filtered, colored glass shone and sparkled. I was staring at the statue of the Blessed Mother holding the baby Jesus. I could swear she was smiling at me, almost as if I could hear her speaking. I knew what I should do. I would ask the Blessed Mother through a Novena to find my mother and to send her to me. I needed a parent. I needed self-worth and self-esteem. Even though momma had only had a passing interest in my life, I needed her.

Every day for six weeks I gave up my books and went to kneel in the chapel for an hour. I prayed with a conviction I did not know I possessed. At the end of six weeks what I considered a genuine miracle occurred. On one very dark stormy Sunday in September, my mother made her one and only visit to the orphanage. I do not know what I was expecting, but whatever 'magical miracle' I was anticipating never materialized.

She brought a bag full of candy and acted like she had never been away from us a day in her life. However, the biggest surprise of all was she had a new boyfriend. Disgust overwhelmed me and I excused myself from the visiting room. I ran to the girl's bathroom two flights up and sobbed for hours. I would not see momma again until I was fourteen years old.

Even while depriving all of us children of any family connections, as far as our siblings went, the idea of family mother, father, sisters and brothers was the one thing that the nuns always threw into our faces. It was used as a defining point to make us understand why we were there. If there were to be any chance of our being together again, it all hinged on the idea of the family unit being together again. The appearance of my mother's new boyfriend dashed my hopes of ever being able to leave St. Colman's. No mom and dad together meant absolutely no chance for us kids

I often wished that school went continuously through the summer. It was as hot and uncomfortable on the playground in summer as it was freezing cold in the winter. I do remember after the summer rains, playing in the mud puddles with worms. I was always amazed at how the worms got on to the blacktop without being fried.

One time, someone had given me jacks and a ball. Linda and I would sit on the hot ground, shake the jacks in one hand and spill them on the ground in front of us and play jacks. This toy was carefully hidden in my clothing but one day Sister Regina saw us playing on the ground and marched over. The ball was in Linda's hand and she did not see it. She bent over, scooped up the jacks and marched away with them in her hand. Goodbye jacks. What she did not know was Linda went into the bathroom and came back with a hand full of toilet paper. She carefully wadded small pieces into ball shapes and lo and behold she showed me how to play jacks using wads of toilet paper. As long as we kept the ball hidden from Regina, we could always play the game.

When I was playing a game that did not include the existence of toys, Sister Regina would come and haul me up for a 'special job'. Sometimes this job consisted of a can of Babo and a cloth and the boy's bathroom. Many times she said a little dirt will not hurt you girl. Sprinkle the cleaner into the bowl, put you hand and the cloth into the bowl and start scrubbing. Of course, the boys never could hit the toilet and it was always on the floor. Sometimes I would even be kneeling in it. Regina would stand there and watch, smirking in her perceived power.

Other times it involved waxing the dorm floors. We would be given old cotton undershirts to place flat on the wooden floor. Next we would dig gobs of Johnson's paste wax with our hands and put them into the middle of the rag and roll into a ball. You had to get on your hands and knees, and start waxing the dorm floor in small circular motions. The fun part was when the wax was dry. You got to use an electric buffer machine to make it shine.

One time when we had the same job to do me and an older girl named Louise started to do it. Riding the buffer was a fun pastime because we were really way too small to be doing this job. Louise would swing it back and forth across the floor while I sat on top of the machine. We needed my body as a counter-weight because it was too powerful for either of us to be doing it alone.

Sister Regina came up to Louise and said, "Do it right girl. Do not be afraid to use a little 'elbow-grease'."

Regina left and went down to the chapel. She turned as she reached the door and said the floor had better be shinny when she returned. Louise raced back to the supply room and looked for over an hour; there was not one single can of elbow grease in the whole place. We looked at each other in mutual terror and sat down and cried. When Regina came back and the floor was not done, both Louise and I were beaten and bruised. When Regina was done and we both lay in a pool of blood, she turned on her heel and as an after thought asked why the floor was not done.

Louise spoke up and tearfully said, "I looked sister really I did. I looked and looked there is no elbow grease in the supply closet."

Sister Regina laughed uproariously and gave Louise a hug and left. It was too little too late, we were both sporting some lovely new black and blue bruises. This is the only time I ever remember Sister Regina genuinely laughing.

On a sunny afternoon the first week in September, all the kids were on the playground. Out on the side of the road came the green station wagon and it stops at the playground gate. There was only one reason that car ever traveled down that road. When boys got to be a certain age, they were taken out that side gate, put in that car and were never seen again. Some kids said they were killed, some even said they were taken into the mountains and let go and some said they were taken to the Hudson River and drowned. I had not been here long enough to know.

I watched with an eerie feeling and saw the nun lining up some boys.

When I saw her pull Willie into the line I started screaming, "Willie, Willie no, get out of that line. Willie they're goanna kill ya. Run Willie, run."

By this time I was running for the boy's side of the playground with Grace and June in hot pursuit. I grabbed Willie around the neck holding on for dear life. Sister Loretta stamped over and pried my hands off my brother. Grace and June are crying and Willie starts marching out of the gate into the car. I stood my ground raging and screaming. I did no good, my brother was gone and I was in for another beating.

I had not helped my brother at all. Willie just looked at me with a very scared expression on his face. What did they do with 11 year old boys? None of us children had any idea. The rumors that circulated were frightening. No one that I know really had any idea of what really happened to the boys. I did not get a chance to see Grace or June.

Sister Loretta picked me up off the ground by my hair dragging me into the girl's bathroom. I was scratching, spitting, kicking and screaming. A mountain lion in heat was probably more tame than I was at this time. Loretta dropped me on the floor and began kicking me. Then she pulled me up and stuck my head under a faucet in the mop utility sink. She turned on the water and held my face under it. I stopped screaming and slumped to the floor.

"Get up?" she ordered.

By then I was soaked in water from head to toe. I was dragged down to the basement play room. Sister Loretta went over to the broom closet and pulled out a radiator brush. It was eighteen inches long and half an inch thick with about eight inches on the end full of black bristles.

"Pull them down," she yelled, "Now!"

I would not do it. She came over and pushed me down backwards and I fell on top of a green bench hurting my back and ribs. A high school girl named Barbara happened to come down the stairs. Loretta ordered her to assist.

Together they wrestled me over that bench onto my stomach. I was hanging in half with my upper body and hands hanging down on one side and my legs and feet hanging down the other side. Barbara was instructed to sit on top of me on the bench. This left my backside clearly exposed on the bench. With Loretta instructions, Barbara pulled my wet dress and slip up past my back and Sister Loretta was trying to pull down my underwear. Because they were so wet, she was having a hard time. She finally got so mad that she just ripped them right off in pieces. She then stood and began to beat me with this radiator brush on my wet, naked rear. I think it had extra sting because my skin was so wet.

The last thing I remember was Barbara screaming, "Sister, Sister I think she's dead."

I would not see my brother again for six long years.

CHAPTER 4

The Wilson Heart

By Halloween I had become so depressed that nothing held any joy or sorrow for me. Nighttime, daytime, bad food, no food, nothing mattered, and I began to slide slowly into the depths of despair that no young girl should know.

Every so often, good Samaritan groups took a passing interest in the orphanage and gave us some of their precious time and energy. It so happened that this Halloween night would turn out to be my salvation, and the only light I would ever see in that God forsaken place.

A group from the Knights of Columbus Club came and took some of us out to trick-or-treat. I do not know why, but this time, I was allowed to go. We walked up and down streets trick-or-treating in groups of six. I had not stepped foot outside the fences of St. Colman's Orphanage for over a year and a half. Although, I had been locked up for a long time, these streets were curiously familiar.

An hour into the evening, we knocked on a door answered by a woman that I instantly recognized.

"Aunt Grace!" I screamed. "Aunt Grace! Aunt Grace! Aunt Grace."

The woman's hand flew out of the treat bowl and up to her mouth. Tears started to flow and Aunt Grace immediately reached to embrace me. I just stood there crying. Years later I would know that Aunt Grace and Uncle Bill had no idea that we were able to come out of the orphanage to visit family. What I also later learned was there was no reason for us kids to have gone to an orphanage at all.

I did not have much time that night to talk to my Aunt and Uncle and pretty soon the volunteer was insisting we had to move along. My feet were glued to the porch and I would rather have died than move. Uncle Bill knelt gently beside me. He promised to come to St. Colman's to see us and make sure that we were okay.

I left with the group crying and looking back the whole way up the street. Returning to St. Colman's was a disaster. As soon as we got upstairs to the dorm, one of the other girls reported what had happened to Regina. She told her that I had badly misbehaved and that the volunteers had to physically remove me from some poor stranger's house. Sister Regina grabbed me by the hair and began dragging me down to the sewing room. When she flung me into the room by my hair, I thought I might just as well bend over and kiss my sweet butt goodbye. I assumed the fetal position but that did not help me much. Sister Regina was absolutely insane with anger. She went over to the drawer in the sewing table and withdrew her paddle.

"Get Up!" she snarled. "Get those underpants down around your ankles."

I stood up and did as I was told. She yanked first my dress and then my slip right over my head and threw them on the floor. I was left standing in my undershirt with my underwear hanging around my ankles. She very ceremoniously pulled out the chair and sat down on it. Over my knee, right now she said. She secured one hand around my waist and brought the paddle down on my bare behind with the other. She used all of her might and she hit and hit and hit. The searing pain every time she hit was unbearable. I counted to fifty whacks but lost track as she continued the punishment.

Finally, the welts on my backside began to bleed and I thought this was the end, but instead she pushed me off her lap and onto the floor. She began to kick me in the stomach. I drew my knees up to my chin and the kicks to my back and head begin.

She kicked me clear across the sewing room floor. I wound up against the radiator. It was on and hot enough to burn my leg. The last thing I remember was the nasty kick to my head that send it crashing into the radiator.

When I woke up the next day, I was in the Infirmary. It hurt to move. I had to go to the bathroom and when I went to get up the ringing in my ears and dizziness sent me crashing back to the pillows. I laid there and cried and wet the bed. Two days went by before I could finally get out of bed. The first time I saw my face in the bathroom mirror, I cried. There was a large black and blue egg on my forehead, a black eye and a split lip. Previous experience told me that I had broken ribs. I remained in the infirmary for a solid two weeks.

Funny thing though, Dr. Haverly made house calls to St. Colman's at least twice a week but at no time was I brought out of the room to see the doctor along with the other sick kids. Twice a day, the nurse came in and changed the dressing on my backside. First she cleaned it and then she put more salve on and finally new dressings. I found sitting extremely uncomfortable. When I finally left the infirmary and joined the general population, Sister Regina had disappeared. My friend, Linda told me she left the night of Halloween after finding me at the bottom of the stairs when I had accidentally fallen down all three flights. She looked at me in a knowing way and said it sounded like you were falling down all of them right from the sewing room.

The psychological scars from that night changed my world forever. Every trace of a gentle spirit was wiped away. Fear lurked in my mind and my heart for ever after. Life without Sister Regina was almost good. There were still beatings going on by other nuns to other kids, but for a reason I could not explain, they stayed away from me.

Two days before Thanksgiving my world turned upside down. Sister Mary Claire came into the playroom and collected the Maloney girls. We went up stairs with her.

"My dad could not be here it was not Sunday," I thought.

We were bathed and dressed once again in clothes that fit and sat down on chairs to wait.

"Girls," said Sister Mary Claire, "you are going home to visit for Thanksgiving." I started to cry but Sister Mary Claire said, "Stop crying, you'll make yourself sick and you won't be able to go."

We waited on pins and needles for about half an hour and then the sewing room phone rang. Sister Mary Claire led us down to the first floor and the front door. I had not seen that door since the first time I walked through it to stay here. In the bright shinny circle engraved in gold were the letters P.A.X.

In the middle of it there stood my Uncle Bill. After what happened the last time I grabbed for him, I stood rooted to the floor until the nun said it was okay to go. Uncle Bill took mine and June's hand with Grace following behind us and walked us through the door. My body began to shake badly my knees about buckled as I climbed into the car. The beating I had received on Halloween night was forever imbedded in my mind and was a direct result of the emotion I had showed for my family.

The words going home for a visit echoed. "We're only going for a couple of days," I had thought.

"Behave, don't cry, don't tell and maybe you can go again," were the words echoing in my mind.

When we got to Aunt Grace's house, we all piled out of the car. Standing in the door, big smile on her face stood Aunt Grace my mother's older sister. I knew that she did not like the way mother behaved when we were home and that something had happened between them. I was just too young to figure it out.

I walked up the stairs and threw my arms around her. Aunt Grace began to sob and I whispered, "Don't cry or I won't be able to come anymore."

She gave me a strange look and we all went into the house. When we took a bath that night I insisted on closing and locking the bath room door.

"I'm too old to take a bath with June anymore," I said. "I'm a big girl now."

Respecting my privacy, my Aunt and Uncle allowed this. If I'd only known then that if they saw the still angry red welts our trials and tribulations would have all been over. A deep abiding shame came over me that I had somehow been bad enough to be beaten half to death and it was something I could not let them know.

Thanksgiving was a wonderful day. We had turkey, mashed potatoes, stuffing, cranberry sauce, and sweet potato pies. Aunt Grace and Uncle Bill had two children of their own; Mary who was six months younger than me, and Billy who was several years younger. Both of them, I knew, had been adopted but I did not know what that meant.

At this wonderful dinner were so many people that my sisters and I were sitting on an ironing board with two chairs on either end to use for extra seating. We were to stay Tuesday through Sunday. On Wednesday morning I sat bolt upright in the bed. It was pitch dark in the room and five a.m. I sprang out of bed and started to get dressed. June sat up and looked at me. She slid out of bed and started dressing too. Then we went into the living room, but the rest of the house was still pitch black.

June and I sat down on the sofa in the living room waiting to go to morning mass. We both fell back to sleep and Aunt Grace found us sitting upright asleep when the rest of the household got out of bed around eight.

When Sunday afternoon rolled around, Aunt Grace told us that tonight after dinner Uncle Bill would be taking us back to St. Colman's. Even though I knew this was going to happen it still hit me with the impact of a speeding freight train. My mood deepened with the day, and by dinnertime I could not breathe. The thought of going back terrified me but clearly these people had their own children and their own lives which did not include the three of us. I would not know for many years that my aunt felt worse than I did.

I had learned to be defensive and I was bound and determined not to let them see my hurt. Uncle Bill drove us back but with one stop on the way, the corner store. We were each given a quarter and allowed to use it on penny candy. Grace and June were happily stuffing their bags with penny candy almost as if they were oblivious to the fact that we were going back to the Colonie Holocaust.

Uncle Bill brought us back through the front door and kissed and hugged us. He also stated emphatically that he would be back for us again. I walked away hanging my head like a dog on death row.

In the middle of December, once again the Behr-Manning annual party came around. This time there was no Sister Regina to cross my name off the party list. The excitement came in waves as we dressed. Most of the kids knew what was coming but I had no idea.

The school busses showed up at the front door and children began filing out and climbing into the bus. The Behr-Manning plant was only about two miles away. By the time we arrived all the kids were in a frenzy hopping, skipping, and jumping off the bus. I walked inside of what looked to be a giant cafeteria. Long tables were set for about two hundred kids. We were shown to our seats and the party began. Men wearing regular clothes with elf hats came back and forth carrying huge bowls of strawberry shortcake with vanilla ice cream. Orange pop flowed like a river continuously into our glasses. There came a point when I was so stuffed I could not move. It was the last time since my Thanksgiving visit that I could remember my stomach being full.

Every year, in honor of Reverend Mother's birthday, the children put on a show of singing and dancing routines that would rival any Broadway show. This same extravaganza was repeated for all the officials of the Behr-Manning Co. and any employees helping with the party. I do remember hours and hours of practicing song and dance routines. When the show was over a quiet hush came over the crowd. The lights went off and there was a pregnant silence for about twenty seconds. When the lights came back on, in the middle of the makeshift stage where we had just performed, stood Santa Claus. Dead silence was followed by a wave of clapping and cheering, yeah Santa, yeah Santa.

Starting with that wonderful class system again, children began lining up to go see Santa. A magnificent chair was dragged out onto the stage and Santa deposited himself into it. One by one the children climbed up into his lap and whispered into his ear. When he heard what they had to say he would ask their age. He would then call out to one of his elves, five year old girl or seven year old boy, whatever the age of the child on his lap. The elf would come out bearing a huge pile of gifts and they would take the child back to their seat at the table and they would begin to open their gifts. The line moved agonizingly slow.

Since this was my first experience with this, I was somewhat nervous. When I was lifted up onto the lap of the man in the red suit, he leaned down and whispered in my ear, Hello little girl, what's your name.

"Susie," I said, "what's yours?"

He smiled and said jovially, "why it's Santa, Santa Claus Miss." Once again he leaned over and whispered, "and what would you like Old Santa to bring you for Christmas."

I looked in his very deep blue eyes and said in a small voice "new parents Santa, parents that will love me, that's all."

Santa blinked his eyes quickly and asked, "how old are you Susie?"

"Eight," I said, "eight years old."

My personal elf came from behind the curtain with a pile of gifts and I slid off Santa's lap. Going back to the table, I could feel Santa's eyes on me and I wondered if I had gotten myself into trouble again. I thought if I could tell anyone my Christmas Wish it would be Santa.

My anxiety temporarily quieted. I began to tear open presents. A doll, a game, a pair of roller skates and a beautiful red sweater were before me. I tried on my sweater at my friend Linda's urging and to my delight it was a perfect fit. I was deliriously happy but the afternoon was coming to an end. As we put on our coats and gathered our gifts, we stood in a long line and elves once again passed out huge Christmas stockings. They were filled with small boxes of hard candy, candy canes, chocolate Santas, large gingerbread men and oranges.

I had never had a Christmas like this in my whole life. Riding back in the bus, the children were all subdued. There was none of the gaiety that was present on the way down. When the buses pulled up at the front door, some of the kids started to cry.

"We just had the best day of our lives," I said, "why in God's name are you bawling?"

No one answered me as they filed out. I picked my gift pile up off the seat and got off the bus with the happiness of the day still bathing my spirit. Once inside the door, a dark trickle of fear overwhelmed me. About ten large white canvas laundry baskets on wheels were lined up in a row down the hall. As each child passed, they dutifully deposited their pile of present into the cart.

I was blinking back tears as I neared the head of the line and I asked the nun standing there, "Why, why? These are mine, Santa gave them to me."

Sister Loretta nodded at me and said that they were going to our overseas missions to children who truly deserved them. It all came rushing back to me. I remembered last year's tears from some of the new kids. Now I understood their questions about their presents. Like a mighty wall of brick crashing on my head, I understood exactly what Sister Regina had deprived me of the year before.

Anger and resentment now owned more of my soul that I did. Anger is such a powerful emotion. It destroys your heart and hollows your soul. One managed to slip by, however, I was still wearing my red sweater. It went back upstairs with me and I kept it under my pillow at night and wore it for over a year almost everyday.

Two days before Christmas, Sister Mary Claire came for the Maloney girls again. We went upstairs, got washed and dressed and again sat in the sewing room waiting for the phone to ring. At five o'clock p.m. we were led downstairs and standing once again in the circle of hope stood Uncle Bill, his hat in his hand waiting for us. Staring straight ahead not daring to look left or right, I grabbed his hand and practically dragged him out the door. Christmas in a family setting again was a painful dilemma for me. I knew that my Aunt and Uncle cared about us, but I was also very aware that they were not my parents. I knew that if it had not been for their unselfishness and their intervention in my life, I would not be alive today. I received many nice gifts for Christmas but I refused to take them back with me to the orphanage. I knew that they would have to be placed at the end of our bed at night and in the morning they would be gone.

On New Year's day it was time for us to go back again. We made the trip to the corner store with our quarter in hand and came out with bulging bags. The three of us waived good bye and walked up the stairs back again into the house of horrors. The sight that met me after stepping into my dorm was enough to send me off the deep end. Standing in the middle of the floor was Sister Regina. Small beady eyes glaring at me, fists clenched in anger.

"Well, well," she said, "and what do we have here?"

She sent Grace ahead to her own dorm and directed June to her area. Snatching my bag of candy from my hand, she looked inside.

"Garbage," she said. "I'll just throw this away for you. Get into bed now!"

As I slid by her my heart was hammering in my chest. I got undressed, put on my pajamas, and got into bed as fast as I could.

In the next bed, I heard Linda whisper, "She's back. She only went on a retreat. She is here again."

I stared into the darkness for a long time. "She's back and I am in mortal danger again," were the thoughts that filled my head.

I knew it is only a matter of time before I was beaten senseless again. My anger boiled, my inner self screamed, my mind teetered on the break of insanity. I was very nervous most of the time. I was making stupid mistakes in school. I could not concentrate. I was continuously looking behind me everywhere I went. I knew she was watching and waiting; one mistake, one misstep, any reason to bring her wrath down on me. Three weeks went by that I had managed to avoid any trouble.

When Friday night rolls around, Uncle Bill was here again to pick us up. I got into his car and dissolved into oblivion. The weekend was great and Sunday morning comes. After church when we go back to the house, my father was waiting there. He was holding a very large box. He and Aunt Grace exchange some pleasantries and she invites him in for coffee and to visit his children. I guess I had not noticed that since we began visiting Aunt Grace and Uncle Bill on a monthly basis that my father no longer felt any duty to visit us.

In the dining room dad opened the box. It contained twelve beautiful, brand new Tiny Town Tog dresses. There were three for me, three for June, three for Grace and three for our cousin Mary.

Aunt Grace asked, "Why don't you go in and try them on girls while the grownups talk."

We left the room and I could feel my father's eyes boring holes in my back. The dresses were beautiful but my feelings for my father had turned to hate. In the years that we were regular visitors to my Aunt and Uncle's house, my father came every six months and brought his armload of dresses for us girls.

He told my Aunt that they were a side benefit of his job as a night watchman at the Tiny Town Togs factory. (Long after I was grown, I found out that he had stolen them.)

Quite the thief my father was. First he stole our happiness, then our childhood, then our clothing. Did he have no shame? If I would have known, I would rather have gone to Sunday morning church naked.

We became very comfortable in our Aunt's house. We used to pretend that we were going to boarding school and coming home for weekends once a month.

I would know as an adult everything Grace and Bill Wilson gave up for us. I would learn of the late mortgage payments because of the amount of food we ate during our stay. I would learn of their painstaking efforts to go into the basement after we all went to bed so they could mix half powered milk and half real milk and put it back into the milk bottles so we wouldn't know. I learned of all of the cost cutting measures that they took in their lives to give us a chance of stability.

I would also find out that in all those times of financial hardship, my father was living a merry little life for himself. He moved back in with his momma. She cooked his meals, washed his clothes, and kept his house. He would come to Grace and Bill's house and boast about taking him and his girlfriend out for steak dinners. Never once did he contribute one red cent to the Wilson family for the things that they provided for his children.

Sister Regina's abuse had become more subtle. To this day, I am sure she suffered some kind of reprimand for the beating that almost cost me my life. I think now, that I was safe from her beatings as long as my aunt and uncle came to visit on a regular basis. The constant bruises would have been too hard to explain.

At Easter the other shoe finally dropped. We came back from a visit with Aunt Grace and I had decided to bring back my beautiful shinny black patent leather Mary Jane shoes. As soon as I walked into my dorm, there she was staring at my new shoes. Without any warning, her hand flew to my head and grabbed me by the hair. I was dragged down the three flights of stairs totally by the hair. When we came to the boiler room door, Regina opened the door, threw me inside, followed me in and then shut the door behind us. She grabbed my hair again and dragged me into the second room. She glared at my shoes and then at me.

"Where did they come from?" she screamed.

"My Aunt bought them for me for Easter," I cried.

"Take them off right now and hand them to me," she said.

I bent down and took them off. She was looking me in the eye as she opened the door to the incinerator. My new shoes were tossed in and gone in an instant.

"Don't you know," she said, "that the boys can see the reflection of your underwear in those shoes?"

My tears were blinding me and I did not see the sneer on her face. "Of course you realize that you'll have to be punished for this offense against God," she said with almost a gleeful glib in her voice.

I was so terrified that all I could do was nod my head. She grabbed me by the arm and we went marching back up the stairs to the sewing room. She closed the door behind us, retrieved the paddle from the drawer and took her usual place on the chair.

"You know what to do," she said as the tears began to slide down my face. "Get them down, I don't have all night."

She pulled me roughly across her lap and pulled up my dress and slip. I only got twenty five pain searing whacks that night and no blood spilled. Things were looking up!

Nothing that Sister Regina could do would be able to take away the very loving and kind things that my Aunt Grace did for me. In the late 50s' and 60s', little girls wore corsages pined on their coats for Easter and Christmas. On this particular Easter, even though I was very young, I remember a beautiful Azalea plant that my Uncle Bill gave to my Aunt Grace. Aunt Grace, very carefully, took out our Christmas corsages and removed the holly berries and bells. She took her scissors and cut and divided her lovely Azalea plant. All four of us girls went to church in the most beautiful corsages. Every time I see an Azalea plant I remember her sacrifices for us.

The rest of fourth grade was a blur in my mind. I was doing well academically although math remained a constant problem. The torturous beatings had yet to cause any brain damage.

Along came the month of June and specifically Father's Day. I understood that Father's Day was important to my cousins and I also knew that it was appropriate for Mary and Billie to spend it alone with their mom and dad.

My sister June had labored long and hard and she made a beautiful Father's Day card. We both stood at the chain link fence, our faces pressed to the metal. At this very corner point of the playground we had a bird's eye view of Bought road. It afforded us a place to watch as my father's station wagon came around the corner and turned up the road to the orphanage. We waited all day long. June just kept watching. I looked every once in a while at her face. Sometimes there was hope, sometimes puzzlement, sometimes disappointment. Finally the 'Angeles bell' rang through the yard at six o'clock in the evening. Two years after our first day of arrival we stood there once again with June crying for a parent.

She would tell me many, many years later how that single event changed her. She would never be a parent. She would never have a child waiting for her to visit and destroy her child with such a callous, thoughtless, selfish act. She was spiritually wounded. She became invisible. Never again would someone hurt her. If you did not love, you could not be hurt. If you did not make any noise you would not been seen. If you were never seen, you would not be beaten. She had finally learned to play the game.

Aunt Grace and Uncle Bill came and took us for two weeks. Our 'little bit of heaven' we called it. June and I are very fair skinned and one afternoon we all went to the park and the Green Island pool. June and I were so excited that we spent the whole afternoon splashing in the wading pool. At five o'clock we gathered our picnic things and started to walk home. By six, we were both in severe pain. By nightfall both of our shoulders were covered in huge blisters. Neither of us had ever spent an afternoon in a wading pool. Nobody even realized that we were burning.

On another day, the parks program had a doll parade and we girls all pranced through the park showing off our dolls. Mary won a prize for the prettiest doll. Aunt Grace took us all to Montgomery Wards to get sneakers. I got navy, June got red, and Grace got white. There was never a question again of taking anything back to the orphanage. I did not tell about my Easter shoes, I just never took the chance again.

Going back after our two weeks was so hard for us kids and Aunt Grace. I no longer doubted that it bothered my Aunt a great deal that we were there. My father would not allow his children to be split up. This is the excuse that he used and told me later as a teenager. This was his reasoning for not granting my mother's family's request for her brothers and sisters to each take one of us to live with them. We could not have grown up more separated if he had placed us all on different planets.

Going back and forth between the two worlds nearly drove me insane. Aunt Grace once made a comment to me "You were such a difficult child Susie. If all the kids were playing outside, you were inside. If they were inside you were outside."

If I could have just opened up to her and told her of my nightmarish existence. I was so fearful of her not wanting me to come anymore. What if she found out how often I had to be punished or how very effective Sister Regina's words made me feel?

She once told me after a happy weekend at the Wilson's how very stupid I was.

"This Aunt Grace is your mother's sister," she said. "June has told me that she adopted both her children. You are so stupid and disgusting that your own family took stranger's children in to love, but she left you here. That's how little she thinks of you."

"Oh God she's right," I thought. She had just succeeded in starting the fire of jealousy that I would feel for many years against my poor cousin Mary. Mary, who was one of the most kind and generous children I had ever known. She shared her parents, her home, her clothes, her joy, and herself. I have always felt guilty about the bad feelings I had against poor Mary Christine.

Even though my Uncle Bill was the only father figure in my life, I was unable to accept him in that particular roll. I did love him without question, but in my mind, if I allowed him into my life in that capacity, I was afraid that I would hate him. My father had so destroyed my ability to love any father figure that I had to keep Uncle Bill at arms length to preserve my ability to love him.

At the same time, my cousin Mary had her fathers' undeniable love. I was so torn about my feelings watching him and his love for his children. It really was a good thing, but for a long time it caused me considerable pain.

What was so wrong with me that nobody could love me like that? Maybe Sister Regina was right. There was really nobody who cared about me one way or the other.

My cousin Mary was just as giving to us as her parents were. Even though she was six months younger than me, she was physically bigger. When we were home with them on the weekend, she would share clothing with both June and me.

Mary taught me how to ride a two-wheeled bike. We would take turns cycling around the block. One day we got the bright idea to teach June how to ride the bike. Mary and I were on either side of her running alongside while she got her balance. She did great until she got to the corner.

She did not know how to turn, worse than that we never told her how to stop. Mary and I stood transfixed as we watched poor June go right up the middle of a tree. The next thing we knew, the bike flew backwards and June grabbed the tree. She slid down the bark on her face. By the time we got to her, half the skin on her face had been scraped off. Mary and I both laughed and cried at the same time. Just too see June try to ride up that tree was hilarious. Seeing her with the bad scrapes on her face was awful.

The Wilson family took us on many outings to Kinderhook Creek. If we did not have bathing suits, they used to let us swim in our underwear. Mary, June, and I would try for hours to catch the pollywogs. We would scoop up the water with our plastic cups and scan for the tiny swimming things.

Some times in the winter months, we all went up to Snyder's Lake. My Grandmothers house was always closed up for the winter months. The grandparents went south for the winter. Aunt Grace always had a key. She would tack up a blanket on the kitchen door and Uncle Bill would turn on the gas stove.

Mary and Billie were the only kids to have skates and we three girls would all take our turns gliding across the ice. Mary was always so patient even though they were her skates. She would just wait until June and I took our turns around the lake.

As young girls, Mary and I were close. When my parents were still together, Mary always wanted to be included with the *Baloney Kids*. The Wilson family was really our 'Saving Grace'.

Time went by with my life strung between these two worlds the pretending everything was alright at the Wilson's and the knowledge that I was horrendously abused at the orphanage.

There are surprises good and bad. It is the summer of the fifth grade. The Knights of Columbus gave their annual Field Day. All of us kids had been told a couple of days before hand that it was coming. The standard *litany of threats* was issued. Any behavior out of line would mean sitting on the center courtyard on the green benches. Watching from this point was useless. We could not see anything. We could, however, hear the cries of joy.

We could sit and close our eyes and imagine that we were eating the hot dogs and chocolate and vanilla ice cream in paper cups with the little wooden paddle spoons. There were three-legged races and egg rolling contests. The nuns played baseball as we all cheered. The one thing that I loved most about the field days was the pie eating contests.

In all the world, blueberry pie was heaven to me. This particular year, I had committed no mortal sin serious enough to keep me from the field day. I waited almost all day for this event. I did not do it so much to win as just to be able to eat the blueberry pie. As I knelt on the grass with my face six inches from the dream, my mouth started to water. The anticipation was delicious. When the man said, "Ready, Set, Go," my face was in that plate in a "New York Minute". I was gobbling so fast that there were berries up my nose and smeared across my face from ear to ear.

When I stood up a man grabbed my hand and pushed it skyward. As I looked around, I realized that I was the only one standing which meant one thing. I had won. I had never won anything in my life so this was pride. I liked the feeling. The funny thing about pride is that I know now that it comes before the fall. I would soon be tumbling down the abyss of abuse.

At the end of my glorious day, I still had KP duty. There were pots, pans and dishes from the nuns dinning room. Sister Regina appeared at the door and stated that I was to follow her. As I left the kitchen and followed her into the next room, I tried to think of what kind of crime I had committed now. She stared at me with a look that withered my soul.

On the stainless steel tables against one wall were the only remaining treats left from the party. Regina told me that she was quite embarrassed about my disgusting table manners at the pie eating contest.

"Oh God, I am so sorry Sister, no one said that there were any rules about how you ate the pie. I thought we were supposed to eat it as fast as we could."

"That does not mean that you eat like a pig", she replied. "Do you see those trays of watermelon on those tables against the wall"?

Fear began to take shape in the form of a lump in my throat. I nodded my head up and down now almost frozen in fear.

"Alright Miss Piggy, start eating them", she said.

I was forced to eat watermelon until I threw up. I have never eaten a watermelon since.

CHAPTER 5

Am I Guilty

Fifth grade was particularly painful for me. Math was a major stumbling block. No matter how much I tried, every time it was my turn at the board it was a disaster. After you got three tries at doing your best to solve the problem, if you were not successful, you had to go and stand against the window. Sometimes I was the only child in the line.

Sister would send a child down to the laundry room to look at the clock. At ten minutes to twelve every child in that line would start to shake and cry. If the child who went to check the time was early, that child would stay looking at the clock until it said 10 minutes to 12 o'clock. When the child reappeared at the door, your time was up.

Sister would pull her chair out from behind her desk and put it in the front of the class. One by one, as you got to the head of the line, you had to pull your underwear down to your knees. Sister would turn you over her knee and pull up your dress and slip. She would hit me so many times with her paddle, that I would loose control of my bladder and I would urinate all over her.

After this happened three or four times, Sister had become disgusted with me. The next time I was up against the wall, Sister went to her desk drawer. She made a big deal out of telling a little boy in the class to reach into the drawer and pull out the rubber sheet.

These sheets were usually used on the beds of children who wet their beds at night. Sister would set her chair up in front of the classroom and this little boy would drape that rubber sheet across her lap.

She would then announce to the whole class, "Alright *baby* Susan, get over here and take your punishment."

I was just as humiliated by the rubber sheet as I was by the bare assed spanking that I got in front of the whole world.

The sixth grade was not any easier and became a particularly dark memory of my life. I was not physically very developed, probably because I did not enjoy the *wonderful cuisine* that we were served. There were other girls my age that had already started to menstruate. I was, however, not one of them.

There was a lay person who worked there and her name was Katherine. She was mostly in charge of the boys. She was pretty hefty and was very mean spirited. I used to see her slapping and kicking the boys on a regular basis. Everyone was afraid of her, boys and girls alike. She had a private bedroom outside the infirmary on the second floor just outside the girl's locker room.

One day after KP duty, I was in the bathroom next to the locker room. As I came out into the hallway, Katherine appeared out of nowhere and instructed me to follow her. She took me into her bedroom. It had blue walls the color of Robin's eggs. There was one bed, a dresser, and a television.

I had never been in that room before. I turned to face her as she closed that door. She did not seem angry, which was unusual as this was her usual demeanor. One thing that always made her seem angry was her severe speech impediment. This impediment was so profound that the word Sister always came out as Sloiter.

"How old are you," she asked?

"I am 11," I replied.

She walked around me in a circle looking at me strangely from head to toe.

"Well," she said, "Sloiter Mary Regina says that one of the girls in your grade has her period and she keeps putting her disgusting, bloody underpants into the laundry cart without first washing them out in the sink."

I knew what a period was. The nuns had just shown us that movie a couple of weeks ago.

"Is it you?" she asked. "Are you doing that disgusting thing?"

"No," I said. "I don't have my period yet."

"Well," she said, I can not just trust you. Sloiter told me to check every girl in your class."

I started to become very uneasy.

"Just lay face down on the bed," she said and let me check.

I told her that I did not want to.

"It is not a choice," she replied, "do it now!"

I laid face down across her bed with a very sick feeling in my stomach. She pulled up my dress and started to pull down my underpants. I started to cry. She yelled at me and told me to stop it.

"I am not killing you," she said matter-of-factly. She was pulling my legs apart and putting her fingers between them, and as far as I could tell, she did not have any kind of examination gloves on.

"I can not really tell this way," she said, "turn over."

"Please," I said, "I am telling the truth, it is not me."

"Over," she said, "now. If it is not you, then there is nothing to worry about."

I could not move. She rolled me over and stood above me. "This will go a lot easier if you would stop that damn bawling," she said.

She pulled my legs apart and bent over me. She kept staring between my legs. The more she tried to see the harder I held my knees together.

Finally she said, "Well if you are not going to cooperate with me you leave me no choice, I am going to get Sloiter Mary Regina and she can find out herself."

"No," I pleaded, "please no."

"Alright then," she said, "stand up and take those underpants off so I can really see, or I am going for Sloiter."

I shook so badly as I stood up that I almost fell over. I very slowly removed my underwear.

"Lay on the bed on your back," she said, "and put your heels on the bed."

I did as I was told. She was staring at me. "You are really nice and young," she said with almost a smile in her voice, "you hardly have any hair on it. I am sorry," she continued, "I can not really see. I want you to spread your legs so that I can clearly see."

I closed my eyes and dropped my knees. The best description I can give of what she did was a full gynecological exam. She stuck her fingers up inside of me and began to move them inward and outward.

"Why are you doing that," I cried.

"Well, I do not see anything outside so I have to put my fingers inside and pull them out to see if there is any blood on them."

I cried loudly.

"Shut up," she said, "shut up now! I am not hurting you. I am just doing what Sloiter asked."

When she was done I jumped off that bed and pulled on my underpants.

"You are not allowed to discuss this with the other girls," she said. "I do not want to warn the girl that is guilty. As a matter of fact, I like you very much. Since you did not give me any trouble about examining you, I am going to see about making sure that you do not get into any more trouble with sister, as long as you do not tell anyone. I will catch the girl who does this. You will be very safe and I will protect you. Have we got a deal now?" she asked.

"I said yes," and ran from that room like my butt was on fire. I felt sick and the next time I saw Sister Regina I cringed and wished her dead.

This same routine went on for almost a year. Once a month she would 'examine' me. On the day that I finally did start my period I went to Sister Regina and told her that I was bleeding. She gave me a belt and napkins. I assured her that I would wash out my panties in the sink.

I also asked that I not be examined by Katherine any more. I swore that I would wash out my panties in the sink every time I needed too. Of course, she had no idea what I was talking about.

When I explained to her what Katherine had been doing, she called me stupid and said it was my own fault. Regina said, "If you let her do that to you, you have no one to blame by yourself."

I never had to go into Katherine's room again. I did, however, notice several other young girls going into her room at different times. All of them had that same sick scared look on their faces.

CHAPTER 6

The Ultimate Humiliation

At the end of the summer in the sixth grade, my world was shattered and I was never the same again. The nuns only taught through the sixth grade and after that you went to the public junior high school. I remember so looking forward to it. I was pretty sure that I could survive until I graduated if five days a week where spent out of the orphanage and we went home once a month to Aunt Grace's.

About two weeks before school started, Aunt Grace took me back to 'Monkey Wards'. I was growing up and she said and it was time I wore a bra. I think she was just being kind to me. All the girls made fun of my body. I was amazingly underdeveloped for my age. (Lack of food will do that to you).

At this time in my life a major torment arrived in the form of three sisters who had been placed in St. Colman's; Sandy, Barbara and Jackie. Sandy was okay to me. Barbara was older and had a superior attitude towards me and then came Jackie. She was my age and she was nasty. (Looking back now I just feel sorry for her.) Life had not been kind to her either. When she walked you could see that she was bow legged. When she talked you knew she was not gifted with intelligence, and when you looked at her she was butt ugly. Her face was covered in deep scarred pits of acne and what was not dark purple was pink and puss yellow. I never could figure out whether her personality was reflected in her face, or whether it was the other way around. She started the other girls in my dorm calling me surfboard and that name stuck for years.

Aunt Grace bought me some training bras anyway. The first week of school something new happened. Since I was now going out into public everyday, our group was moved to the junior high dorm. We thought we were *soooooo cool*. We had spent our time in the pits and it was our turn to crow!

Welcome to the bottom of the pile, again. Of course, the older girls looked at us as one step above babies and one step below animals. We suffered the usual sling and arrows of the superiority complex. Once again I was on the bottom clawing my way up for respect. The only population we could dump on were the kids in the lower grades, and dump we did. In their eyes we were the cool ones.

Junior high, big deal, I was just old enough not to know that the feudal system goes on throughout your life. There is always somebody above you that is better, smarter, stronger, richer, and prettier. If I had gained this knowledge in my life sooner, I would have been better off.

Just before we transferred to the junior high dorm, Sister Regina had to have a crack at me again. If your family brought you an article of clothing and you wanted to keep it for yourself, you were responsible for its upkeep. Aunt Grace had purchased me bras, but my underpants and slip still came from the communal laundry.

On this particular occasion my locker held a yellow transparent slip. It was what I was given so it was what I wore. When you got into the higher grades you stood in the hallways in your underwear and slip standing in the two great lines waiting for your turn in the shower. This particular Sunday evening I was standing in the line with everyone else inching my way forward wearing this yellow slip. We were lined up by grade so I am pretty far in the back. Sister Regina came strolling down the lines eye-balling everyone. When she got to me she stopped dead. An evil look spread across her eyes together with a gleam of triumph mixed in.

"Oh my God," she screamed at me, "you disgusting little tramp!"

I was not sure what the word meant but I knew from her tone that it could not be good.

"What? What? What could I possibly have done now?" I thought.

I was just standing here in the line waiting to shower. Heads snapped around as if on command. The girls in front of me moved ahead, the girls behind me moved back. There I stood shaking, not knowing what mortal sin I had committed now.

"You filthy pig," she screamed.

Sister Regina reached over and grabbed me by the hair pulling me into the middle of the lines.

"You can see your underwear and bra right through that slip. How dare you!" she ranted.

"Sister please, it was on my locker. Please I did not do anything" I was pleading for my life.

"Where," she demanded "did you get a bra?"

"My Aunt bought it," I said. "Please sister," I was sobbing now. "Tell me what I did wrong."

So she shouted, "You're wearing a slip that everyone can see through. You're so proud of your little body you want everyone to see that you are wearing that stupid little bra, Okay, then let's see it!"

My face was drained of color and there I stood with everyone watching in silence.

"I said take off that slip, Now!"

I could not move. I would not do it. For the first time in my life I openly defied her. I was beginning to grow more backbone that my small body could handle and it seeped out of me in the form of attitude.

"No," I croaked! "No I won't do it."

I thought I knew what was coming and I did not care. Sister Regina was furious.

"You filthy, rotten, ugly little snot," she said.

She put her hands on my shoulders and began to rip the slip from my body. I dropped to the floor and curled into a ball.

"No," I screamed. "No, No, No, No!"

It was not long before the slip was shredded into many pieces, then my bra was also ripped off. I was left lying on the floor in a heap in nothing but my underpants. After several sharp, painful kicks into my ribs, I was hauled to my feet, shoved to the beginning of the line and made to stand in the middle of the two rows.

I stood there, naked from the waist up with my hands tied behind me. I stood this way for two hours. When the last girl had gone in, Sister Regina dragged me into the shower room. She yanked off my underpants and shoved me under the shower head.

"I'm going to teach you some respect for your body," she snarled.

She went to the supply cupboard and returned with a bottle of Lysol and bar of Felsnaptha brown octagon soap. She poured the Lysol on the washcloth and began scrubbing my face with it. My eyes burned, my nose burned, and my skin felt like it was on fire. She soaped the cloth from the brown soap then soaked it in more Lysol. I was huddled in the corner of the tiled shower. She brought the cloth between my legs and shoved it up my vagina. I started screaming. The more I screamed, the harder she shoved.

"It burns, it burns!" I was begging.

"Good," she said, maybe this will teach you not to flaunt your body ever again. The burning was so bad I fainted right there in the shower. I returned to consciousness with cold water pouring from the showerhead. I was shaking from shock and cold. Sister Regina was sitting on a stool a couple of inches from the shower stall.

"I hope that I have taught you a valuable lesson today," she said with a kind of satisfaction in her voice. "Turn off that water."

I stood on rubbery legs and did as I was told. She threw me a towel and said to get dressed. When I came out of the shower, my clothes were waiting for me in a wet pile in the hall. Underpants, undershirt, skirt and blouse, but no slip; what now! Oh God, what was I going to do now? I did not have a slip that you could see through, I did not have one at all. Some things are not easily forgotten and the slip humiliation was definitely one of them.

The distribution of clothing changed in the seventh grade. We were issued three personal dresses, one pair of penny loafers and three pairs of bobby sox. This was great as far as I was concerned. I had never owned a piece of clothing in this place in my life. The only problem was my size. I was in the seventh grade and only weighed fifty-five pounds which meant a size eight or ten dress. In these sizes, of course, were only little girl dresses. Still, they were new and they fit. I did not think that I looked bad.

The night before school was to start I was beside myself with anticipation. Sister Annunciata came into our dorm room and set down the ground rules for behavior. We were to only mingle with other St. Colman's girls. We were to conduct ourselves as ladies. We were told that we were a direct representation of the Sisters of the Presentation and that any embarrassment to them would be dealt with in the harshest possible way. Under no circumstances were we to voice our opinion about anything. There were to be no friendships made with anyone. We would not participate in any after school activities and under no circumstances were we to leave the school grounds. We were never to discuss anything that went on in the orphanage with anyone for any reason. We were not to join in any communal showers after gym class. We would not expose any bruises that we had.

We were expected to bring all A's home on our report cards. Homework would be done Monday through Friday, seven until nine PM in the cafeteria. School dances, football games, basketball games and pep rallies were out of the question. We were never to speak to anyone about the Sisters ever. We were now responsible for the upkeep of our own clothing. It would go down into the communal wash and when it came back you were to go into the laundry cart and retrieve it. Ironing was to be done on Saturday afternoons. The use of the library on the basement floor was open to us on Sunday. We were to eat the lunches provided for us and not throw them away and skip lunch as some St. Colman's girls had been reported doing.

Last but not least, the topic of 'boys'! There would be some at this school and they were all *wicked* and *evil* and they were only interested in 'one thing'.

Of course, living in this closed environment for so long, I did not know anything about boys and could not imagine what that 'one thing' was.

My first day at public junior high was yet one other horrible day that I would shove into the back of my mind. When the school bus arrived, we all stood in a line to collect our two cents literally. Sister Regina was handing out two pennies and someone else handed you a paper sack. I climbed into the bus thinking this was great. Since I really had no idea of fashion, I thought I looked okay.

When the bus pulled up in front of Watervliet Junior/Senior High School my smile disappeared. There were kids standing outside the front doors of the school. Others were crossing the parking lot with still others leaving their parents cars.

Their clothes were dramatically different than ours. Each and every one of the junior high girls on that bus was absolutely a stand out. The difference was so apparent that my face turned a beet red. When the bus doors opened and the girls started to file out, I heard the first snickers. The words the 'orphan bus' rang clearly in my head. Other kids were staring and pointing, some openly laughing and snickering behind their hands. I do not believe in this lifetime, that I have ever been so embarrassed.

I followed the other girls into the school with the sound of laughter echoing in my mind. I found my locker and my class schedule without much problem. For the entire day as I went from class to class, I knew for the first time what it felt like to be a second- class citizen. I was behind academically from most of the other kids in my classes except, of course, for the other St. Colman's kids. I walked around that whole day trying to hide my tears.

When it was lunch time, I sat in the cafeteria with my sack lunch. When I opened it there was a sandwich wrapped in waxed paper and an apple. I did not have the heart or stomach to eat it. I walked slowly over to the garbage can, making sure no St. Colman's kids were watching, and pitched it into the trash.

After the first three days of school I suddenly realized that I would need to wear the same clothes again during that week. Of course, on the fourth day when I wore the same dress that I had worn on the first day, the cruel remarks started.

"Okay on the three day route I see!" "Don't you have any other clothes?" "Where did you get that dress? It looks like you robbed the kindergarten class!"

I was more miserable and depressed than I had ever been. Public school was not great. It was a great big nightmare.

My first report card was not good. I did not get one single A, but there were probably only one or two girls that did. For this reason, we were not allowed to go to the Behr-Manning party that year.

I had always been very athletic and gym class for me was a lot of fun. I was very good at tumbling and in the winter Mr. Nash, the gym teacher, sent me home with a note. There was to be a spring tumbling show and he wanted me to be in it. I brought the note to Sister Regina thinking, well maybe! If the teacher was asking and not me, just maybe!

Sister Regina looked at the note and stared at me, she then started to laugh. "I can see why he would want you to do this," she said, "you do sort of look like a monkey."

Of course, it is out of the question. You were told at the beginning not to try anything like this."

"But Sister," I said, "I did not ask for this."

She just looked at me and said, "I have just the right thing to show off your wonderful athletic talent. After home work tonight, you will come directly to me, understand!"

I walked away and would not let her see the tears in my eyes. After home work, I went to her.

"Since you *so* like to show off your body strength," she said, "go and kneel in the middle of the dorm with your hands outstretched just like you were hanging on the cross. If this exercise was good enough for Jesus, it's good enough for you."

I knelt on the hard wooden floor for hours with my arms straight out at my sides. Every time my arms started to droop, Sister Regina would come up behind me and kick me in the back which would knock me on my face.

She would laugh and say, "Still think you're able to perform for a group of people."

After that night, gym class held no allure for me. Whatever natural abilities I had possessed became a burden. I watched the rest of my team perform their routine like a choreographed ballet. With every step, my heart sank a little lower.

I began to believe Sister Regina was right. I was not now nor would I ever be as good as the rest of the performers. Whatever the gym teacher, Mr. Nash, had seen in me no longer existed. All that I had left was a lot of shame and another shattered dream.

There were so many questions asked by the other kids about our lives.

Some, I do not think I would every consider asking another human being. When someone asks if you can come to their house on the weekend or can you join the debate team or volleyball team the answer was always a reluctant 'no'. I could live with that but not the more personal question about what is was like to live with the nuns.

What if I could tell them, my God, what would they say? What if they knew about the beatings, the torture, the humiliation? If just one time they were the ones to step on the so called 'orphan bus' they would know. If they could feel the ridicule and the scorn that we feel when other kids laugh at our clothes and our same lunch everyday if they had to rise at five AM every day and were forced to go to mass they might stop the insults. If they knew how much I wanted to scream out what was really happening up there what would they think? If they knew any of this, what would they think of me? I kept quiet, I knew better.

It took me some time to realize that the methods of discipline were changing. They had to. If people saw us constantly sporting bruises, someone might actually question their methods.

With my new found life came other changes. All the while telling us how wicked boys were, several of the high school girls went to dances about every three months to another orphanage called LaSalle Institute for Boys. After all this time, I finally found out that this is where all the boys magically disappeared to at ten or eleven years old. You had to jump through many hoops to have the luxury of attending these dances. You had to refrain from upsetting any of the nuns, you had to refrain from getting into any trouble in school, and you had to keep your possessions in military style order.

Usually two days before a dance, the nun in your dorm would come while you were in school and go through both your locker and the two-drawer night stand by your bed. If things were not lined up in a row neatly, the drawer was turned upside down on your bed when you came home. If your drawer was on the bed, you could not go to the dance. To add insult to injury, your personal items were confiscated at that time and placed in the nun's cell. This was a separate area in the dorm about 10 X 12 that contained a bed, chair and a locked door. The walls, however, only went up about eight feet leaving two or three feet from the end of the wall to the ceiling open so that the nun could hear what was being said and done at night.

The taking of personal items was cause for great dissension in the ranks. For each item that you wanted to retrieve from the large cardboard box in the nun's cell, you had to pay her five cents. The five cents came from the ten cents you got through the week for milk money. This money was then donated to their overseas orphanage to help the children who were *truly* needy and worthwhile.

On this particular occasion, it was almost Christmas and the excitement was palpable. On Wednesday of that week when we got home from school, we learned there was going to be a dance on Friday night. We all looked in confusion at one another. What? No overturned drawers on beds? We would soon know of an even crueler punishment in a very short time.

We went to bed thinking how all of us were going to this dance. Unbelievable! Our own little Christmas miracle! The next day we went into our lockers to choose something to wear for the dance and all of our decent and personal things were missing. Stockings which had a value equal to gold, skirts, blouses, and dresses provided by families and the only fashionable clothing around were gone. All gone! Sister Annunciata stood there gloating; a look of great satisfaction glowing on her face. Every one's spirits hit the ground. Great! We had a dance with nothing to wear. No one wanted to go. Mind you, we were not being told not to go, we just did not want to.

Who can say for sure when the human spirit breaks? There was power in numbers. We were all sitting in the junior/senior high hangout room and the anger and grumbles kept getting louder. Brave talk bounced back and forth about someday getting enough guts to stand up to the nuns. No time like the present I decided. So the great plan was hatched.

Linda was to fall down the stairs and make her acting debut. She was to make sure that she kept Sister Annunciata busy with her twisted and possibly broken ankle. The other girls were to let me stand on their shoulders and I would jump over the wall onto sister's bed, unlock the door and push the cardboard box with our belongings into the middle of the dorm floor. Every one would go as quickly as they could and take what belonged to them.

Oh the sweet smell of success! Everything in the box had disappeared. Oh happy day! When Annunciata returned and found the empty box, the steam started pouring from her ears. Her eyes slanted into hard beady marbles, her face grimacing and snarling like a rabid dog.

Most of the girls had already fled the room. There were a few of us left. She whirled around, her massive bulk looming larger, the heat from her face glowing fire ball red.

"Who took that box from my cell?" she screamed.

"I don't know sister, I just got here I have KP duty remember?" I said.

She pivoted from face to face glaring and searching each girl's eyes.

Broadway producers would have been proud. Each face in the dorm was a blank. Annunciata went back into her cell and slammed the door so hard I thought she broke the hinges.

Sister Annunciata came out of her cell when all of the girl's were back in the dorm, a triumphant look on her face. The perpetrator of this crime had left a clue. It seems on her pillowcase where my feet had landed, I had left a perfect shoe print. So Sister Annunciata of Scotland Yard was about to play detective. She had a whole tablet of blank white paper and one by one we all had to go up to her cell and step on the piece of paper. She would then compare the print to the pillowcase. God help the kid whose shoe print matched that pillowcase. Linda was in the front of the line and I was towards the back.

After she came out of the cell she came back to me and said, "quick, change shoes with me."

"Why?" I questioned.

I still was not aware of what Sister Annunciata was doing in her cell.

Linda said, "Just do it. Hurry up."

I knew better than to ask questions. I changed shoes with her. When it was my turn I stepped inside the cell where Sister Annunciata was kneeling on the floor. In front of her was a pad of white paper and on the side of her a pillowcase with a footprint.

"Put your foot on the paper," she growled.

I started to put my left foot forward.

"Not that one," she snapped, "the other one."

I pulled back my left foot and extended my right.

"Step firmly on the paper and then step back," she said.

I did as I was instructed and she then snatched the paper off the floor. She was carefully scrutinizing the paper against the pillowcase.

"It's a good thing for you that you weren't the stupid one," she stated. "Next," she screamed as I was summarily dismissed.

When I got downstairs to the cafeteria, Linda and I changed shoes again under the table. We thought we had pulled it off.

Lesson one - never be cocky in your success and; Lesson two – never show gratitude to someone who has helped you with a problem with the nuns.

We all went to the dance in appropriate clothing. I can not say it was all that great, but I had fun.

The junior high school dorm had a Christmas tree and each of us had to pick a name off that tree and wrap a present for the girl you chose. The present had to be one of our personal possessions and it had to mean something to you. According to the nuns, this was the only way to truly observe Christmas. The gifts we had to share were small things usually collected from a different party that some social club gave to the orphans. Nothing on the scale of the Behr-Manning party, but parties never the less.

One such party was the Allegheny-Ludlum Steel party. We usually got two or three small gifts. If they were not anything special, you were allowed to keep them. On this Christmas dorm party, I got more gifts than anyone else small things like Christmas pins, hair ribbons, shower caps, and lotion. It was enough to give away the fact that all the girls were grateful to me for rescuing their things from sister's cell.

When Sister Annunciata saw my pile she went crazy. First of all, she weighed about 300 plus pounds and she came steaming towards me and I almost shit my pants. She resembled a Brahma bull in a fight. She pushed me and I went flying backwards and landed on my ass. Next she jumped on top of me expelling all the air from my lungs. I started to see stars. She then grabbed my hair on both sides of my head. The first time I feel my head being slammed into the dorm floor I was pretty sure that I was going to die. She was sitting on top of me bouncing up and down. She kept slamming my head on the floor until I passed out. Once again, I ended up in the infirmary.

There are lumps all over the back of my head and it hurts to lie on the pillow. My rear, thighs, and legs are a solid mass of black and blues. I am in the infirmary for a week when it got to be two days before Christmas and Aunt Grace and Uncle Bill were coming for us. The bruises were now a light shade of green and yellow.

"You're going to have to be more careful," Sister Annunciata said as I was preparing to leave, "you just can't keep running and skipping down the stairs three at a time. Someday you'll be seriously hurt doing that."

Her snapping angry eyes bored into my face.

"Yes sister," I said and ran for the first floor when the sewing room phone rang and announced my family's arrival.

When we arrived at my Aunt's house, I was tired. I remember Aunt Grace asking me if I felt alright. Yes I said, just tired. During this visit, they did notice some bruises and I repeated the usual, I was running too quickly down the stairs and fell down. The next morning, Aunt Grace was helping me to comb my hair and I winced.

"What's wrong," she asked?

"Oh, it hurts when you comb my hair," I said.

She is more careful with the comb the second time and then she said it.

"Susie, where did you get those bumps?"
"Oh, when I fell down the stairs," I replied slowly with my heart about jack hammering out of my chest.

Annunciata had warned me about this. Oh God, why did I not just kept my mouth shut? Why did I have to say ouch? For the rest of the Christmas break, I tried to stay away from everybody tried not to step out of line, and tried to become invisible. We went back to school in January and I tried to be good. Really I did.

One day on my way back from KP duty alone, I went up the seldom used back stairs. On the landing of the first floor the maintenance man appeared. His name is Guy. I never liked the way that he looked at me. It gave me the creeps. I try to squeeze as far over on the stairwell as I can, it does not help.

He is standing so close to me that he is touching me. He put his hands on my shoulders.

"Hello girlie," he says to me. "Where are you going?"
"To the dorm," I said.
"You're a pretty little girl aren't you?" he smiled.
"No," I said, "no I'm not, I'm really very homely."

I dodged left and right trying to get away from him. It was no use. He was bigger and stronger than me.

"Get away," I said, "get away from me!"

He brought his mouth down on mine. It was disgusting. I squirmed and twisted trying to get away. He just pulled me closer. The next thing I knew, this man sticks his big ugly thick slobbering tongue into my mouth, so I bit him hard. He gave me a shove and sent me flying into the wall. Gasping for breath, I ran for my life.

Of all of the people in that orphanage, I had to run smack into Sister Regina. I was so hysterical that I did not even see her. I was crying and incoherent. Sister Regina grabbed me by the arm and dragged me into the sewing room.

"What is wrong with you girl?"
I stood there staring at her unable to speak.
She finally stood in front of me and screamed, "Tell me what's going on I said?"

"That man sister, that man, he grabbed me in the stairwell" I managed to spit out.

The look on her face changed instantly her face turned to a frozen mask of anger.

"What man?"

When I did not answer she grabbed me by the shoulders and started shaking me violently. All the while, I sob uncontrollably. She finally got so mad because I could not talk that she started slapping me across the face. She slapped and slapped and slapped until I fell down. Once on the floor she started kicking me, fury in her face. When my ribs are broken again, she yanked me to my feet.

"Now tell me what happened." She was screaming at me.

"Sister oh sister, that man, Guy he cornered me in the stairway. He grabbed me and stuck his tongue in my mouth."

She slapped my face again so hard that I flew across the room and landed on the floor.

"Don't ever let me hear you say such filthy lies again," she said. "Get out of my sight."

When I got up for school on Monday morning, I had a black eye and split lip.

"I do not know why you are so stupid that you can not keep from falling down those stairs," says Sister Regina as she hands me my two pennies for milk and I get on the school bus.

Everybody is staring at me in the halls. I have an English teacher by the name of Mrs. O'Grady. She had befriended me at the beginning of this school year. She has daughters, one of which was my age and she used to bring me her hand me downs which were usually better than anything else I owned.

When she saw my eye she took me outside the classroom. She looked me straight in the face and asked what happened.

"What do you mean?" I said.

"What happened to your face?"

"Oh that, I just fell down the stairs on Saturday," I tried to explain.

She looked at me and I knew that she knew.

"These stairs did not happen to be black and white did they?"

"Please, I begged, "don't, please I don't want to get into more trouble, please, please leave me alone."

As I turned to go back into the classroom, I saw that Mrs. O'Grady had tears in her eyes. At some point during the day, I was summoned to the Principal's office. When I went in, there stood Mrs. Hanrahan, the principal and Mrs. O'Grady. I started to shake. Oh God! What was I going to do? I was trapped like a rat. I lowered my eyes and just stared at the floor.

"Susan," Mrs. O'Grady said, "I want you to tell Mrs. Hanrahan what happened to your face."

"I fell down the stairs," I whispered.

"I can't hear you," the principal said.

"I fell down the stairs," I repeated.

Mrs. O'Grady said "listen Susan, if someone is hurting you we can help. We can keep you safe. We can stop it."

I started to laugh loudly. Did she know how absurd that sounded? Protect me from the nuns now **that** was funny.

"Really," I said. "I fell down the stairs but thank you anyway for thinking about my safety."

I left with the feeling that they knew I was lying, but as long as I did not tell I would be safe. When I got home it was not even half an hour before I was summoned to the sewing room. I ran and hid. I stayed in the closet in the small dorm off the sewing room. I hid in the woolen coats. The mothball smell was overpowering, however, it was not enough to make me come out of hiding. I stayed there. I heard different people calling my name the nuns, the older high school girls everyone was looking for me.

Time seemed to be drizzling by much like a misty rain. I waited for hours and finally fell asleep. My eyes were blinded by light. Staring straight into my face was Sister Regina. She was furious with me.

"What are you doing in here?"

"Nothing sister, nothing!"

"Do you know how many people are looking for you?"

Not only did I not know, I did not care. I started to shiver and cry.

Regina said, "Knock off the water works and stand up now!"

I raised slowly, my legs cramped from curling into a ball for hours. I was escorted into the sewing room. There must have been 10 nuns in there. Every eyeball in the place was on me. I scanned the room looking for even one sign of compassion from anyone nothing. I was prepared to die.

I dropped my eyes and just stood. It was amazing everyone except Sister Regina and I just filed out of the room. There was not even one word spoken. From the color of the sky I could tell it was late. I was hungry, scared, and tired.

"Go to the bathroom," Regina said.

I did and when I came out of the stall there she was.

She looked me up and down and said, "You've been nothing but a little troublemaker from the get-go. We have ways of bringing you little snots into line."

I spent the entire night kneeling on the hardwood floor in the dorm. I was in the middle of the dorm with my arms out, like I was hanging on the cross. Sister Regina went to bed and left me there. In the morning I was still there. I was cold and tired and woke up curled into a little ball still on the floor. I jumped up, got dressed and slid into line to go to morning mass.

I could not believe I had gotten away unscathed. That thought did not last long, it was coming.

After breakfast, as I was gathering my things for school, Sister Regina grabbed me from behind and pulled me back up to the small dorm off the sewing room.

"Well," she said, "since you can't be trusted and you don't know how to behave outside these walls, you'll be staying here for awhile." She opened up the closet door and said, "Get in."

I stared at her.

"For how long?" I asked.

"Until I say so," she replied.

She gave me a shove and slammed the door. I heard the lock click behind me and there I stayed. For an entire week I spent my days locked in the closet during the day and kneeling on the hardwood floor at night praying for God to end my wicked existence.

When I was finally allowed to back to school, I was a basket case. I jumped at every sound. I did not look anybody in the eyes. I sat through my classes but heard nothing. Everything about me at the time was mechanical. I ate little and was losing weight. When it came our weekend to go with Aunt Grace, and Uncle Bill they were told that I was sick in the infirmary and only June and Grace could go.

I was looking out of the third floor window crying and waiving trying to get his attention. I started screaming as his car drove out of sight. Sister Regina came after me. She took me to the sewing room, stuffed a sock in my mouth and tied another one around my head to keep me from pulling it out. She then tied my hands behind me and tied me into a chair which was behind the door. I spent the whole day tied to that chair.

I struggled continuously in my life day to day. Nothing that I accomplished that year was ever right. Sister Regina continued her damming ways to try and destroy my soul, as I continued to watch how normal children lived.

I prayed to God for the strength to go on in one breath, and looked for answers as to why I was so distraught in the next. I tried hard to learn what other children took for granted and refused to acknowledge the reality of my own existence. I do not know how I managed my classes but I passed and I was grateful for that.

The summer was different, we went to Aunt Grace's house about every three weeks and I was happy. Somewhere near the end of July, Aunt Grace dropped a bombshell. It seems my sister Grace was not very happy about her living arrangements. Aunt Grace decided to take her to live with them all the time. Our time would come as we got older she assured us.

My memory of the end of our visits is not very clear but there came a time when school started again and Aunt Grace and Uncle Bill disappeared from June's and my life. There are a lot of things about the fall of 1963 I can not remember clearly.

Something happened to me in early September that would nearly destroy me. In all my years of torture, beatings, and humiliation at the hands of these nuns, this was unthinkable the worst fear that each and every child lived with everyday in the holding cell of hell. When I would go to sleep at night I would hear the screams. When the lights went out, I would hear the pleadings. It was real I knew, but I could not put my finger on it. I had begun to slide into oblivion, the fear that I felt was painful. I had never in my life been so frightened. I was literally scared to death.

Everywhere I looked, any place I walked I was getting paranoid. I took to running down the halls after KP duty with my eyes shut. When I ran past that room, my heart beat so fast that I could not breathe. This was the room that I used to sneak into to steal books. Never again would I be able to enter this library. What I had witnessed there, in that room, was slowly driving me insane. I was afraid to close my eyes at night because of the nightmares. Since Aunt Grace and Uncle Bill were no longer around, there was no one to take notice.

I spent many weekend days hiding. Sometimes I hid in the coat closet, sometimes under the stairs next to the playroom. I spent a lot of time with Linda. She knew something was really wrong but I could not tell her what it was. I knew that if I gave voice to what I had seen, I would then have to admit that it happened.

I can remember lying in my bed crying at night. I would roll my head from side to side, the tears covering my pillow. I watched this play and repeat over and over. I went into the chapel and sat in the back by myself. The Virgin

Mary had granted me a novena once before when I was younger and this time I really was asking for a miracle.

"Please Blessed Mother, I will do anything. I'm only twelve years old, I want to live, please protect me. Make me a good girl. Make me be respectful to the nuns. Make me roll over and take it. Please take all my spirit as it only gets me into trouble. I swear on my life that I will never again offend you. I will listen when the nuns speak to me. I will not glare with hateful eyes. I will not wish these sisters dead. I will even become a nun if you want me to".

"Oh Blessed Mother please, I will be so good that I'll probably turn into a saint. I would like a place in heaven just not today before I have really had a chance to live."

I thought of every sin that I had ever committed and begged forgiveness for each and every one.

My pleas to the Virgin Mary were answered. The dreams were not as vivid. The screams were muffled and one day I woke up and I had forgotten what had so terrified me.

"Thank you Mother Mary, you have saved my life."

This horrible secret had the power to destroy me. It almost did.

As with everything evil, it strikes you at your most vulnerable.

I am no longer a child. The fears that kept it hidden no longer exist. The adult Susanne was able to remember it in 1995.

CHAPTER 7

Enough is Enough

One day after school had started, there was a notice posted in our dorm. There would be absolutely no straight skirts allowed. Anybody whose family had given them one was to turn it over to Sister Regina. I did not own one so it meant nothing to me. There was however, a great deal of screaming going on in the dorm from other high school girls.

This year I was finally a freshman. Wow! The ninth grade only four more years to go! Only four more years of insanity, I would graduate and would be let out of this children's prison.

My Uncle Earl was my godfather and a confirmed bachelor or so I thought. He came the weekend of my birthday and introduced me to his wife MaryAnn. They had a baby girl named Cheryl who was only about two months old. They lived in a tiny two bedroom trailer, but he would try to fill the void left by my Aunt Grace and Uncle Bill.

We went home with them for the weekend. On Saturday, Aunt MaryAnn took me shopping for my birthday. She went to Two Guys Department store and let me pick out my own blouse and skirt. I tried it on and twirled around. This was the very first outfit that I had picked out by myself. The blouse was white with small blue flowers and the skirt was aline Royal blue wool. I was as happy as I had ever been in my life. I thought I looked great.

I was so looking forward to going to school on Monday. I was going to Watervliet High School, with clothes that fit, and looking like everyone else did. Some dreams were just never meant to be I guess.

We went back on Sunday night with my new clothes in a paper bag. We were too old to be going to the candy store and we were so grateful to my Aunt and Uncle just for being there for us. After I put my new clothes into my locker, June and I went to the auditorium where the nuns were showing the movie *Pollyanna*.

It was a great Disney movie which embodied everything that I ever yearned for, family, friends and a happy ending. I could see a light at the end of my tunnel. Once you graduated from high school, you were set up in an apartment, given two hundred dollars and told get a job and were on your own now. That dream kept me going a long time.

On Monday morning, I put on my dream outfit and went to church. I do not remember the last time that I looked forward to going to school. My feet did not touch the floor all the way down to the chapel. I was not aware that the dream was about to turn into a nightmare.

After mass, when we began trooping into the dining room, Sister Regina appeared as though out of thin air. She wiggled her finger at me and said to come with her. I followed her up three flights of stairs, my blood running cold and my lungs taking in huge gulps of air. Into the sewing room we marched.

"Close the door," she said.

I moved as if my shoes were made of lead. What had I done this time? I turned around and she was glaring at me.

"Where did you get that skirt," she barked?

"It's a birthday present from my godfather," I managed to croak.

Regina spun on her heel and headed for the drawer in the sewing table. I was not holding my breath but I could not breathe. When she whirled around in her hands she has a very large pair of black scissors. She headed toward me with a most malicious smile on her face.

"You know that you are not allowed to own straight skirts here," she said.

"Oh Sister," I pleaded, "this is not a straight skirt, it is an Aline with a pleat that goes from the waist all the way to the bottom."

"No," she smiled, "I think that we really have to call this a straight skirt. As you know they are clearly forbidden."

All the while she was advancing on my position, and I did not know what to do or think. Surely, she was not going to stab and kill me because of my skirt. When she reached me she bent over with the scissors and cut my skirt right in half while it was still on me. She cut through the belt that was holding it on my hips. When it fell to the floor, she snatched it up and turned to the back and cut the skirt into two pieces. I started to scream.

"Shut up, Shut up, you filthy tramp!"

One slap sent me ass over tea kettle across the floor. My mouth was bleeding but I did not have any bruises on my face. Sister Regina left the room and returned shortly with a black straight sack dress with huge Kelly green flowers on it. She threw it at my face and screamed at me to put it on now.

"This dress is your best friend now. You will take if off after school every single day and put it back in your locker. Every morning for school you will put it back on. You will wear this dress to school every single day until I tell you to stop. Do you understand me?"

I was staring at her with so much hate that I thought she moved back a little bit. I put on the shapeless dress and stormed out of the sewing room, down to the school bus. The dress was way too big but that was not the worst thing I had been given to wear to school.

When I returned home, I hung it in my locker. The next day, I put it back on again. This went on every single school day for all of October, November and up to school break at Christmas time in December. I had endured so much taunting and insults from the other kids at school I do not think I can count that high.

Day in and day out I heard, "here she comes 'Susie Orphan'. God don't you own anything else. Do you ever take that dress off and wash it?" The taunts went on and on for months.

On the last day of school before the Christmas break as I was getting on the bus, a boy walked up to me and said, "I really hope Santa brings you a new dress for Christmas, that one is really ugly."

The laughter followed me on to the bus and I began to cry. I don't think I can remember ever being so mad. When I got off the bus I went straight upstairs to the locker room, took off that dress and ripped it apart. I gathered up the pieces and stormed down to the basement, walked into the boiler room, opened up the incinerator door and threw in the rags that had been the green and black dress.

When I went down to dinner, Sister Regina was in the hallway and said, "Bring me your dress after you get back upstairs."

I glared at her. If looks could kill she would have died on the spot. I stomped away from her and into the dining room, anger so fierce that I could not control it. Linda looked at my face and she knew something was very wrong.

"What" she said, "what."

I was not about to cry. This was the first time that my anger took precedence over my fear. I told her what I had done with the dress. At first she laughed. Then she asked if I had realized what you have done? I knew but I did not care.

When KP duty was over, I went back to my dorm. I did not go to Sister Regina. I went straight to my bed and crawled into it.

I prayed, "stay away from me you bitch, stay away."

She never came looking for me that night and I could have cared less. I knew it was only a matter of time before she came. For the first time in my life I did not feel fear, just anger. In the middle of the afternoon she appeared in the doorway of the hangout room for the high school girls.

She pointed her finger at me and growled "you".

The anger still had the top spot. The cruel remarks of the other kids the laughter, the boy who wished a new dress for me for Christmas all of these thoughts were exploding and going around and round in my head. I rose from the chair and followed her. When we reached the locker room, Sister Regina said to get my dress.

"I can't," I said "it is not here."

"What do you mean it is not here," she said "where is it?"

"It is gone," I said "and it will never come back."

"Where is it?" she screamed.

"Gone," I said, "just gone."

She slapped my face hard and I fell face forward into my locker.

"Get that dress and get it now."

"No, I won't," I said, "it's gone forever."

Sister Regina shoved me aside and started throwing things out of my locker. The dress was not there.

"Where," she screamed into my face, "where is your dress?"

"Some place where you'll never find it," I replied.

We stood facing each other, her in absolute fury and rage, me in absolute defiance.

"You have made a laughing stock of me for the last time," I said. "I don't care what you do to me. I will never wear that dress again."

POW!

The fist was in my face before I could blink, but still I had no fear. A mighty, burning, ferocious, hell bent anger took over. I snapped around to face her, my own fists were clenched. I shoved her so hard that she fell down. I started kicking at her. The look on her face was shock.

""No," I said, "no more. Don't you ever touch me again."

I left her staring at me in disbelief. She was still on the floor. I should have looked back but I did not. I had not quite gotten to the door when I was yanked backward off my feet by something wrapped around my throat. The nun's habit had a black leather belt that went around their waist and hung to the floor. Sister Regina's was curled around my throat. She pulled it tighter and tighter. I could not breathe. I was slapping and scratching and kicking. I did manage to bite one of her arms and she let go.

I whirled on her and began hitting back. I was in a fist fight with a nun. All her years of beating me were going around in my head. We were both on the floor. She was pulling my hair, slapping my head, screaming at me and I was hitting back. She was stronger and eventually got the upper hand. I started to curl into a ball on the floor. Still I was not crying. There were handfuls of my hair everywhere. There was blood from my nose and my mouth smeared on the floor. She reached down and grabbed my arm and twisted it behind my back. I heard my shoulder pop and dislocate while she was twisting my arm. She started kicking me in the side. My ribs broke again. I actually have bald spots on my head from her pulling my hair out of my scalp. I am a bloody mess but the beating continues.

I am sure that I am to hurt not to die and as I loose consciousness I am prepared to meet my maker. When I next open my eyes, it is Christmas day. There is a nun sitting on a chair next to my bed. When I blink my eyes she made the sign of the cross on herself, got up and left the room. Everything hurt; my head, my face, my jaw, my ribs, my shoulder, everything. I tried to move but it hurt too much. I lay there and now the tears started to flow. I remained there for almost three weeks.

When I finally did go back to school, kids were looking at me. There were still faint yellow bruises around my eyes but they were hardly noticeable. What they were staring at really were the bare patches of scalp on my head. There were at least six plainly visible bald spots. The excuse, I fell asleep with gum in my mouth and the nuns had to cut it out of my hair.

The anger in me was spilling over everywhere. I was disrespectful to the teachers. I swore at everybody. I just did not give a damn about anything or anybody. I began to make friends with the wrong crowd at school. I left the school campus at lunchtime and got on a motor cycle with Jimmy Whitehall and rode around with him. What was left of my hair freely flying in the wind.

I got into fist fights in school. Every time I heard the other kids making fun of the Orphans, I would walk up and punch them. I only weighed 80 pounds but I had a five hundred pound chip on each of my shoulders. I found myself in Mrs. Hanrahan's office a lot. I think that she knew why and she did not tell on me. I do not think the nuns ever knew what I was doing.

My Uncle Earl and Aunt MaryAnn came intermittently. They just did not have the room for us to come that often. I know our interruptions into their lives were a lot for them. Earl would have moved heaven and earth if he knew what was going on but it was engrained in me that if my family ever found out how many times that I had to be punished for my evil, sinful ways, they would most likely disown me.

No one ever explained to me why Aunt Grace and Uncle Bill had stopped taking us home. Sister Regina told me it was because I was so evil. I was garbage and they were embarrassed to death by me. I believed her and got even more depressed. At the end of the school year I barely managed to pass. I think I got a D average in every class. I did not care. What were they going to do, beat me?

I had learned a valuable lesson with that last beating. If you are going to go down, go down swinging. I would never again stand and let them do anything to me. I would fight back. I would kick and scream and slap and bite and spit and scratch. I would do everything in my power to physically hurt them just as much as they hurt me. My days as a punching bag were gone forever.

CHAPTER 8

The Beginning of the End

When school ended in June I was overwhelmed. I could not think about another endless summer with no chance of getting out of here for another two and a half months. Just the thought was extremely depressing. As it turns out, I need not have worried at all. The catastrophe that happened to me next caused me to think for the first time about ending my own life.

I was walking down the basement hallway after KP duty. I do not remember why but I was alone again. I turned at the boiler room to go up the stairs to my dorm. Before I put my foot on the first step, a hand grabbed me around my waist and the other hand clamped over my mouth. I was being dragged backwards into the boiler room. I knew it was a man he had a big hairy arm. I was kicking and trying to get away. He dragged me clear to the back of the second room. I had been in this room before with Sister Regina when she burned my new Easter shoes and I burned my dress. I was forced to the floor on my face. I started to scream as soon as the hand left my mouth.

"Shut Up. Shut Up. If you do not stop that screaming, I will pick you up and throw you into that incinerator and you will burn to death. No one will ever know where you went."

My blood ran cold and I just knew that I was in terrible trouble. I was lying on the floor, my face on the ground, my arms pinned behind my back. He tied them tight and I started to cry. He shoved a dirty white cloth into my mouth then he flipped me over on my back. I lay on the concrete floor looking at him. His eyes looked like glass and he was rubbing his hands together. He reached down and tried to pull off my underpants. I started kicking him. I got him good once and he stumbled backwards. I was scrambling trying to get to my knees but he was faster than me. His hands were not tied like mine. I saw him undoing his belt. He pulled it off and tied my feet together. Now I could not move at all.

This time he was successful in pulling down my underwear. The tears were spilling down my face crying in a strangled silence. "Oh God, please help me, what is he going to do?" He got down on all fours like a dog pulling up my dress and started sniffing on my crotch. I tried to wiggle to get away but this seemed to make him happy. He started licking me and all I could do was pray. As suddenly as it started, it stopped. I opened my eyes and he stood before me minus his pants and underwear. I had never seen a naked man before and I was horrified. He started stroking his penis and smiling at me. I shut my eyes again and lay there in silence. He grabbed me again and turned me onto my stomach. I was wiggling and thrashing but it did no good.

The shock of what he did then almost made my heart stop. He was trying to stick is penis into my behind. I bucked like a bronco trying to force him off me. I succeeded.

I twisted my head around trying to see what he was doing. He stood beside me with a broom in his hand. He dropped on top of me straddling my back the broom still in his hand. He was very heavy and I was having trouble breathing. The pain, the incredible pain! He took that broom handle and shoved it up my behind. The pain was equal to any of the beatings I had ever had there. He kept pushing and pulling it in and out.

Finally, he threw it down and turned over and lay on top of me. His groaning was loud in my ears. He shoved his penis into my behind and started pumping up and down like he was doing pushups. When I came to I was still on the ground but he was standing up. He pulled me to my feet. The belt was gone from my legs but the rag was still in my mouth and my hands were still tied behind my back, his pants were back on and he was doing up his belt. I was filthy dirty from being on the floor. He came at me again another white cloth in his hand. He rubbed it on my face and was trying to brush the dirt from my clothes.

He looked me straight in the eyes and said "I think you are going to have to die girly."

I began shaking my head violently back and forth trying to scream no. He looked at me and then at the incinerator. Back and forth, back and forth for what seemed like forever. He finally began to speak.

"If I let you go will you promise not to tell?"

I shook my head up and down. "Yes. Yes. Yes."

"Just remember girly, I can get you anytime. If you breathe one word of this, I will stuff you in that incinerator and no one will ever find you, okay."

I shook my head up and down again. He took a small black comb out of the back pocket of his pants and combed the front of my hair. Then he took off the gag and I spit the dirty rag out of my mouth. He combed the back of my hair and untied my hands.

"Git," he said, "and remember our bargain."

I crashed blindly out of the boiler room. By the time I got to the second floor I could no longer suppress the screams. Sister Regina met me at the double doors at the entrance to the girl's dorms. I was filthy dirty and screaming. She dragged me into the sewing room and slammed the door shut. The frosted glass on the door nearly shattered.

"Stop that. Stop it right now. What is wrong with you? Where have you been, you are filthy?"

I do not know why but I was suddenly absolutely calm. No sound was coming from me at all.

"Well she said tapping her foot on the floor, let's hear it."

What should I say? How could I say what just happened to me? Had she ever seen a naked man before? Did she know what they had in their pants? I sat on the floor and began to rock back and forth and then I laughed. I just kept laughing louder and louder. Was this that one thing that Sister Annunciata was talking about that boys wanted? I laughed harder and louder. Sister Regina led me to the infirmary and I remember the needle going into my arm.

When I was awake again, it was morning. I am in the infirmary but not the regular one. I am across the hall in a room by myself. I am in bed but still in the filthy clothing from last night. The night before unfolds instantly in front of me. Again, I hear the screaming in the distance. It sounds like it is a long way off. The nurse and Sister Regina appear in the doorway.

"Stop that. Stop that right now? Stop screaming."

It is then that I know the screaming is coming from me. I curl into the fetal position in the bed and rock, rock, rock-a-bye baby in the tree top. I am singing and the world goes away again. I do not know for sure how many days I stayed there. One morning the door flew open and Sister Regina stood there glaring.

"That is enough of this behavior," she said. "Get up out of that bed and go get some clean clothes."

She followed me to the locker room and threw some underwear and socks and slip at me.

"Come with me she ordered and we marched to the sewing room."

Regina closed the door and turned to confront me.

"Now," she said, "tell me what happened to you last week."

I stared at her. I was there a whole week and did not even know it. When the memories came flooding back, I started to shake.

"Stop it," she screamed. "Tell me what happened."

"That man, that man again."

"I told you before," she said "I will not listen to any more of your lies."

She picked up the broom from the corner and began to beat me on the back and the head. School is out so she can bruise me. There is no one to see it. She slams me all over my body, head, shoulders, stomach, and legs. I scrunch into a ball smaller and smaller until there is no more me.

The cold water is hitting me so hard in the shower that it stings. Sister Regina was standing there with the brown soap and the Lysol. I stood up like I was dead. I let her pour the Lysol all over me and shove it everywhere private. As far as I was concerned, I probably needed all of it. I was filthy and contaminated and I would never be clean or decent again. She became really incensed when I did not scream this time. No I was different now.

She slapped me in the face four or five times and kept yelling you filthy tramp, disgusting little tramp. Still I just smiled at her. Then I spoke.

"No matter what you do to me, there is not one thing that you can do or say that will change this. When my father or my Uncle comes to visit, I am going to tell. I will tell everything. You can kill me too, it does not matter, and I am going to tell."

Her eyes were little slits.

"Are you threatening me" she asked?

"No, just telling you. I will not be quiet anymore. The next person from my family that comes to visit, I will tell. You might keep me from seeing them a few times but you can not do it forever."

By this time I was screaming at her. "Do you hear me, I am telling."

She threw me a towel and said, "put your underwear on and follow me."

Down the hall into the small dorm off the sewing room we go.

The closet door opened and I am shoved inside. It is June and stifling hot in there but the lock clicks behind me. I pounded on the door for hours. My resolve was stronger than ever.

"I will tell, I will tell everyone who will listen and I will keep telling until someone hears."

I wished to God that I had told Mrs. O'Grady the truth. I wished I had told the principal, Mrs. Hanrahan. I wished that I had told all the kids in school when they asked and I had the chance. Sometime in the late afternoon, the door is flung open. There stands Sister Regina with a blouse and a very tiny pair of green shorts. I know I am little but these were probably meant for a four year old. More than that, shorts and pants were forbidden at the orphanage. Dresses or skirts were all we were allowed to have.

"Get out here," she said. "Now"!

As I stepped out she threw these clothes at me saying put them on.

"This is ridiculous I said these are baby pants."

"On" she said, "now."

I actually had to lie on the floor on my back to get them on. When I stood up I could neither breathe nor walk.

"Now," she said "we are going to see Reverend Mother Bernadette and you are going to show her what a little tramp you really are. If you repeat one word of your filthy garbage lies, I guarantee that you will not live through the night."

"Angie is Reverend Mother's personal secretary and Guy is her brother. He would never touch a little child. Your lies will be the death of you yet."

As I stood in front of Reverend Mother, I knew it would do no good to tell her anything. She was a nun and she did run this place. There was not a snowballs chance in hell that she would listen to what happened to me and know that it was the truth. Mother Mary Bernadette is looking me up and down with such a disgusted look on her face that it makes me cringe. She was scrutinizing me like a bug under a microscope. I stood there in defiance glaring back at her and I never said one word. She might be Reverend Mother but she too would not be able to keep me quiet. I was going to tell no matter what the consequences were.

I was definitely not prepared for what happened next. I was escorted to the play ground and out the side gate there stood the green station wagon. There was dead silence on the playground as I was led out to get into the car. I searched the crowd of faces for June but she was not there. There would be no chance to say good bye or give her a message to tell anybody who came to visit us. I was leaving and she was alone. What would happen to her now?

CHAPTER 9

Hidden in Disgrace

A shove from behind sent me stumbling into the back seat of the car. The door closed and it started to move. I was petrified with fear. Where were they taking me? I did not care though. If I died today, I could not be any worse off or so I thought. We drove for a long time some place out in the country. We finally pulled up to the front of some Iron Gate's Prison and I thought, I did not know that there were prisons for bad kids.

The station wagon pulled up a long driveway and stopped at a large green house. I have seen this house before I thought, but where. I was pulled out of the car and dragged up the front steps. When the door was opened from inside, I was shoved in. I remembered now, this is Cobb Memorial School for retarded children. I was pushed forward into the living room. The appearance of two nuns that I did not know startled me. In comes Sister Regina with a smug look on her face.

"This," she said "is your new home. Only retarded people live here and this is where you will spend the rest of your life. There will be no one to visit you here. As you can see through that window, not everyone here is a child. This is a place were retarded people live forever. Mother Bernadette and I have spoken to your father. We have assured him that you are mentally unbalanced. Very much like your mother and that you need to be confined here. This will protect other people as well as yourself from all of your disgusting delusions."

I was staring out that window. There were, indeed, grown women out there. This was how they intended to keep me from telling anyone. This was how they were going to get away with it. They told everyone that I was emotionally and mentally disturbed and a danger to myself and others.

I slumped to the floor and started to scream. Hands were pulling me up and dragging me out the door. Through the front door, across a lawn and up into a fairly new brick building we went. The door that we just went through closed behind me and I heard the click of the lock.

This was obviously a communal gathering place. There was a television set on and the room is full of retarded children. I recognized a lot of faces from St. Colman's. My mind was racing. So my father finally knew that I was a disgusting filthy girl. He was so ashamed of me that he decided it was better for me to exist in oblivion rather than acknowledge what had happened. Nothing that happened after the assault really surprised me. Here I was in a room full of retarded children and I would never see the outside world again.

I began to seriously consider ways of ending my life. I stood in one spot for about ten minutes. There was a rustling noise behind me and I jumped. The voice behind me said to follow them. I followed them down a hallway and watched as the nun unlocked a door.

"In," she said not in a mean way just matter-of-factly.

I walked into a room which held one bed and chair and a dresser. The nun said to turn around and I did.

"I know all about you," she said. "Every day you will get on your knees and ask God for his forgiveness of your mortal sins. This is not a free ride and you will be expected to earn your keep. You will rise at six and help with preparing breakfast for 'Our Holy Angels'. You will clean up the dining room, do the dishes, sweep the dining room floor and set up again for lunch. These same things will be done after lunch."

"After these things are done you will be escorted back here to the dorm. You will then begin your chores over here. Every bed that is wet will be washed down with Lysol and clean bedding put on. The rest of the beds are to be made neatly and the floor swept. On Thursday and Tuesday they will be mopped. You will then proceed to the bathrooms. They are to be cleaned including inside the toilet bowls everyday. When the children have gone to take their naps you will clean and dust the common room. You are not to talk to or touch any of my children. I will not have you contaminating them."

"When you have done these things you will report directly to me. Do you understand?"

"Yes, Sister," I said.

"You may begin now and do it right."

When I was done it was nearly 5:30 p.m. Sister unlocked the door and took me back to the dining room. I was led to a back corner and told to eat facing the wall.

"Do not even look at 'My Little Angels'" she warned.

When dinner was over, I had to collect all the dirty dishes, wash them, clean the tables and reset the table for breakfast. The floor had to be swept and moped. When I was done I was so tired. I went back to the kitchen. Sister pointed to the sink full of pots. I think it was somewhere around 10 PM when I was finally finished. Sister silently led me back to my bedroom.

"Go to the bathroom," she said.

I did and then she looked me directly in the eyes and said "it did not happen."

The door closed and locked without another word.

"It did too," I screamed at the retreating figure. "It did too."

Every single day for two and one-half months this same routine went on. I never learned the names of the sisters in all the time that I was there. The only words ever spoken to me during my sentence of solitary confinement was to do this or do that. Most importantly, every morning when sister came into the room and every night when she locked me in, she would look me in the eye and say "It did not happen" and everyday I would look her right back in the eye and say "It did too."

I was very tired at the end of each day however, I was not unhappy. There I was an unpaid slave but on the other hand no one was beating me on a weekly basis. The food was both recognizable and edible. If I was to be punished everyday for the rest of my life, this place was as good as any. By the last week of August or the first week of September, I had resigned myself to this life sentence. I wanted to have a decent relationship with the nuns.

They never screamed at me or hit me. True they treated me like I did not really exist, kind of like a working ghost. Still there was something to be said about the peace I now found in my life. I often wondered what would have happened to me if I had not opened my mouth this particular night. Sister was backing out looking at my face.

She said her usual "It did not happen."

"All right," I said "It did not happen."

The next morning after breakfast, sister came over and escorted me out the front door. My heart sank into my chest hitting a new low. There in the driveway was the green station wagon.

"Come along, she said "it is time for you to go back where you belong."

I ran the gambit of emotions; disbelief, joy, anger and the final one that settled on me, fear. If I just had said my usual "it did too" would this be happening now?

I thought I might die right here and now. I was going back to St. Colman's. The cruel irony of it being, that at first I did not want to be here and now I really did not want to leave. I stopped and looked at sister.

"I do not want to go," I said.

"Yes," she said, "you do, you really do."

The trip back was in absolute silence. My stomach was rebelling big time.

When we stopped and pulled up in the familiar circular driveway, I stepped out of the car and threw up. Welcome home I thought. Welcome home.

I trudged up to the third floor and to my dorm. When I went in I was told by Jackie that my bed had been assigned to someone else. I was not to be sleeping with decent girls anymore. I had this insane desire to slap that stupid grin right off her face. I went out to the locker room to retrieve my clothing. My locker has been emptied out. Every single thing I owned was gone. I started to laugh. An orphan among orphans for some reason I laughed until I cried.

After dinner I was assigned a new bed. I climbed under the covers and went immediately to sleep. Five a.m. came very early the next morning. Sister Annunciata saw me in the line and raised her eyebrows never saying a word just glaring at me. I followed the line down to chapel. My mind was a jumble of emotions. I liked it better at the retarded school. Nobody there judged me or acknowledged me in any way. Here I stood as if in a spotlight. All the girls were staring at me as if I were a disease. After breakfast I learned someone else had my KP duty and I was free to go. I followed my friend Linda outside.

"Come sit on the swings with me," she said. "Where have you been? What happened to you?"

I held up my hand, "no first what happened to my sister?"

"Oh my God you do not know do you?"

"What? Where is she," panic rising in my voice.

"She is gone. She left last week. I do not know where," Linda said. "About a week ago Sister Annunciata come and got her. She told June to pack all her things. Her father was coming and she was going home for good. She would not be returning."

I sat there on those swings frozen. First my Aunt Grace took Grace to live with her and now my father had taken June. I was totally alone in the world now. The feelings flooding me now were undeniably anger and hate. I would hate my father till the day I died. At last I understood I was a Throwaway Child.

The death of your body was one thing but the death of your spirit was painful beyond words. I sat like a stone absolutely quiet all morning long. At lunch time I could not even consider eating. I went back out to the playground into the blistering heat of the sun. I stood against the fence staring down the road. Sister Carmel's hand slapped hard on my shoulder.

"Come with me," she said.

I followed silently not knowing or caring where she was taking me. We went up the stairs into the locker room.

"Go," she said "get all of your things out of your locker."

I laughed uproariously.

"What things," I said. "They were all stolen. I have nothing."

As if she did not believe me she went to my locker. She turned to look at me, a blank stare on her face.

"Where are your things?"

"I do not have any thing," I said. "Not one single thing."

I was then taken to the shower room.

"Bathe," she said "this afternoon you will be leaving."

Oh good I thought I am going back to Cobb Memorial School. I really did not want to be here. At least at Cobb they did not beat you. I was surprised that the prospect of going back there pleased me.

When Sister Carmel brought me down to the front door, I stood there. Staring at me big as life stood my father.

"Come on," he said "we are going home."

He turned away and started walking out the door. Just like that, we are going home. Where the hell was home? I did not know this man at all and he was here to take me home. No one spoke during the ride home. He pulled the car up in front of a gray two story house, turned off the car and got out. I sat there and he turned around to look at me.

CHAPTER 10

Reunion

The door of the house flew open and June came tearing out. She threw her arms around me.

"Where have you been," she asked "I thought you died. Where did you go without me?"

"Nowhere special," I said and followed her into the house.

June practically dragged me up the stairs.

"Who lives downstairs," I asked.

"Oh dad's girlfriend Carolyn and her daughter Meg".

When I walked through the door, there was Grandma Julie sitting in the living room smiling at me. I ran over and hugged her. I had not seen her in over eight years. She looked the same to me maybe just a little older.

"You will be sharing a room with your sister," dad said. "Where are your things?"

"What things I said?"

"Your clothes, where are your clothes?"

"I do not have any," I said. "Somebody stole the few things I did have"

"Well share with your sister," he said. "You are both the same size."

Amazing, yesterday I was retarded, left in a school for retarded children. Today I was normal and living at home with my sister, father and grandmother. Absolutely amazing!

June dragged me to our bedroom a small room with a double bed and a dresser.

"We will be sharing the bed just like when we were little," she said.

She went to the dresser and tossed me some shorts and a shirt.

"Here, put these on."

For the first time I saw she was also wearing shorts.

"Are we allowed to wear these," I asked.

"Yes everyday if you want. It is great here and you will like it. Nobody screams at night, nobody hits you and you do not have to eat anything you do not like.

"I have been sleeping until about eight every morning. There is no mass every morning only on Sunday. "Isn't this great."

"Yeah," I said, "just great."

My father spent most of his time down stairs with his girlfriend. This was just fine with me. I was still unable to control my feeling or my facial expressions. The next day, we went shopping at J.M. Fields Department store. My father would point and the sales person took the clothes off the racks and brought them to the dressing room. I walked out with six brand new outfits plus underwear, socks and shoes. These were mine all mine, and when grandma washed them she gave them back to me. I could keep them forever.

School started and the relief that I felt was undeniable. There were no taunts about my clothes. Nobody here came on the *Orphan Bus*. There were no disgusting baloney sandwiches for lunch. I should have been sitting on top of the world. I should have been happy beyond compare but I was not. I was angry all the time.

The living conditions were better. However, my feeling toward my father remained the same. He never mentioned the abandonment or the retarded children's home placement ever. It was just as though it never happened.

I did alright in school nothing great. I was intelligent enough but I just was so overwhelmingly angry most of the time that I just could not concentrate.

Around October, I began to realize there was nothing to stop me from participating in after school activities, school football games or dances.

My father's girlfriend did not like me and I knew it. I did not really care. She had a daughter Meg about four or five months younger than I. I felt sorry for her. Her mother made her a freak.

The hairstyle in 1965 was long and straight parted down the middle like Mortica Adams. Poor Meg, about every three months her mother would drag her to the beauty shop and get her a big frizzy perm.

When she got on the school bus with me in the morning, I stayed as far away from her as I could get. I went to the public high school and she went to the Catholic high school. In the morning we both rode the same Fifth Avenue bus to school.

When you looked at Meg, you just had to laugh. She was made to wear uniforms, a blue plaid pleated skirt, white blouse, gray blazer and knee socks. When she would get on the bus with me, I would just move away from her and shake my head. She wore maroon colored knee sox up past her hemline. Her mother made sure that no knee was ever exposed. She had a bright flourescent thick orange headband around the front of her head. Her hair stood straight out behind the headband. The effect made her look like her hair was a giant tangled bush.

The kids on the bus sniggered and laughed. I would never take part in such cruel behavior I had had my turn in that spot. At the same time, I just could not be associated with her. The pain of that position was just too much for me to bear.

When the first school dance and pep rally came around, I was excited beyond words. I had decent clothing. I did not ride the orphan bus. I was in a new school. Nobody knew about my previous life. When I came home from school dad was downstairs in Carolyn's part of the house.

This was a very respectful arrangement. Carolyn and Meg lived in the downstairs flat and we lived in the upstairs flat. Still dad spent most of his time downstairs. I went down and knocked on the living room door. Meg opened it beaming at me.

"Come on in" she said. This was the first time I had ever been in there.

Dad was sitting at the kitchen table with Carolyn cups of coffee in hand and a cigarette curling in an ash tray beside each one of them. Carolyn looked me up and down a look of absolute dislike on her face. I began to feel the old gnawing in the pit of my stomach. I had met her a few times in my life. She always made me uncomfortable. She had a way of making you feel inferior. This was not a good feeling to foster in me.

"Dad," I said, "there is a school dance on Friday night. May I go please?"

He looked at Carolyn and she back at him.

"Well I don't know," he replied, "let me think about it."

"Okay," I said and walked away out the door and back upstairs.

Was this life really going to be any better? I am a sophomore in high school and have yet to go to any school extracurricular activities.

On Thursday night dad came into my room and said "Yes, you can go but you need to take Meg with you."

"Why," I asked, "she does not even go to my school."

"Carolyn thinks it is best," he said "and so do I. You do not really know anything about the outside world. Until you understand all the things that you need to learn, you need to bring Meg with you. She is a good girl and if you are with her I know you will not get into any trouble."

So here it was. I was going to be punished for the rest of my life for the assault. Somehow I must have done something bad to make that man do what he did to me. Somehow it was my fault. I was not a good girl and I could not be trusted.

There was irony in my dad's sentiments. He had trusted the nuns to teach me and keep me safe. However, in their care I was beaten, brutalized and raped. Where does any of this translate to being my fault?

"Never mind," I said "I don't really want to go any more."

"Your choice," my father said and walked away.

I cried into my pillow that night. When would things change? When was it my turn to be normal? I was not asking for the moon just a normal existence.

About two weeks after the dance, there was a football game at school. I asked dad if I could go.

"Sure," he said "just remember you have to take Meg."

"All right," I said, "all right."

On Saturday we walked the five blocks to the football field. As we started up the bleachers, Meg got a very tiny cut across her leg. She stared at the cut, a worried look on her face.

"Come on", she said "we have to go."

"Go where," I asked "we just got here."

"I have to go home right away I cut my leg."

I looked at her like she was crazy.

"Are you nuts?" I asked? "It is a little tiny cut about an eighth of an inch long. You can go home if you want but I am staying right here at the football game.

"I think you have to come," she replied.

"No way! I am staying."

She turned around, went down the bleachers and disappeared into the crowd. I stayed until the game was over. On the way home I thought what a strange girl Meg was running home like a baby for a very tiny scratch.

When I arrived back at home the house was strangely quiet. Where was everybody? I found my grandmother upstairs in the kitchen.

"Where is everybody" I asked?

"They took Meg to the hospital," she said.

"I do not understand," I said. "She had a very tiny cut on her leg. It was barely bleeding."

Grandma shrugged her shoulders. "I do not know why only that they went," she said.

I went to my bedroom, got my books and took them to the dinning room table and started my homework. A couple of hours later I heard the foot steps on the stairs and my father bellowing my name. As I moved toward the stairs I met my father. He looked like he was ready to kill.

"Downstairs right now," he shouted! "Why did you let poor Meg walk home alone," he screamed.

"As soon as we got there she wanted to go home. She got a little tiny scratch on the bleachers and she ran for home like she was a two year old."

"She could have bled to death," he yelled. "What is wrong with you?"

"You can not bleed to death from a scratch. We are not talking about a gash or a cut, were talking about a scratch."

My father led me into the living room. Meg laid on the couch her face dead white. Her leg raised on a pillow. I could see that the stitches went almost all the way around her leg. I was dumb founded.

"Where did that come from," I asked? "I swear to God she had a scratch a quarter inch long nothing more."

"Meg has a rare disease," Carolyn said. "Her skin is elastic. Anytime she gets a cut it just spreads across. She always has to have every single cut stitched. She could have bled to death today and it would all have been your fault."

"No one had ever said anything to me about Meg having some strange disease. How was I supposed to know?"

Carolyn looked at me with such a disgusting look on her face like I was stupid, ugly and evil all rolled into one. I fled the room and ran up the stairs.

"It is not my fault," I sobbed to my grandmother. "I did not know. If I was supposed to be watching her they should have told me."

Grandma nodded her head and I ran into my room slamming the door and I cried for hours. For the next month I lived a very strained existence. Dad barely acknowledged me. He spent most of his waking moments downstairs. I felt so guilty about what happened I could not even look at Meg.

At Thanksgiving we all had dinner downstairs. My brother Willie was in the US Marines and he came home on leave. He was tall and I barely recognized him. I had not seen him since the day they took him out that side gate at St. Colman's. Gone was the boy and in his place stood this young man. I did not know him any more. I stared straight at him for a long time. Finally he stepped forward and gave me a bear hug.

"How are you doing trouble maker?"

So the word had even reached him. I pulled away from him, walked to the table and sat down. It does not really matter I thought. I do not really care not anymore. He would never know about the beating I had suffered in my pathetic attempt to save his life. This was just one more thing to stuff into my simmering pot of injustice.

Christmas came and went. The only think I asked for was a pair of black corduroy jeans and I got them. I got other things too but this was the first time since the Wilson's disappearance that I got anything I asked for at Christmas.

Spring brought surprises that once again changed my life. A woman appeared at the front door one day and identified herself as my mother. She had a bag full of gifts in her hand. My father came down the stairs. His face showed the most anger I had ever seen. He pushed me aside, grabbed the bag and pushed it and the woman out the door slamming it behind him. He ranted and raved like a lunatic at this woman for a long time. When he came back inside, he marched me up the stairs. He yelled for June and summoned us both into our bedroom.

"Sit girls, I have to have a serious talk with you."

We both sat on the bed the tension in the air so thick you could cut it with a knife. He looked particularly at me.

"That women," he said "was your mother." I mean she gave birth to you but she was never really your mother! Did she come to see you all those years in the orphanage? No only once! Now that you are practically grown up she wants to be a part of your lives. This will never happen he stated emphatically. Never! She abandoned you as babies" he continued, "never once thinking about you. Now she wants to come back with gifts like nothing was ever wrong."

I was thinking what a hypocrite. He did exactly the same thing except for the little bit of monthly concern thrown in.

"I sent her and her guilt gifts away. Susan you know what she looks like. If you see her on the street you will ignore her. You will keep walking and not acknowledge her in any way. Understand?" he said?

I said "yes" but in my heart he was not any different from her. They both went on living their merry little lives without a thought to their children. I would find out years from now that they only reason he took us home was because the nuns wanted him to pay more money towards our care and he figured out it was cheaper to take us home.

CHAPTER 11

No Bed of Roses

I saw my mother on the streets many times. When she tried to speak to me each time I turned and walked away. I would not give her the time of day. When school ended I discovered the Knickerbacker pool. It was a public pool and you had to pay ten cents a day to use it. I had a babysitting job on Friday night with the Tobin family who lived next door. They had a whole passel of kids and that is where I made my spending money.

June and I spent the whole summer at that pool. Poor Meg rarely came with us. That mysterious skin condition also did not do well with sunlight either. I was developing compassion for Meg. Her life was no bed of roses either. Her mother was not any nicer to her than she was to me. Never once did I see her show any love to her daughter.

"Maybe I got it wrong," I thought. "Maybe parents did not really kiss and hug their children."

Then I remembered Aunt Grace and Uncle Bill. Their love for their children was readily apparent. There were generous amounts of praise and genuine concern for their well being.

"It was just me, and poor Meg," I thought.

June showed no sign that she was unhappy in any way. It was many years before I would know that she suffered from attachment disorder. All those years with no one to care about us had taken a toll on us that was beyond any measure.

That entire summer June and I hung out at the pool. We went home for dinner and came back afterward until the pool closed at 7:00 at night. I was relatively happy most of the time. I did not make any close friends because I was so different. All the girls in school knew each other forever. They shared stories of childhood, play dates, birthday parties, barbeques and picnics. I had nothing to share nothing or contribute to these conversations. I just did not fit the normal mold.

When school started again, I thought I knew enough about the world to go to school activities alone. It was, however, Carolyn's opinion that I still was not ready to be that grown up. I was a junior in high school and I could not go anywhere without my shadow. There was a dance coming up and I badly wanted to go but the Meg rule was still in place. I asked her if she wanted to go and she said yes. Permission was granted but dad and Carolyn were also going out. Carolyn looked at Meg and said you know the rules. She nodded and we both walked away smiling.

On Friday night after dad and Carolyn left, I looked Meg in the eye and said, "may we do something about your hair."

Her eyes lit up like a Christmas tree and she said, "Yes. Yes please!"

I went upstairs to get dressed and so did Meg. We were the same size and she picked something out of my closet.

"Okay let's start. Get the ironing board Meg."

We set it up and plugged in the Iron on high. She leaned down and laid her hair in sections on the board. We ironed her hair as straight as we would get it. We applied a little bit of mascara and a little cheek blush. Meg had beautiful almond shaped eyes. When she stepped back I looked at her, she was beautiful. For the first time in her life she looked normal like everyone else. She was looking in the mirror and smiled. When we put our coats on and went outside on the walk to the dance I do not think her feet touched the ground the whole way.

It was my school that the dance was at and a lot of boys wanted to know who the new girl was. Absolutely no one recognized Meg. She was having a ball and danced almost every dance. It seemed no time at all and the dance was over. I do not think that I had ever seen her so happy nor ever again. We walked home chattering the whole way. The plan was Meg would go upstairs with me. She would put on her own clothes, wash her face and go back downstairs. If it were not for bad luck, I would not have any luck at all.

Parking the car in front of the house were dad and Carolyn. Too late, they had already seen us. Carolyn stood in the middle of the sidewalk staring at Meg.

Dad said, "Well Meg don't you look nice."

Carolyn turned in rage.

"Look at her," she screamed, "just look what your daughter has done to my Meg."

We both ran for the front steps with dad and Carolyn sprinting fast behind. Meg ran into her apartment and I made a dash for the stairs her mother still shouting her litany of filthy language at me. Grandma Julie met me at the top of the stairs.

"What is all the racket," she asked.

"Trouble Gram, big trouble," and I hurried by her into my room.

In about two hours dad came up stairs and said, "you need to talk to Carolyn right now lets go."

I walked stoically down the stairs. I did not hear any more screaming. I assumed Meg was either dead or permanently confined to her room. Carolyn's gaze was so malicious that I involuntarily flinched.

"Sit," she pointed at a kitchen chair.

My father sat across from me. There were several minutes of complete silence.

"You are the devil," Carolyn stated. "I had my reservations about letting you come into my house. Against my better judgment I let your father bring you here. I am so sorry for that decision," she spat. "Imagine taking my daughter out in public looking like a filthy whore."

I blinked a couple of times. What the hell was she talking about? She was wearing some of my clothing all picked out by my father. We ironed her hair put a little color in her cheeks that is all. For Christ's sake we went to a school dance. We did not go to downtown River Street and stand on a street corner. Voicing my opinion was probably not the best idea right now but I could not help it. We had done nothing wrong. I lost my temper totally and completely. There was so much pent up anger in me that I exploded.

"You are a freakin' idiot," I screamed. "What the hell is wrong with you? Do you see what you're doing to your daughter? You're making her into a freak. Do you know kids point at her on the bus and laugh? Do you know that the other kids call her Maggie Aggie the Moron? You saw her tonight. The kids at the dance wanted to know who the new girl was. She's beautiful and you're destroying her. What gives you the right to make her feel so miserable about herself that she won't even go to any of her own school functions? You are a hateful, mean, nasty bitch and I hope your die!"

She smashed me across the face and then whirled around to face my father.

"Did you hear what she just said to me, did you hear it?"

My father sat there his face a mask of green. For the first time I looked at him and thought he looked pathetic. Carolyn faced me again.

"I told him you were trouble I told him from the beginning but did he listen to me, oh no! Just look what has happened. You bring my daughter home to me looking like a filthy slut. I warned him," she continued "you look just like your mother and you act like her. "She is a filthy whore and so are you!"

A surge of anger coursed through my body and I could contain it no longer. I raised my hand and in an instant I slapped her so hard she fell over.

She was staring at me from the floor. I hated her enough right then to kill her.

"Don't you ever, *ever* again speak of my mother with such disrespect! Who the hell do you think you are? Do you think I am stupid? Do you think I don't hear my father creeping back upstairs every night between three and four o'clock in the morning? Guess what! I am pretty sure that you are not down here playing patty cake with him. As far as I know my mother and father are still married. You are the one sleeping with a still married man. When you next look in the mirror, go ahead and scream whore. I guarantee you will be right on the mark."

I turned on my heel and stomped up the stairs. Both of them, him on the chair, she on the floor looked at me with their mouths hanging open. I stomped up the stairs as angry as I have ever been in my life. Grandma Julie was sitting in the dark in a chair by the window.

"Susie," she said quietly "come talk to me."

I sat on the sofa unable to stop the flow of tears that had begun to fall on the stairs.

"Tell Grandma what happened," she cooed softly.

I poured my heart out. I told her everything, everything that had happened to me for the past ten years. I heard her sniffling; she was sitting on the chair crying like a baby.

"I told Billy in the beginning he should have told you where he was taking you. I told him but he did not listen to me. Go to bed honey," grandma said, "things will be better in the morning."

I refused to go to mass on Sunday morning. Dad finally gave up and they all left without me. I still hadn't seen Meg all weekend and I was beginning to worry about her. Sunday evening after I went to bed, I heard my father's footsteps on the stairs un-characteristically early. I heard my grandmother call his name.

"Billy, I need to talk with you."

I heard him turn toward the living room. They spoke in hushed tones for a long time. I could not hear what they were saying however, I did hear the last bit of conversation.

"You know she is right Billy, you have young girls living with you now. You can not act in one way and expect them to act entirely in another."

I heard my father's steps again on the stairs. I put the pillow over my head and went to sleep. Meg was out on the corner for the bus on Monday morning. She looked alright but the bush was back on her head, her smile was gone and her spirit was missing once again. I felt sorrier for Meg than I did for myself.

I at least had a choice as to whether or not I saw Carolyn. She on the other hand did not.

CHAPTER 12

Good-Bye Grandmother

Coming home from school in the afternoon, when I started to get off the bus people were craning their necks out the window looking at something. When the bus doors opened and I stepped off the sight in front of me was indelibly etched into my brain forever. Bag and baggage, furniture, lamps, clothing, pots, pans and dishes everything my grandmother owned including herself were sitting on the middle of the side walk on fifth avenue.

Carolyn had purchased this house with a renter's insurance policy when her apartment burned down two years ago. She threw my almost sixty-five year old grandmother out into the street. My spineless, pansy-ass father let her do it. It did not matter that when his own marriage broke up that she lovingly took him in. She let him live with her no questions asked. She took care of him, cooked his meals, washed his clothes, made his bed for years and this was her thanks. He made her the laughing stock of the neighborhood.

The humiliation was painted in bright scarlet across her face. People going by pointed and laughed. For standing up to my father's mistress, she was homeless. The guilt from that is still with me today. I sat on the couch with her outside waiting for my Uncle Jimmy and Uncle Jack my father's brothers to come with a truck and get her.

I waited with her sitting on the sofa for about another hour. Uncle Jimmy and Uncle Jack came to pick up grandma and her things. Jimmy went up and knocked on the front door.

"Don't," grandma cried. "He's not there he went to work."

I saw the lace curtains part in the downstairs living room window and Carolyn's smiling face was revealed. The curtain dropped back into place. It was a good thing to. I thought that if I could have sprinted over there fast enough I would have grabbed her through the same window and strangled her.

When grandma and all of her things were gone, I turned and faced the house. The front door opened and there she stood in all her glory. My face must have conveyed my anger. She stepped back quickly. I walked up those stairs with murder on my mind. At least she had sense enough to go back into her apartment.

When I walked into our living room it was empty as was the dining room and kitchen. Not so much as a dish was left. Okay dad had gone to work and there's no grandma and no pots or pans, no way to cook. I went into my room and sat on my bed. My God, what a mess I had made. June came trudging up the stairs. She looked at me stupidly.

"Oh no, are we going back again," she asked.

"I'm not sure," I said.

June sat on the bed and cried into her hands. Meg came up stairs and knocked on the bedroom door.

"Mom says you guys have to come down for dinner."

"Where's Grandma," June asked?

"I don't know," Meg said "but mom's happy."

"Go on down June and tell her I am not hungry."

By Wednesday night I was really hungry. When Meg came upstairs and announced dinner I went down with June. Carolyn's cooking was a disaster. Not just because I hated her, but it genuinely was awful. June wrinkled her nose in disgust and I pushed mine around the plate.

After school the next day I went downstairs and offered to cook dinner. I generally did this about three times a week after that. Between canned soup and school lunch I was not starving. I watched other girls in school. I listened to conversations about their mothers. All my life I had been told your mother is sick. Never once did anyone ever hint about anything else. What she had said about my mother could not be true. It just could not. My father refused to discuss it.

His standard response was, "don't you think you've caused enough trouble already?"

The guilty arrow aimed and hit my heart every time. My grandmother was gone and it was my fault. If I had not told her she would not have spoken to my father and he would not have spoken to Carolyn. Grandma would not have been thrown out. My fault, all my fault! It began to fester inside of me. How much would it take to send me over the edge?

Thanksgiving came but Willie was not coming home. He had gone to Vietnam. Carolyn could not cook any better now than she did before. I did not really care. Everything tasted like cardboard, kind of like my life.

About a week before Christmas the doorbell rang. I opened the door and there stood two US Marine officers. My heart hit the floor and I started backing up.

"Dad," I yelled, "dad."

He came out of the living room. I think he heard the panic in my voice. He stared at the men. His face turned ghostly white.

"Mr. William Maloney Sr.?" one of the men asked.

Carolyn came out the living room door into the hall. When she saw the officers she turned on her heel and went back in closing the door.

"I regret to inform you that your son William D. Maloney Jr.—"

I put my hands over my ears and started shaking my head. Dad asked a few questions, shook hands with them and closed the door behind them when they left. I was sitting on the floor in the corner sobbing. My father walked right past me into the living room and went to comfort Carolyn. I do not know how long I stayed there in such a state of shock that I could not move. I think it was hours later when June came out into the hall.

"It's okay, sissy. He'll be okay. When he comes out of the hospital he'll be coming home."

I stared at her in disbelief. They do not put dead people in hospitals I told her. They send them home in a casket.

"Oh no," June said, "he's not dead just shot."

"What? What?"

"Dad says men came and told him Willie got shot and he's on a hospital ship. When he is better he is coming home."

Son of a bitch!

I stomped into the living room.

"What's wrong with my brother," I screamed?

My father turned to look at me.

"Calm down you were out there you heard what they said."

"I did not. I had my ears covered. I did not hear."

"He was wounded just wounded. He will be coming home after he gets out of the hospital."

I was raging inside. I had just spent hours crying for my brother and my father was in here with Carolyn not even bothering to check to see if I was alright. It was abundantly clear to me where my father's feelings were.

CHAPTER 13

Truth Revealed

I spent a lot of time brooding. My mother is a whore, God a whore. My father is playing house with the woman downstairs but my mother is a whore. Did my mother take money from men? Is that what made her different from Carolyn? I had to find out. I just had to.

I began walking up and down the streets every chance I got looking for her. I knew she lived somewhere in the neighborhood I just did not know which house. I needed answers badly. I could not stand it. I had to know what the difference was.

One day in April my chance came. There was a woman walking down the street pushing a baby carriage. I thought it looked like her from the back but no how could it be. This woman was pushing a baby carriage. Maybe it is her, maybe she's baby sitting.

I walked behind her just following to see where she went. Three blocks later she crossed to the other side of the street. I did not cross, I watched her from the corner. She went into the red house fourth one from the corner. She picked up the baby and went upstairs and came back empty handed and picked up the stroller. I could see her face clearly. It was definitely my mother.

A baby, my God where did she get a baby? My life was so sheltered the only thing I knew about sex was what had happened to me. If dad was living here with Carolyn, where did my mother get a baby?

I walked across the street and knocked on the door. She opened it and stared at me then she stepped aside and I walked in. There was a baby girl lying in a wooden playpen. She looked to be about six months old.

"Hello," she said, "remember me."

"Barely," I replied.

"Sit down and let's talk."

I raged and screamed at her. She just sat and listened. She never interrupted. She cried a little and laughed a little.

"I knew some day you would come looking for me," she said. "Of all the kids, I knew it would be you who came. You were the smartest and the most curious. You questioned everything and every body with you. There always had to be an explanation for everything."

I'd had been there a couple of hours and had not even realize it.

I stood up and said, "I have to go."

"Will you come back," she asked.

"Please, I need to sort some things out," I said.

I got up and walked out. She was not the devil incarnate as my father and Carolyn implied but I would need time to get to know her. I went back after school every day for weeks. We talked for hours. In a month I had all of the answers that I needed. My father was just as much to blame as my mother.

My mother admitted to being a very headstrong teenager. When she was younger the Great Depression was going on. Grandmother had eight children and momma was somewhere right in the middle. My grandfather worked on the railroad and Grandma opened a restaurant. The older kids worked with grandma and momma babysat for her younger siblings. She hated it and did not want to be tied down by the younger kids.

She met my father when she was fifteen. On the day that she turned sixteen she married him. By the time she was seventeen, she had Willie. At eighteen she had Grace and at twenty she had me and at twenty-one she had June. Twenty-one years old with four kids. My father's idea of a husband and father was to come home eat his dinner and read the paper. Under no circumstances was it his job to do a dish, change a diaper or do anything that was his wife's job.

It was also his right to have sex whenever he wanted it. Momma said after four children her body was not so curvy anymore and he began to criticize and complain about her shape. He would tell her she was fat and not very attractive any more. She said her world started to cave in around her. Dad took a second job and then he was never home. Four kids, no money, no breaks, no help all sent her into a depression. She finally went to the doctor and he prescribed diet pills otherwise known as amphetamines. On these pills she began to loose weight but the side effects were a problem. She was up for days on end and then she would sleep for days. Up, down, up, down, up down! My Aunt Grace and my grandmother Catman tried to help but it was no use. She was addicted.

She would lock the doors and they could not get in. My father lived in this mess in oblivion. He got up every morning stepping over dishes, toys, and dirty diapers and went out the front door and locked it behind him. He locked his drugged out wife and four hungry, dirty children in the house drove across the bridge into the city of Troy and ate his breakfast at the diner.

Eventually my grandmother got us out of the house through the dinning room window and took us to her house at the lake. My mother was sent to the Poughkeepsie State Mental Hospital. These were all the details that I could not remember before and it explained why we wound up at Grandma's house in the summer of 1957. When momma was released from the hospital, she came looking for us. That was the night that we spent at home with her for the last time.

Now I was really mad at that self-righteous bastard. When he was telling us the story of how my mother was never around for us as children, he knew full well that he had caused most of her problems. They were both responsible for the mess. I finally got around to my all important question. Was she a whore?

"Depends on how you look at it," she said, "I never took money if that is what you are asking."

"Well then," I asked what makes you a whore?"

She began to tell me about her sordid past. When my father took us away and put us in the orphanage, my mother was distraught. My grandmother tried to talk him into each of my aunts and uncles who were married taking in one child. My father was furious. Absolutely not he said. You can not guarantee me that she will not be able to see them. She must not ever be able to have any contact with them ever again. Grandma could not stop him, we were his children and he had the power to place us anywhere he wanted and he chose St. Colman's. He told mamma when she got out of the hospital that she would never see her children again. Momma felt so much guilt that she could not stand it.

She met a man who was nice to her and she moved in with him and she had a baby. After the baby, she gained weight again so she started the pills again. It was the same trap! When the addiction fried her again, the state came and took the baby. She went back to the mental hospital again. When she got out and the state would not give back her children, it would start again, another baby, more pills, more hospital stays, around and around. This baby she had now was number thirteen. I was horrified, thirteen kids, oh God. My head was turned around backwards. Neither of them was any better than the other as far as I was concerned but at least my mother was honest with me about it.

Around the first of May all hell broke loose. I was leaving my mother's house and Carolyn was driving down the street and saw me. Oh Lord, I thought the roof was going to come off the house. By the time I got home Carolyn was already there. My father was standing there shaking his head at me. Carolyn was screaming and yelling about sluts and whores. I walked right up into her face and started screaming to shut up.

"Don't you dare say one more thing about my mother. You have only his version and I have both sides." I whirled around to him shouting, "You pompous, arrogant little bastard. Who the hell do you think you are? You are just as much to blame as she is! I hate you, I am leaving this house now and don't you dare try to stop me. I am sure all your little buddies at the police station would like to hear the real story of what goes on here. I bet they would love to hear about your nice respectable little arrangement here and all the rest of the crap that you've been shoveling into people for ten years."

I walked up the stairs, put my clothes in a garbage bag and walked away. Never once did I speak to my father again.

I wish that I could say that life with momma was any better, however, that would be a lie. The pattern was so ingrained in my mother. She had begun her decent into drugs again and I was powerless to stop her. Everyday before I went to school I fed and changed the baby and put her in the playpen with toys. I came home for lunch and did the same thing. After school I would race home and take care of Gidget.

School was almost over. It made me nervous to go and leave the baby like that but I had to get an education for without one I was going no where and I knew that. In the last week of school, disaster struck. I was walking up the street to our apartment and there was smoke billowing out of our window. Oh God, a fire. Gidget was in there and the house was on fire. I raced up the stairs two at a time threw the door open and heard Gidget crying.

The place was full of smoke but I did not see any flames. I picked up the baby and started opening windows. It was the iron. Momma had gotten up in a stooper, and started to iron Gidget's dress. She passed back out on the sofa but she left the iron down on the dress. I was shaking with fear and Gidget could have died. It would have been my fault. I was the one who left her here alone with momma. I skipped the last three days of school.

The summer was a very strange one for me. I was a welfare case. Even now a normal life was not possible. I spent the entire summer taking are of Gidget and momma. As summer was coming to an end, I had some very heavy duty decisions to make. If I did not graduate, I did not have a prayer for a decent life. I was too young and inexperienced to make these kinds of decisions. I called my grandmother.

"Gram what should I do? Call the welfare office and they'll come get the baby. What will happen to her," I asked?

"A foster home or maybe St. Joseph's Home for Infants is where she will go," she said.

Oh God a life just like mine. I was unable to stop it in any way. Could I do this? Would I walk away and leave her to fend for herself. What kind of person did that make me? I spent a week ripped in half. I was job hunting. I tried in every way to think of a safe situation for Gidget. When you only fifteen, there just are not many options.

CHAPTER 14

The Best Year of My Life

My mothers' younger brother Ronnie came to get me. He was living in Newburgh. So was my Aunt Grace and Uncle Bill and my mothers' younger sister Alice Jean. Come with me for the weekend he said. Just to think about things.

While I was there one hundred miles from momma, the welfare department came and took the baby and momma took her usual trip to the state mental hospital. Uncle Ronnie did not have room for me to stay there neither did Grace and Bill. Alice Jean and her husband had six kids in a three bedroom trailer. Alice Jean's husband was in the air force stationed there in Newburgh. He was gone on TDY (tour of duty) for three months at a time. I approached her with an offer. If she let me stay with her through my last year of high school, I would work for her. I promised to clean the house, which I was obviously very good at. I would cook, do the dishes, the laundry and watch all the kids for free. I would do everything she asked for a chance to live with her and complete high school. She very quickly said yes.

Later in life, I would come to understand how very lonely she would become when Uncle Al was gone for months at a time. The responsibility for so many children was a daunting one for both myself and her.

Alice Jean took her credit cards and me to the mall for school clothes. I did not know that they lived so close to the line, but still she bought me school clothes. High school here was very different. I had the normal life that I had always dreamed about. I joined the cheerleading squad. I made friends and I started dating.

"So this is what it was like to be normal," I thought.

My grades went up to A's and B's. I will remember that year always. I worked hard for my Aunt and she appreciated it. Just to have someone say thank you to me was enough to make me cry. I was almost sorry to see school end. Just before school ended, I found out that I was awarded a New York State Scholarship which I could use at any state college. This was a possibility that I had never even considered.

The idea, now that it was presented, was a very good one for me. After graduation I got a summer job and planned my future. Apparently, other people had seen potential in me that I was unaware I possessed. At the end of August, I boarded a Greyhound bus and headed back to Troy, NY.

I was not at all sure that I had the brainpower to attend college so I decided to get a job and monitor some classes at Russell Sage College for Women. I could do this I knew I could. I worked for New York Telephone Company and lived at the downtown Y.W.C.A. Life was good and I was happy. I dated occasionally nothing serious. I had a plan and every intention of being successful. Life was smooth. I went along my merry way going to school and working full time and it was what I wanted. It was too good to last though.

One day around Thanksgiving, I was downtown shopping for a winter coat. Just ahead of me walking down the street pushing a stroller was a familiar sight. It was momma. I raced up behind her expecting to see Gidget. Surprise, this was a little baby. Oh shit, number fourteen. I was in shock but momma was happy to see me. I gave her a dirty look and she asked me not to be mad.

"Please don't judge me. You left, I had no one to help, I could not do it alone."

The baby started to cry. I picked it up. His name was Bruce. Blue eyes and clenched fists stared up at me. You poor little boy I thought, you do not have a chance. How many times would you need those little clenched fists in your lifetime? We walked two blocks together to a restaurant and had coffee.

"Momma," I said, "you're alone again with another baby. Don't you ever learn? You had no right to bring another child into this world. Look at the mess you've made of all you children's lives.

"I can do it if you would only help me," she said.

I just turned eighteen last month momma, that's not my job. I am going to school and I work full time. I am going to make my life count for something momma. Don't you understand it's my turn to live?"

Big tears were coursing down her face and Bruce started to cry. My resolve slid away with momma's tears. She looked from Bruce to me so I picked him up caught up now in my heart trap. Only ten pounds or so but he pulled at me with the force of a grown man. I took her address and wrote it down. I promised to come for Thanksgiving dinner. I went and spent a lot of time trying to see if there were any changes in her. Bruce grew to know me quickly, too quickly.

It was not long before he looked to me instead of her. There were little telltale signs that everything was not okay.

Finally one day in January the roof fell in. I knocked on mommas' apartment door. No answer but I could hear Bruce screaming. She had given me a key in case I ever needed to get in she had said. I opened the door and walked into the mess. Déjà vu! Here we were full circle again.

I went into the bedroom. I could hear Bruce screaming but his crib was empty. Where is he? Oh sweet Jesus where is he. I finally found him hanging upside down between the wall and mommas' bed. She had gotten up in the middle of the night and put him in bed with her. He had slid down between the bed and the wall. God only knew how long he had been hanging there.

I fished him out and checked him all over, changed and fed him. What the hell was I supposed to do now? Bruce was laughing and slapping at me. Too late I realized this child had bonded with me and vise versa. I felt the noose begin to tighten around my neck. I was not going to be able to let the welfare department take this child. Choices would have to be made. If just one time, I could make a decision without having it affect another child. Could I bask in the glory of selfishness for an hour? The stone was already cast. There was no way out for me, I moved in with momma.

I searched the apartment for her stash of pills I knew that they had to be here somewhere and after two days I found them. In a two pound coffee can full to the top, were glistening white pills with green sparkles. This had to be them. In the bottom was a note from the doctor.

I called his office. At first he pretended not to know my mother or anything about the pills. I was enraged.

"I have your note to my mother," I stated.

Sleeping with my mother in exchange for diet pills was disgusting not to mention highly illegal and a breach of his professional ethics.

"If you so much as give her one more pill, I swear to God I'll bring this note to the police and then the newspapers," I told him. "Your behavior is criminal. I'm living with my mother now," I said, "and I am not a child anymore. I understand what is going on here and I will expose you for the leach and sleaze that you are."

By this point I was screaming at him on the phone and I hung up shaking in anger. He was a professional man and he was luring my mother into a drugged out stupor and sleeping with her. Apparently, St. Colman's did not have the market cornered on disgraceful, deceitful, disgusting people.

I hired a woman to watch Bruce for me during the day. I worked at night trusting and hoping that momma would be okay with him at night. Working full-time and going to school, being responsible for my mother and my brother was too much. Something had to go. The idea of giving up my dream of a college education hurt but really there clearly was not any other choice. I let the scholarship go.

I worked hard at making my choice work. I watched momma like a hawk. By Bruce's first birthday, momma had finally been drug free for six months. For the first time in twenty-one years she was a mother again in every sense of the word. She cared for Bruce and loved him. I was happy for both of them. I had given up my dream to early it seemed. If only I had been able to hold out for another six months. Hindsight was always 20-20. Momma was okay and so was Bruce. I had no more scholarship, however, financially college to me now was out of my reach. A deep depression slid over me and I created my own path to hell.

CHAPTER 15

My Fall From Grace

Eighteen was the legal drinking age in New York State. I no longer felt a need to be responsible for anyone. I switched my work schedule to days. This left long lonely nights. I began to join my coworkers after work in an area of downtown called the strip. My favorite place along this street was Peter's Club Morocco. I found drowning my life in alcohol made all of the pain go away. I drank myself stupid every weekend.

One Friday night I had a date so after work I stopped at a sandwich shop to get something to go. I asked the man to hurry because my bus was coming and I had a date. I had already stood this man up before so I knew that if I was not there at my apartment when be came he would assume that I was standing him up again. The guy behind the counter was a real jackass. When I asked him to hurry he just went slower. If I had not already paid for my sandwich, I would have left without it. I looked out the window of the restaurant watching for my bus and then watched him. He also occasionally looked out at the street. The bus pulled up to the corner. Please mister, that's my bus I said.

"Okay, okay," he said.

The bus started to pull away quickly. There was no one else standing at the bus stop. Oh for Christ's sake, the man turned around and smiled at me.

"Oh, you mean that bus that just left, that was your bus?"

I glared at him.

"Thanks a lot I said, thanks a lot."

"I'm sorry lady, does this mean you lost your date?"

"Very funny," I said. "It was not that I really like the guy I was going out with it was just a date. I really just wanted to go out and have some fun. The guy behind the counter started to speak.

"I'm sorry lady really. Let me make it up to you, I'm off in an hour. Let me drive you home."

"I'm not going home anymore," I said. "I guess I'll just walk the couple of blocks over to the strip. All my friends from work were already over there."

I stormed out of the restaurant into the night. About two hours into the evening the man from the restaurant came up and sat next to me at the bar.

"Can I buy you a drink," he asked?

"Drop dead," I replied and moved to the back of the bar.

My friend Christine came back after a while and said, "See that gorgeous guy with the black hair at the bar, he wants to know who you are."

"Forget it," I said, "the guy's a creep."

"Well if you're not interested, I am," she said.

"Go ahead, if you want to," I said, "but the guy's a jerk."

So back she went to the bar. It was not long before I saw the two of them drinks in hand coming toward me. By this time I had drunk enough Black Russians not to care. We partied into the night and I got very dunk. I was wasted enough to let him and Chris drive me home. After that, it seemed that every time I went to the Club on the weekend, this guy was there. I would drink myself into oblivion and he would drive me home. It did not take long for Chris to disappear into the back-ground.

I did not care about this guy one way or the other and he knew it. One Friday night I got so drunk that I passed out on the bathroom floor of the Club. My drinking was seriously out of control. If, I had been a bit more worldly, I would have known better than to trust this man. He took me home and started taking off my clothes. I was drunk and I passed out again. I came to with the guy on top of me but it was too late. He had taken advantage of me in the worst possible way. In the morning, I was filled with a dreadful shame.

I was now the same as momma. I had allowed a man to do things to me that should have been saved for marriage. I was now truly a spoiled woman, second rate and dammed to hell for eternity. Paul did not seem to have any conscience at all. I had already done that with him so what difference did it make if we did it again. He was right, the damage was done. I never associated pleasure with sex and this was not any different. I also did not know anything about birth control and on my nineteenth birthday I became pregnant. The repercussions were disastrous.

My grandmother and mother went nuts. Shame on you a good catholic girl pregnant and unmarried.

"This can't happen," grandma said, "you have to marry him."

"Oh no, Gram, never, I don't love him in any way. I can't have this baby and give it up for adoption either."

This is a fine kettle of fish. First stupid, then irresponsible, then pregnant, not a pretty picture for only nineteen. What was I going to do? The pressure from my family was overwhelming. I did not have any choice with both my grandmother and my mother never letting up.

"You have to marry him, you have too."

They were right. I had no right to bring a child into the world as a little bastard so on December 13, 1969 I married Paul. I would, however, never again be out of control. Alcohol had gotten me into the mess and I would never drink again. Paul on the other hand remained a party boy. The whole time that I was pregnant, every night, after work he headed for the bars. He would come home smelling of booze and cheap perfume when the bars closed at 2:00 a.m.

So many things to remember and so much pain revolved around my childhood that I wanted to forget it all. I would occasionally talk of that time in my life but not often and never without severe emotional pains. During my first marriage, I did tell my husband about some of the abuse. He would never believe me. He always said "catholic nuns would never do things like that." The marriage was a disaster and because my son has asked me not to write about that period of my life, I will honor his wishes.

We divorced in 1983.

PART TWO

The Treasure Box

On darkest nights of deepest woes
Of tales as yet unsung
There comes to me a different voice
A child's voice very young.

She looks at me with saddened eyes
In her hand she holds a box
But when I try to look within
Something makes me stop.

My treasure box says the child
For in it lays my life
But please you mustn't open it
It must not see the light.

What secrets must this young child hide
That make her cry in the night
I know this box I know it's use
This box holds memories of child abuse.

No matter where you run or hide
The box is always locked inside
If anyone else hears this voice
Try your best to listen
Remember every treasure box does not
Hold things that glisten.

By Susanne Robertson
Published March 1996

CHAPTER 16

The Treasure Box

There are so many scattered memories associated with my childhood besides the things that personally happened to me. There was a young lady named Jenny. This poor girl could never stop wetting the bed. Every single day I would watch and listen. You could hear the screams start at the beginning of the Dormitory as each bed wetter suffered her own fate. Jenny was in my section and she would begin to cry as soon as her feet would hit the floor. Sister Regina would appear at her bedside and Jenny would start to shake. Regina would bend over and pick her up by the hair. Jenny would scream and Regina would push her face into the wet, nasty bed. Her whole head would be dragged across and pushed back and forth face first in the urine.

She was then picked up by her hair and flung across the floor. Regina would begin to kick this little tiny girl who was curled up in a ball. She would kick her five or six times, all the while this little girl would be screaming. Sister would pull the sheets off the bed, wrap them around her neck and head like a turban and drag her down to the supply room at the end of the hall. Jenny had to stand up unwrap the pissy sheets from her face and neck and throw them into the laundry cart. Regina would then hand her a cloth and a bottle of Lysol. She would kick Jenny in the back and send her flying on her face. She continued with her kicking as Jenny scrambled to her feet to try to get back to her bed to wash it down.

Some other memories included hair cuts. You did not have any choice in the matter until you got to the junior high school age. Every other month by groups in your class grade, Sister Delores had you come up and she would cut your hair. It always looked like she put a bowl on your head. No matter what, you were not allowed to keep your hair. I saw children crying and begging please don't cut my hair, please. It never mattered. The more you cried the shorter it got. I remember one time, I had no bangs left at all and my hair was as short as a boys. I cried for weeks. I learned very early on not to cry when I was forced to get a hair cut.

This is the memory of my younger sister Michelle about hair cuts. "When I first went to St. Colman's I was four years old. I was told that I had older brothers and sisters at the home. I remember someone pointing them out to me but I must honestly say I did not ever remember seeing them before. I came from St. Joseph's Infant Home in Troy. I saw these same relatives when my father came once a month to visit me. I was there about two weeks and one afternoon, a nun, Sister Delores, came into the playroom and the kids just went straight into two lines. I got into a line also.

Some of the girls were crying and I did not know why. All of a sudden my older sister came flying up behind me and grabbed my by the arm. She dragged me out of the line and took off running with me. Sister Regina pursued both of us. When she caught up with me, my sister and Regina had a tug of war with my body. Sis was on one side of me and Regina on the other. I thought I might be ripped in half. I heard my sister screaming "no, no, my father said no".

Sister Loretta came up behind my sister and started beating her with a stick and she let go of my arm quickly I fell on my butt. I covered my eyes and cried. I did not want to see the blood that was flying everywhere all over the floor. I was dragged to the head of the line and lo and behold there is Sister Delores cutting off children's hair.

I had two braids that went down to my waist. I was scooped up onto the stool and Sister Delores did not even take out the rubber bands. She cut off both of my braids and they fell on the floor. I was scared to death. I saw them fall onto the floor and I just thought that was so funny to see them there all by themselves.

Next thing I know I hear the buzzing sound behind me. I jumped because the noise scared me. Then the pressure was on the back of my neck. Sister took her hand and shoved my head down into my chest. The feeling on the back of neck was weird. She worked for a while longer on my head and then pushed me off the stool.

My sister was dragged kicking and screaming up next. She would not sit in the chair so Sister Regina sat on top of her on the floor. I heard the funny buzzing sound again and saw my sister kicking and screaming. The blood was everywhere. When Regina got off my sister, I started to cry. There she was, that girl who was my sister, only she did not have any hair left.

Her head was shaved almost bald. I put my hand up on my head and realized that I was also bald. Sister Regina kicked my sister in the ass one last time as we left the room. When I did finally get a look in the mirror, I cried a lot. I went from waist length hair to looking like a bald monkey in a matter of minutes.

Even though my sister is in her fifties, she still wears her hair almost to her waist. My sis – ever the defiant one!"

There were a very few girls who's parents wrote a note and made very plain to the nuns that they were not to touch their girls hair with a pair of scissors. One of these girls had long blond hair to her waist. She was the envy of most of the other girls. I don't recall this girl's name. She was much older than me. She had been abused one day to the point that she ran away. When the nuns caught her running down the road, they dragged her back kicking and screaming.

When she finally reappeared that evening in the cafeteria every voice rang silent. She was led to the center of the room and stood in front of us for all to see. She was bald. The nuns shaved her head. Let this be a lesson to each and everyone of you the nun said. For running away they cut off all of the young girl's hair. I don't remember anyone laughing, not one sound. We all looked into our plates and began eating again.

They were all powerful, they could do anything they wanted with you and there was nowhere to turn. There was no one who would save you. The excuse her parents received from the nuns was "Oh she had head lice so bad that we had to shave her head." I wondered if the parents were blind. Did they not know that head lice are highly contagious? Why weren't any other girls head shaved?

Some parents just buried their head in the sand. I can't believe with all the beatings going on and all the bruises that kids had that absolutely nobody said one word about it. "Discipline by the catholic nuns was an accepted practice" but did they know about the torture and humiliation? Most likely not!

Sister Regina had warned me many times. Just one word to my family about how very many times I had to be disciplined, about how disgusting and stupid I really was or if they even thought about the terrible things that I did that I would be completely disowned. A new threat started about junior high. "If you don't behave, there is another place where we can send you, St. Anne's prison for children."

This place according to the nuns was so much worse than St. Colman's. Every time we began to show any kind of backbone, some inkling that we weren't going to submit to any more of their insanity, this was the threat paraded in front of us. St. Anne's had bars on the windows and prison guards with bilyclubs. You could never go outside. There were no visitors allowed ever. "If you thought you have it bad here, just think about being there."

Up until the early 1960's, a lot of people were advised by their doctor's to place their severely retarded children into institutions. Many people did this absolutely unaware of the things that were happening to them. The attorney for the orphanage had a son in St. Colman's. His name was Michael. He was a handsome young man by anyone's account with gorgeous blond curly hair and startling blue eyes. I think he may have been autistic. This attorney was and still is a very staunch supporter of St. Colman's. I wish with my whole heart and soul that I could talk with this man. The faith that he placed in these nuns to care for his son was sadly mistaken. I never in all of the years that I was there saw Michael treated with any dignity, kindness, love or respect. I felt so sorry for him. Michael was a child who could never be still.

One of Sister Loretta's unbreakable rules was absolute silence and military style marching in two straight down to the dining room for dinner. Michael had a very large two-toned teddy bear which he always carried under his right arm. It went everywhere with him. On these evening marches, Michael would break out of the line and begin galloping down the hall with this teddy bear under his arm. With his other hand he would slap his thigh as he ran. It drove Sister Loretta nuts.

She frequently would run up behind Michael and grab him by the back of his shirt. She would try to make him stay in the line. When he could not do it she would grab his bear away from him. When he would try to grab his bear back, sister would shake her head no and point for Michael to get into the line. He would reach and reach and sister would slap him hard in the face, shake her head no and point to the line. This would go on all the way from the playground to the dinning room. Slap, grab, slap, grab, poor Michael just did not understand.

Finally on one such occasion, Michael managed to grab onto the bear and yank it back out of Sister Loretta's hand. The consequences for Michael were catastrophic. Loretta became so incensed that she chased Michael right to the end of the hall and grabbed the bear back. She stood in front of him and began to tear it apart. She ripped off his ears and poked a hole into the middle seam in the back. She then proceeded to pull out the stuffing and finally the head was ripped off. This great, huge bear was decimated, ripped into a hundred pieces. Great fat tears began rolling down Michael's cheeks. The startling crystal blue eyes that should have seen only kindness and comfort watched Sister Loretta gather up the pieces of his beloved bear and throw them into the incinerator.

For as long as I can remember after that, Michael ran in circles on the playground and galloped down the halls with one or two telephone books under his arm. I often wondered if he did not want to just reach out and call someone who cared.

There was another little girl named Mary and she stuttered. Mary was also brain damaged and not Down's. Her father was an eye surgeon. She was very easily confused and excited. When she got that way, Sister Regina would walk in circles around Mary repeating and mocking her stuttering. Mary would cry and Regina would slap her. "Talk right" Regina would scream but Mary could not do it. It was not something she was able to control.

Another young retarded boy was Philip. I was in the infirmary one time after a severe beating and Philip was in the same room with me. This young child was Down's syndrome. He had been in the hospital for an operation and come home with some kind of drainage bag on his abdomen. Every time he would touch near his stomach, the nun sitting by his bed would slap him. Sometimes he would just cry in pain and she would slap him. If my memory serves me right this young man had a remarkable talent.

If you mentioned any date in any year, say July 4, 1906, he would tell you what day of the week it fell on. He did it instantly he did not even spend 5 seconds to figure it out. You could say a date and he would give you the weekday it fell on. A couple of times I would check it out and he was absolutely correct. He was amazing.

My birthday is October 2nd. Sister Joelcum, the teacher for the retarded children invited me into her classroom for the day. October 2nd is the Feast Day of the Holy Angels. This was how she referred to the retarded children. She called them "her holy angels." I think that I helped her a great deal and I did enjoy working with these children. Sister Joelcum really was a woman of God. When these special children were in her classroom and in her care, they were treated with a kindness and reverence that was seen no where else in the godless place.

There was another girl in this group of children whose name was Ellen. She had a terrible habit of sticking her whole hand into her mouth and sucking on it all day. It drove sister crazy. Her hand smelled unbelievably bad and it was slimy. It became my job to keep Ellen from sucking her fist whenever I was not doing Sister Regina's "Special jobs" or my daily KP duty. To this day, slime is still the one thing that will turn my stomach. I found myself drifting toward these children on the playground. There was a great satisfaction in being able to teach them something or help them out.

I remember a brother-sister team of Patty and Tommy. Because they had different last names, the nuns kept telling them that they weren't really brother and sister in God's eyes. A number of years after my first Behr-Manning Christmas party I was in church with Aunt Grace and Uncle Bill and I thought I recognized Santa Clause's deep blue eyes in church that Sunday. This man was staring at me and when he winked I knew. The next time I saw that man in church with his wife, sitting in the pew next to him were Patty and Tommy. He had gone to St. Colman's and took these kids into his home as foster children.

Barbara Ann was also a young lady with waist length hair. One day she made the unfortunate choice of bringing her new doll back to St. Colman's. From the ruckus that was raised, you would have thought that she had brought home a porn flick. She had a new Barbie doll. Sister Regina flew into an insane rage. She grabbed the girl and the doll, dragged them down to the kitchen and sawed that doll into pieces with a knife. The next stop was the boiler room and the incinerator. Barbara was lectured in front of the whole dorm about the disgusting item that she had brought into God's house. She was instructed to never touch such a filthy doll again.

My best friend, Linda was a very quiet girl. She rarely got into trouble because she never opened her mouth. When they said jump, she said how high. Only once did I see her lose it. Sister Regina was yelling at her about something and Linda had that face on. Like I'm not really listening or drop dead. Sister Regina walked around her in a circle. Linda's dad had committed suicide and she had found him. She had nightmares about it and Regina knew that. "I'm talking to you she screamed, look into my eye's." Linda still had her face toward the ground. "You remember what happened to your father" she yelled? "Well I am pretty sure that I can arrange for it to happen to you."

Linda's face turned a pasty white. I was close enough to see her face harden and her lips turn pale. Linda turned slowly to face her, "Don't you say one more God Dam word" she spitted. 'Don't you ever say one thing to me about my father again, or I won't be the only person hanging from a doorway" she screamed. Regina grabbed her by the hair. Linda was like a wildcat, spitting and scratching and kicking up to the sewing room and then the door slammed shut. I had had my turn in that room so many times and with every smash of the paddle and every scream from Linda I cried. I did not see her again for over a week. She was just another child sent to the infirmary beaten to a bloody pulp.

While sitting in the auditorium one Sunday night, where we were watched the Disney movie Toby Tyler someone behind me started to giggle and whisper. We were not supposed to talk during the show. Like a hawk in the night swift and silent, Regina swooped down on the girl and began to pound on her back. I remember hearing the girl sitting next to her crying and screaming "please sister, can't you see you are killing her!"

Another unpleasant memory is the time in the fifth grade when we were learning the multiplication and times tables. We went over and over them. For some reason the majority of the kids in the class were not understanding them. One day sister got so mad about it she took first the girls and then the boys out of the room. The girls were marched downstairs into the playroom. One little girl named Joanne did not live at St. Colman's. She lived directly across the street from the orphanage. She and her brother Johnny and cousin Jimmy all went to elementary school with us. Joanne was always left in the room with the boys.

The rest of the girls walked single file into the playroom. There were long green benches that followed the perimeter of the room. We all had to face the benches and pull our underpants down to our knees. We were then instructed to lie over the bench. There were probably fifteen to twenty girls in this class. Sister came down the line and pulled up your dress and slip. She took the radiator brush from one of the lockers and starting with the first girl began to spank each of us. How many whacks you got depended on how much you did not know. You could always tell how close to your turn it was by how close the screams of pain were.

One of these sessions scared me so badly that when sister was paddling the girl next to me, I just lay there and pissed all over my dress and all over the floor. My extra punishment for this was to wear that same dress and slip for rest of the day. When she was done paddling all the girls, we went back to the classroom and then the boys were marched down. I can't say for sure what happened to the boys. I was not there to see but they all came back in tears also.

My memory of something called the party list was particularly painful. Different groups of social organizations would occasionally give a party for some of the orphans. I am sure that if these good intentioned people had any idea how much pain they were causing the children not chosen to attend, they wouldn't have done it. The kids who went to these functions were always the same chosen few. This happened seven or eight times a year. The rest of us were told "you are not good children." "You are an embarrassment to our good name. We don't want anyone to know that we have this kind of garbage here in God's house. Maybe if you learn to behave you will be chosen next time." In the whole time that I was there, not once did my name ever make it to the party list. The Behr-Manning and the Allegheny Ludlum Steel Christmas parties were for everyone so I did get to go to them unless Sister Regina could manufacturer some horrendous mortal sin I committed.

CHAPTER 17

Vengeance Belongs to God and Justice Belongs to Me

When my brother Bruce was eleven years old, my mother died. She was only forty-nine. She had moved to Texas some time earlier. We had momma's body flown back to New York and she was buried somewhere near her brother. I called Texas and spoke with Bruce. I asked him if he wanted to come and live with me again he said no that he wanted to stay there. He would live with my brother Paul and his wife and children. He wanted to stay in his school and be with his friends.

My brother Paul had ultimately wound up living at St. Colman's when he was younger. He was also horribly abused. He was one of the people to be forever damaged. He turned to the circle of abuse. Bruce ran away and called me from Pennsylvania and I arranged to have him brought to me. He began to tell me horrible stories of what my brother Paul had done to him. Thank you St. Colman's for the damage done to Paul which he in turn did to Bruce.

When I took Bruce, I needed another child like I needed another hole in my head. I was a single parent with a little boy of my own to take care of. His father did not pay any child support and I worked hard to make sure that he had a decent life. With the addition of Bruce into my household I needed to take a second job, so after I left my office at 4:30, I would go and clean other people's houses at night and on the weekends. I was so tired most of the time, but I had saved Bruce from an orphanage or a foster home.

In 1982, I met a man while walking my dog. He was younger than me but very mature. He was kind and decent and loving. Never once was he mean or unkind. It was easy to fall in love with him. In March of 1984 we were married. For the first time in my life I felt the magic of real honest to God love and to have someone look at me in that special way and not see the look of "I am better than you are on his face". Too be on an equal footing with a man who was willing and able to share his heart and his soul and is still a wonder to me to this day. The difference between a loving man in this marriage and the abusive childish man in my first marriage is astounding. Of course, never having been anything but abused for most of my life, I had no way of knowing that not every relationship had to be based on forced sex and violent behavior. What might my life have been, if I had met Scott first? Scott was attending

Rensselaer Polytechnic Institute (RPI) and when he graduated with his Engineering degree he was offered a job in Seattle, Washington with the Boeing Company. We moved to Kent, Washington in August 1984. We were blessed with a little boy in February of 1987. Welcome to the world Orion Scott William Robertson. This child has a life so much different from mine or even his brother.

In today's society, pretty much both parents have to work. Property on the West coast is sky high. I could not bring myself to leave Orion and go back to work. I needed to find a job that I could do at home. I had not brought another child into this world to be brought up by a babysitter. I had a friend who cared for elderly people in her home. She told me all about the business. We had an extra bedroom in our house. I decided to give it a shot.

I started with just one little lady. Our house was on a main road in Kent and the area was expanding rapidly. The traffic became very heavy and noisy. Scott and I discussed moving out to the country. I love peace and quiet and we began looking for property. We found 5 ½ acres in Enumclaw and bought it. We purchased a modular home and set it up on our property. I was happier than I had ever been in my life. Orion was thriving and we were happy.

Our first little lady died about a week before we moved. My next client was a young man in a wheelchair. He had been involved in a tragic motor vehicle accident which left him a quadriplegic. Since I had five bedrooms and 3 bathrooms, I decided to expand and open a licensed Adult Family Home. This license allowed me to care for up to six adults in my home. I thought why not, in for a penny in for a pound. My first client was totally dependent on me and I had to be there all the time anyway. We had a series of older people and the problem with this was they did not live very long. When the deaths of my clients began to adversely affect Orion, I decided to change the population of the clients that I took in. I chose to take developmentally disabled people. For the most part these clients were much younger and not as likely to die in Orion's childhood.

On Christmas Eve in 1995, my son Pete and his family were visiting. He asked if he could use my phone to call his dad in New York and wish him a Merry Christmas. He spoke with him for a few minutes and then said Mom Dad says he needs to talk with you. I was not crazy about the idea but it was Christmas. As I took the phone, the familiar voice made me a little nervous. I hadn't seen or heard from him in many years. The faceless voice said, "I guess you weren't lying after all, the papers are full of it." "What the hell are you talking about" I said. I thought he was forgetting the fact that I now lived

3,000 miles away. How would I see a local NY paper? "The nuns at St. Colman's" he said, "the papers say they killed a kid." I said absolutely nothing and just handed Pete the phone and walked away.

My first stop was to the bathroom to empty my stomach. I had earlier toasted the season with some eggnog. It is Orion's favorite drink on Christmas Eve. I have never liked the stuff, but it seems important to him so I drank it. It is a part of his Christmas ritual to toast the season. After I went to bed that night, I had nightmares so intense that I got practically no sleep at all. The dreams were all the same. A young boy of ten or eleven was lying on a black and white filed floor. He was curled up in a ball and he was screaming over and over, please, please, please. I sat bolt upright in my bed bathed in a cold sweat. The dreams were so real and for some reason absolutely terrifying.

Trying to go back to sleep was useless. I got up and sat in my chair in the living room. A dreadful fear was oozing out of every pore in my body. I sat in the dark scared to death in my own living room. What was making me so afraid and fearful? I sat there most of the night waiting for Orion to wake up and see what Santa had brought him.

Christmas day did not get any better. I thought that I was losing my mind. I was sitting in my living room and it was broad daylight. All of my clients were having a great Christmas morning. Wrapping paper was flying everywhere. The clients were in full holiday mode. Voices were exclaiming thanks Auntie Sue, I love this or oh boy this is great it is just what I wanted. Still, I sat with images that burst in front of me like flashbulbs going off in my face. All of the images were of this dark, curly haired boy lying on the floor and a pointed black shoe was kicking the hell out of him. If I were to lay odds on my sanity right then, I would have had to say zero to none. God what was wrong with me? What did this mean? It did not matter if I was awake or asleep, it followed me everywhere. As the week went along, the images stayed and got longer.

By New Year's Day, I knew all of it. The words spoken to me over the phone on Christmas Ever had triggered a memory block that God and my novena to the Blessed Virgin Mary had mercifully allowed me to forget. I had witnessed the murder of Mark Longale, a little retarded boy at St. Colman's when I was twelve years old. I buried it so deep in my head that I did not ever want to have it come out. Unfortunately, this hiding for me was now over. I now questioned my own sanity.

Who in the name of God could see a child beaten to death by a nun and not remember it. My hold on my sanity was tenuous at best. When I remembered the whole thing, I was shocked and appalled. How the hell could I be forty five years old see a catholic nun beat a child, murdered and not remember it? Now that I did, I could not make it go away. It just kept playing and replaying every time I closed my eyes, the same thing it did in the fall of 1963.

It was a Sunday in September of 1963. There was another burned pot after dinner time and I spend my customary two hours with my trusty paring knife scraping the burnt gunk off the bottom. When I was done, all of the other KP duty kids were long gone. I was going by the library which as a high school girl was now open to me. I stepped into the room closing the door behind me. I heard the sound that I will never forget in my life again. At the other end of the library was another door that connected to the retarded children's classroom.

There I saw Sister Regina standing over Mark Longale. I don't know why she was there with him. She did not have anything to do with taking care of the boys or the retarded children. Mark was curled up into a ball on the floor pleading and crying, "please, please, please." Regina just kept kicking Mark in the stomach and yelling "shut up, shut up, shut up!" I could see that Mark had vomited. His hand and face were smeared in it. He was squirming in the vomit trying to get away from her. I think I must have made a noise because Mark's head came up about 3 inches off the floor and there were strands of slime sticking between his face and the floor. Sister Regina slammed her foot on the side of his head and I heard it slap back down on the floor. She was now glaring at me and said, "I don't really think that you should be in here minding other people's business, do you?"

I made a beeline for the door and ran like a disgusting coward. I ran all the way to the basement playroom. I climbed the stairs to the girl's bathroom. I sat in the stall with the door locked and my feet up on the wall so no one who came in would see my feet and know I was there. To this day, I can't explain why I did not try to help Mark. Sister Regina had brutalized and beaten me severely many, many times. It was a sure bet that she would do it again. So why did not I help Mark? That single cowardly act will now haunt me for the rest of my life.

After the New Year I could not cope anymore. I could not concentrate or effectively run my business. I did not seem to be able to do anything. So many people depend on me my clients, my son, my husband, and my employees. I went to a therapist. I was almost destroyed by my feelings of helplessness. The therapist did help me to see that the only way for me to survive after

Mark's murder was to hide what happened.

About three days after Mark's murder, I was emptying trash down next to the boiler room when I felt a very sharp jab to my ribs. When I turned around, I was face to face with Regina. The scowl on her face was awful. "Mark Longale is dead she spat and he died of a ruptured appendix, do you understand me" she said? "It could happen to any child here, you got that!" It did not take a rocket scientist to figure out that threat. She had gotten away with Mark's murder. There was absolutely nothing that protected me from the same fate. I was scared to death.

The therapist helped me to understand that the human mind can only take so much. If you fear for your life everyday, your mind will make you forget it. It would be too much to carry around everyday. Either you will blank it out as I did or you would have a nervous breakdown. Now that I had a plausible explanation, it made a little more sense to me. I began to grow angry again, very angry.

I made a call to the Colonie Police Department in Latham, New York. I tried to tell them what I saw. They were not interested. I was shocked. I was telling them about a beating I saw administered to a child who died three days later and they were treating me like a moron. I contacted the *Troy Record* Newspaper for a subscription request and copies of the previous months' back issues. I read several articles in the paper and then I realized that the articles weren't talking about Mark Longale at all.

These stories were about another little boy named Gilbert Bonneau. He was struck on the head with a stick according to a witness and taken to the infirmary. He was dead in about a week. There are many discrepancies contained in his autopsy report and multiple diagnoses for his death. The mystery surrounding this little boy will most likely never be solved. He has three surviving brothers who have spent years and all of their life savings trying to find out the truth about the death of their youngest brother.

I called a reporter at the *Troy Record* and talked with him about the young boy that I had seen beaten. I only remembered his first name and the time of year that I had seen him beaten. This reporter went searching in the public records and found the report on Mark's death. When he called me back and said Mark's last name, I remembered it. I also told him that Mark's father worked for the Fort Orange Vending Company. He came once a week to refill the candy vending machine down in the basement. He was a nice man and sometimes if you walking by when he was refilling the machine, he would give you a free candy bar.

I felt terrible now that I remembered what I prayed for in my novena to the Blessed Virgin to forget. It was eating away at me. I could not live with myself. I called information in New York and got Mark's brothers' phone number. He put me in touch with his mother. She told me she always knew that there was something more about Mark's death that the nuns were not telling. This was 1964 and women did not have many rights about what went on in their lives or their marriages. She said she always knew that something was wrong with what went on up there but her husband made her keep quiet.

I called television news stations and news print reporters. I told them what I saw. Another investigation was started. I was, however, 3,000 miles away. My older sister, Grace told every one including the media that I was a nut case. She got on a public radio show in the Capital District of New York and told every one I was crazy and had been seeing psychiatrists for years. Some one from New York sent me a tape of the radio talk show. When I heard my sister's comments, anger so hot came over me that I exploded. I flew to New York and hired and attorney. My intention was to bring a law suit against her for slander. No wonder the police were ignoring me. My sister had convinced them that I was nuts. That was the second time that someone from that hellhole had tried to hang that label on me and I was furious beyond words.

Grace had gone home with my Aunt Grace when she was in high school. She could not stand living there any more. If this place was so warm and wonderful, why then did she beg my Aunt and Uncle to take her to live with them? She left June and me there, like my father did and she never looked back. When I was raped there and beaten nearly to death, she was not even living in the area. How the hell would she know what went on after she left?

I had many letters of recommendation and character references from everyone from my sons' second grade teacher to Washington State Social Workers who had placed their developmentally disabled clients in my care. I paid for a complete Mental Evaluation by a New York psychiatrist. I was now and have always been as sane as most every one else in this world.

My lawsuit was never about money. It was about truth and justice. It was about accountability for your words and actions and the damage done to other people by your very wrong opinions. I settled the lawsuit with my sister out of court. I made her pay for all my legal expenses and print a public retraction in the newspaper. I wanted that retraction and apology to be just as public as the lies she shouted out on a radio station for half or New York to hear. After the apology appeared in the *Times Union* newspaper the Colonie Police Department took a statement from me. It was too late. The investigation was over and once again St. Colman's home had gotten away with murder.

As an adult, I would later find out that the state of New York had a new requirement for teachers in the late 1960's. For my Uncle Bill to keep his job, he had to get a Master's Degree. The only way for The Wilson Family to do this was to sell their house. They moved three hundred miles away so he could go back to college. Aunt Grace could not bare to tell us this and I can't blame her for that. I think that kind of an emotional wrench might have been more than she could take. The family slipped quietly away. In retrospect, it was the only way for them to go. Had they told me what was going to happen, I know that I would have broken. I would have told her that she was the glue that was holding me together. If I had only known that she really did not have any other choice it might not have taken so much of me when Sister Regina so cruelly continued to strip off all my feeling of self worth.

When the reporters told the stories of what had happened to Mark; when I saw on a tape that someone sent me from New York my sister's face as she was being interviewed the absolute belief in what she was saying about the nuns' I was floored. What was wrong with her? Ever so slowly in my mind I began to think back. Most of the beatings were done in a room without other children present. Each dormitory had a different nun in charge of them. Grace was never once in the same group as me. As far as I know, she never had any dealings with Sister Regina or Sister Loretta. Still, she could not possibly be that blind. Denial is a classic example of emotional pain. While I do feel sorry for her, I will not allow any one or any thing to stand in my way of the truth.

Yes, Regina, as I screamed at you thirty eight years ago, I am telling. I will tell every one what you did. I will keep on telling until some one hears until every one knows the truth about what you did. I will tell until the Albany County Department of Children's Services admit what they knew about what was happening up there. Bishop Hubbard refuses to return my phone calls. The Catholic Church and you are responsible for what you did to us. **MURDER, RAPE AND ABUSE ALL DONE IN THE NAME OF GOD.**

CHAPTER 18

The Great Controversy Begins
The Saint Colman's Saga

The story of St. Colman's broke in the newspapers in 1995. Since that time, former residents have come forward to tell of their experiences at the orphanage.

I have and am using documentation from these former residents. Some of it is from newspaper articles which are a matter of public record by their very nature. I have e-mail correspondence from several former residents who have given me their permission to use any and all of their writing too me, in my book. I have also included some official correspondence again given to me by those former residents for inclusion into this book.

The purpose of these next chapters is to share with you, the reader, just how much influence the orphanage had on these children placed in its care. I hope to give you a clear picture of what orphan life was like not only from my own point of view but by other's who have had a similar background.

Child abuse is a crime and should be punishable to the full extent of the law. Unfortunately, this does not always happen as you will read. All of the following is true. I have included those stories from former residents who had a great life at the orphanage as well as those who have termed the place "orphanage of horrors".

In all of my conversations, correspondence and e-mails with my fellow former orphans at St. Colman's, our goal is the same. WE WANT VALIDATION OF OUR CHILDHOOD. WE WANT TO BE HEARD. WE WANT THE LABEL OF TROUBLED CHILDREN AND DYSFUNCTIONAL ADULTS REMOVED WHEN OUR NAME IS SPOKEN. WE WANT TO BE BELIEVED AND NOT CALLED LIARS EVER AGAIN. WE WANT THOSE RESPONSIBLE FOR THE ABUSE WE SUFFERED TO BE HELD ACCOUNTABLE. WE WANT THIS NEVER TO HAPPEN AGAIN.

We survivors of St. Colman's have used every channel and avenue available to us to meet our common goal with no resolution in sight. Those reading this book will finally have this whole story. We are being heard.

METROLAND-The Capital Regions
February 29, 1996
Alternative Newsweekly #854

Children's Crusade by Mike Goudreau

It is a gray bone-chilling morning on Bought Road in Watervliet, and the group outside St. Colman's Home looks like a funeral gathering. If not for the protest signs and the TV remote trucks parked off the road, all the tears and grieving faces certainly would lend any passerby to thing it was some type of memorial assembly. The men and women bundled up in heavy coats and sipping coffee to stay warm are clearly mourning something. The only question is what.

In fact the gathering is equal parts press conference, protest and support group meeting. All of the people assembled once lived in the unassuming brick building across the street when St. Colman's was a home for orphans. Many of them tell stories of horrible abuse at the hands of the Catholic Sisters of the Presentation, who continue to run the facility, which has existed for well over 100 years and is now a center for autistic children and teenagers. The press conference, organized by the newly formed St. Colman's Survivors Group is to announce two women's allegations that they were repeatedly sexually molested by a male chef in St. Colman's for many years.

Though the group's members are there to show support for the women, carrying signs protesting alleged abuse at the home, they are also there to exchange stories of a painful time and to build unity. The memories and tears flow – for some, it is the first time they've seen the building in many years – but the process of opening old wounds produces some fresh pain, too. St. Colman's denies that any such abuse went on within its walls, so the survivors are, as they claim was the case many years ago, being accused of making up stories.

That has essentially been the home's argument since speculation arose late last year that a young boy named Gilbert Bonneau was beaten to death at St. Colman's 42 years ago; that such allegations are the concoctions of "troubled" people looking for a scapegoat for the pain they suffered as orphans.

But this argument doesn't quite answer a critical question, the one that many never be answered: *Can all* of those stories be made up!

Seattle is in the midst of a much-needed dry-spell, and rays of early-afternoon sun shine through the windows as Susanne Maloney Robertson sits at a table in one of the city's countless cafes, nervously fiddling with the rings on her fingers as she rehashes the events of the last few months and the distant past.

Robertson had a ruddy complexion that she owes to years of living in a rural town 40 miles outside Seattle, where she runs two state-licensed group homes for disabled adults. It is difficult for her to recount many of her experiences at St. Colman's without her voice cracking and eyes welling up with tears, including the story that may soon have her flying to Albany to give statements to local authorities.

The 45 year-old Robertson claims that in 1963 she saw one of the nuns at St. Colman's, Sister Regina, kicking a 10-year-old boy named Mark Longale repeatedly in the stomach as he lay on the floor of the home's library. Longale died several days later of a ruptured appendix, according to an autopsy report.

Robertston was 13 years-old at the time, and she was making her way down a long hallway to report for kitchen duty. She decided that she wanted to get a book from the St. Colman's library along the way, when she opened the door, she saw Longale lying on the floor and Sister Regina standing over him. The nun allegedly was kicking the boy in stomach and at least once put her foot on the top of his head and slammed it to the ground. Robertson vividly recalls that Longale had vomited and was crying "please" and screaming for her to stop.

She remembers Regina yelling at Longale to shut up before she spotted the girl at the door and said, "I don't think you need to be minding other peoples business, do you?"

Robertson quickly retreated, and a few day later – she thinks it was three, but she's not sure – the nun supposedly came up to her and said, "Mark Longale is dead, and he died of a ruptured appendix, do you understand me? And it could happen to any child here."

"If I told, it would've happened to me," says Robertson. "She'd gotten away with killing him – what protected me?"

Robertson left St. Colman's a few years later, and she says she repressed the memory of what she'd seen until only last December, when a chance conversation with her ex-husband sent her life into chaos. For years, she had told him of other experiences at St. Colman's, abuse she'd suffered at the hands of the sisters. He never believed her, however, until he saw a TV story on the Bonneau case. When Robertson's son called his father from Washington for Christmas, she was summoned to the phone.

"I guess all those things you told me about St. Colman's weren't lies after all" her ex-husband said. "They killed a kid."

That night, Robertson began having nightmares about St. Colman's. The nightmarish images stayed with her in the form of flashbacks the next day, and they haven't stopped since, she says. Robertson has always carried with her memories of abuse at St. Colman's, but she claims to have suppressed any recollection of the Longale beating and being repeatedly sexually molested by a maintenance man at the facility. All of that comes flooding back when she spoke to her ex-husband, Robertson says.

At the time, Robertson thought he was talking about Longale – little did she know the St. Colman's controversy had been ignited by the death of another little boy, Bonneau.

THE LOCAL MEDIA HAVE JUMPED all over the St. Colman's story since the *Troy Record* broke it in December, and the controversy has sparked questions about at least three deaths, those of Bonneau, Longale and 6-year-old Andrew Rada, with a fourth case possibly on the way. The Colonie Police, the Albany County District Attorney's office and the state Department of Social Services are all now involved in investigations of the institution.

But the furor might never have started had it not been for a mysterious call Bonneau's older brother, Williams, says he received in 1978 from a woman calling herself Marion Maynard.

The woman told William that she had seen a nun beat Gilbert severely in the head with a stick, the day before he died. Maynard would not leave a number or any other way of contacting her, and she never called back. The Bonneau brothers, William, Michael and Danny – the last two of whom had been at the orphanage with Gilbert – placed classified ads searching for an eyewitness. Though they received a number of responses from people who told stories of abuse at the orphanage, none had any information on Gilbert, so the Bonneaus put the matter to rest.

Their suspicions remained dormant until last year, when a local woman and former St. Colman's resident allegedly approach Michael, saying that she was doing a book on her experiences there and that she had witnessed the beating. The brothers say she also arranged a meeting with Albany Bishop Howard Hubbard, but they became suspicious of her motives, so – thinking she might be "an informant from the home" – they asked her to sign a notarized statement containing her eyewitness account, but she refused.

That led the Bonneaus to place more classified ads in the paper, once again hunting for witnesses, which triggered a wave of media coverage over the last few months.

Gilbert Bonneau's autopsy and infirmary records have been released by St. Colman's, thanks to the state's waiving of a confidentiality law that had prevented the home from doing so; Mark Longale's records have not been made public. Based on the official and anecdotal evidence to this point – and assuming it is accurate – it seems unlikely that allegations of murder could be proven, but there remain questions and inconsistencies that may keep the families of the two boys from ever believing they died of natural causes.

The autopsy report on Bonneau indicated that he died of a bacterial infection, a conclusion supported by Albany Medical Center pathologist Dr. Barbara Wolfe and St. Colman's attorney Al Sabo. The autopsy mentions both "possible" meningitis and the bacterial infection. It is possible, according to Schenectady County Medical Examiner Thomas Oram, for bacteria to cause meningitis, but it's "extremely unlikely" that head trauma would cause bacterial meningitis to kill someone.

Can the records supplied by St. Colman's be trusted? The Bonneaus don't trust them, pointing to several inconsistencies. For example, both the county and state death certificates list "meningitis" and "cause undetermined" in the blank for cause of death. And the autopsy report seems to indicate that the postmortem was conducted six hours before the time of death listed on the death certificates.

Sloppy record-keeping? Perhaps. But don't tell William Bonneau that. He thinks the records were falsified years ago to protect the nun who beat Gilbert.

"It's a cover-up," he says. "It's sickening. The Catholic church against the little guys – that's what going on here."

St. Colman's isn't the only party that has earned the Bonneau's wrath. The Colonie Police Department is on the family's list as well for its alleged handling of a statement by witness Tony Periard, who was at St. Colman's with Gilbert. Periard claims he saw Sister Regina hit the boy in the head with a stick in the infirmary, before he died – "Quite hard", Periard recalls. "You could hear a crack."

Periard says he told that to a Colonie Police detective in a recent interview at his home with several relatives present, but the account of the blow somehow did not end up in his statement. When William Bonneau and Periard discovered that at a later date and tried to amend the statement, they claim, they were rebuffed by the detective.

Colonie Police Lt. Steve Heider says the department won't identify anyone it takes statement from, but in general, once one is obtained in front of witnesses and the document is signed and sworn to, the department doesn't take second statements.

In the Longale case, the allegations of murder – at least the way Robertson says it happened – are equally unlikely, according to medical experts. Sabo says it is impossible for an appendix to burst from a blow without other organs that surround the appendix, like to spleen, being destroyed first. Oram agrees that it is "almost impossible" for a blow to cause an appendix to burst.

Sabo goes on to contend that he spoke with the boy's father, Don Longale, who lives locally, and he denied that his son had been beaten. According to Sabo, the father claims Mark came home that weekend and did not complain of anything but "intermittent stomach pains" before returning to St. Colman's and experiencing the problems that killed him.

But anyone who saw Don Longale interviewed on WNYT (Channel 13) recently would have a hard time trusting his credibility, given that he acted "erratically," as reporter Bill Lambdin put it. Longale made strange sounds in the brief piece of video WNYT showed, and Sabo admits that it appeared as though Longale had been drinking. Sabo, however, claims his conversation with the father took place "earlier in the day" when he was "clearly not intoxicated."

The boy's mother, Phyllis, has not responded to calls from METROLAND on the advice of an attorney, Martin Smalline of Albany. Though Mark's younger brother, Kevin, has also stopped returning calls, he did speak to METROLAND briefly a few weeks ago.

Kevin Longale, who was only 3 at the time of his brother's death, notes a few things that have made the family suspicious. According to him, St. Colman's kept the young boy in the infirmary for 12 hours before bringing him to the hospital, and when they did, it was not in an ambulance. More important, he claims his mother was told at that time by the doctor who treated Mark that he had injuries caused by a fall or blow to the area. He says the doctor is still alive, and his name is Agopovich. (There is a local physician by that name, but he was on vacation and unreachable.) Kevin notes that his mother had a "funny feeling that something was awry back in 1963 but that she "did not have too much say as a woman" and let the issue go.

Though the theory that kicks to the stomach caused the boy's appendix to burst may be bogus, it's not hard to imagine a scenario in which the real cause of death was covered up. Smalline is also representing Robertson, and he appears confident that there is something to her allegations, but he is hesitant to get into details.

"The cause of death is disputed based on what I've heard from Sue and the family," he says. "I am optimistic at this time that once all the witnesses are interviewed, the DA's office will be able to go forward (with the murder allegations)."

WHEN TIMES UNION COLUMNIST Dan Lynch interviewed Sister Regina in December – one of the few times any of the nuns has spoken publicly during this saga – she told him that in 45 years at the institution, she had never seen a child struck.

"Look into my eyes," Regina told the columnist. "I'm telling the truth."

The nun's comments may have been largely responsible for the dozens of angry calls from St. Colman's residents to local media, the Colonie Police and Paul Koren, a father who once had three children in the facility and has become a sort of one-man clearinghouse for abuse complaints. That's because Regina probably is mentioned more than any other nun when it comes to allegations of abuse.

Nancy McGrath a spokeswomen for St. Colman's Survivors and a former resident herself, says that Regina was the only nun who ever beat her while she was there. "That one Sister Regina," – says McGrath "has destroyed more lives than is imaginable."

To hear Robertson tell it, Regina was her nemesis at St. Colman's, beating the girl on several occasions – once badly enough to break her ribs. Just as disturbing, however, are the stories of psychological abuse that Robertson and others tell. She claims that one day, when she was waiting in the line for the shower, Regina became enraged at the kind of slip Robertson was wearing, so she tore the garment and Robertson's training bra off, making her stand there wearing nothing but panties as the other girls passed for two hours.

"Sister Regina," Robertson spits, "was the worst nun that ever lived."

Sabo disputes that characteristic of Regina, pointing out that she did not mean to indicate that she'd never seen anyone struck, but that she had never witnessed a *beating* at St. Colman's.

"It was an inartful way of her describing it," he says. "I don't find it difficult to believe that she would've frightened these kids or scared them in an attempt to get them to behave, but (I can't believe) that she physically abused them."

Still when the sister told Lynch to look into her eyes, it struck a chord with many former residents, because the nun, according to Robertson and McGrath, was always saying the same thing to kids in her care as a means of manipulation. Robertson says Regina could not stand a child looking away when she was talking, and she also remembers the nun often admonishing children by saying, "You look at the ground and don't date look at decent people."

Manipulation and denial were the standard modes of operation among at least some nuns, according to critics of St. Colman's. That may be no surprise to anyone who has had a bad experience in a Catholic institution, and survivors are quick to say they don't necessarily discount the opinions of former residents who say the home was a sometimes tough but ultimately positive environment. The survivors don't doubt that many orphans may have seen it that way. But the stories of abuse at St. Colman's go far beyond the usual knuckle-rapping and paddling. Robertson and McGrath, along with Nancy Barootjian and Judy Fowler – the two women who alleged they were sexually molested by a chef at the home – all say that, in one way or another, allegations of sexual abuse they made while under the care of St. Colman's went unheeded by the nuns. Robertson says that at about the age of 12 she told Regina she'd been molested by a maintenance man at the home, and the nun "took me into the shower and scrubbed every inch of my body with Lysol ... and told me I should never repeat that again."

Barootjian and Fowler talk of a similar reaction to the charges. Barootjian, 32, claims that the chef began fondling her when she first started working in the kitchen at age 7 and that over a period of years the abuse eventually turned into violation with a foreign object and, ultimately, sexual intercourse.

"I had a uniform dress on," Barootjian recalls, "and he pulled down my panties, took a hot dog, went like this (Barootjian mimics rubbing the object between her hands), and you know the rest. That was the most traumatizing thing he did to me – until he started having sex with me."

Neither woman could get the sisters or anyone else to believe them, they say. It should be noted that the man who they say was their institutional psychiatrist at the home, George Cuttita – who did in fact work for St. Colman's for many years and who the women claim did nothing about their allegations – voluntarily surrendered his license in 1998 amid charges from the state Board for Professional Medical Conduct that he had forced sexual activity on two female clients in his private practice.

Two complaints to the Colonie Police, one by Barootjian alone in 1985 after she'd left St. Colman's and another by both Barootjian and Fowler in

1990, eventually yielded an arrest of the chef but any charges filed apparently were either dismissed or reduced to violations. Barootjian and Fowler don't know for sure, because the records have been sealed, a relatively common procedure in such cases when an outcome favors the defendant.

McGrath wonders whether the police ever did question kitchen workers when Barootjian filed her '85 complaint – because they would have run across the worker named Judy Fowler there at the time. But police spokesman Heider says he can't discuss any specifics because the records are sealed.

THOUGH MOTHER CARMEL, director of St. Colman's, and Sister Regina did not return METROLAND'S phone calls, Sabo had plenty to say in defense of the institution.

Critics wonder why the chef was let go by the home, even though Sabo has contended that St. Colman's officials believed he was innocent.

"If you 99.9 percent sure, that isn't even enough," he responds. "If there's one-hundredth, one-thousandth of a percent possibility that there was something to it, you can't possibly take the chance of him, being associated with children again. It's terribly unfair, but they did not have any choice."

Sabo has for the most part not investigated allegations of abuse – though he did talk to one kitchen worker who served with one of the alleged victims and claims she saw no evidence of abuse. He's concentrated on refuting the murder allegations, which are the only ones not precluded by a statute of limitations. He's convinced, however, that the controversy can be blamed on a "primarily dysfunctional population of people" whose resentment toward their parents has been "transferred to St. Colman's." Those people, the lawyer believes, have succeeded in creating an unwarranted media feeding frenzy in order to get back at the orphanage.

"I'm not going to say the nuns did not rap some knuckles or smack some fannies," says Sabo, "but that's not a beating, and that's not savagery, and that's nothing I did not get at home ... I think the press and the media, frankly, are being taken advantage of by these people."

Is it a case of mass fabrication of memories? When the St. Colman's Survivors cry in front of the building, are they remembering an abusive atmosphere, or are they remembering the pain of being sent there in the first place?

Clearly, many former residents of St. Colman's have been and continue to be deeply disturbed people, but many also say the atmosphere there made them that way. And then there are people such as Liz Carey and Susan O'Connor, sisters who spent some 10 years at St. Colman's starting in 1955.

Like many former residents, they did not suppress memories of abuse – they've carried them around for years, with no public forum in which to air them until now. They seem rational and well-adjusted; Carey owns a local florist, O'Connor is a veteran state worker. Both have kids.

So when Carey says that a nun once forced her into the shower and burned her on an exposed pipe or that she saw a nun jumping up and down on her sister's stomach or that the nuns made them eat regurgitated oatmeal when they could not keep it down, are her memories to be dismissed?

"The fear was unbelievable," says Carey.

Robertson, too, resents the argument that her allegations are the delusions of a "nutcase." She admits to being "emotionally unhinged" right now and is seeing a psychologist twice a week in an effort to deal with her horrible memories of St. Colman's. But in some ways, the ordeal had made her defiant.

The St. Colman's Survivors recently put out their first manifesto, and one of their objectives is to "meet with those responsible for the abuses." Robertson is asked how she'll react if she has to confront Sister Regina, in a court or elsewhere.

"I can tell you one thing," she says. "I will not be looking on the floor."

SUSANNE ROBERTSON

December 12, 1995

New York State Department of Social Services
Albany Regional Office
Attention: Wanda A. Austin-Peters
Family and Children Services Specialist
Attention: William McLaughlin, Director
40 North Pearl Street (3 City Square)
Albany, NY 11243-0001

RE: St. Colman's

Dear Ms. Austin-Peters and Mr. McLaughlin:

 This letter is in response to yours dated December 6, 1995. As we all know, children are abused every day and it goes on everywhere. In light of these "allegations" which I assure you are very true, I would think your department would conduct its own investigation immediately into the "current practices" and to verify the "current relevancy" even before you speak with me or any of my siblings. I can be reached at (phone number) after 5:30 p.m. to discuss this further.

Very truly yours,
Tracey A. Koren

cc:Paul A. Koren, Sr.
Paul A. Koren, Jr.
Arlene Gladstone
Brian J. Wang, Acting Commissioner

THE THROW AWAY CHILD

Albany *Times Union* Article
Sunday, January 7, 1996

Perspective Section – Investigate St. Colman's

THE ISSUE - Former residents complain of physical and emotional abuse.
OUR OPINION - The community has a right to know what really happened.

Police and medical investigations have determined that Gilbert Bonneau's death 42 years ago probably resulted from infections, not from a beating by a nun at St. Colman's Home in Colonie. Yet ever since Dan Lynch's December 21st column reported on the charges surrounding that death, the letters to this page have been pouring in. They are from readers who say they spent years of their childhood at St. Colman's Home and suffered either physical or emotional abuse, or both, at the hands of the Sisters of the Presentation, the religious order that staffed St. Colman's for nearly a century.

There are detailed descriptions of defenseless children who were literally living nightmares at St. Colman's. When they tried to protest to relatives or outsiders, their cries for help went unheeded. Even now, years after they have become productive, respected citizens in the community, they recall the anguish of their past. A few days ago, some of them gathered to protest outside St. Colman's, angered by one nun who denied any abuse and dismissed the accusers as troubled children who have grown up to be troubled adults.

While the accusations are numerous, detailed and graphic, there are other adults who also spent time at St. Colman's who have very different memories of their years there. They recall a nurturing environment provided y nuns who cared about their future.

Any further inquiry into Gilbert Bonneau's death is up to law enforcement officials, but the statute of limitations has expired for criminal prosecution of charges of abuse. Thus, absent civil suits filed by the accusers, there may be no way for the public to learn what really happened inside St. Colman's.

That's one reason why the state Legislature should intervene and demand an investigation. For nearly 100 years, St. Colman's opened its doors to orphans and neglected children. The state has a legitimate interest in finding out what kind of care was provided. St. Colman's has an equal interest in preserving a reputation it claims has been unjustly tarnished.

SUSANNE ROBERTSON

Albany *Times Union* Article
Saturday, January 20, 1996

Main Section - KIDS SHOULD BE SEEN AND HEARD

THE ISSUE – An investigation into a former orphanage shows no one heeded cries for help.
OUR OPINION – State lawmakers should provide a way for authorities to follow up claims of abuse

Medical records released Wednesday have all but put to rest the claims that eight-year-old Gilbert Bonneau was beaten to death by a nun at St. Colman's Home more than 40 years ago. The documents, which had remained sealed because of state confidentiality laws, reveal that Gilbert died of a viral infection, not trauma, as one of his surviving brothers had believed.

Even so, the brother, who sparked interest in the case after he ran newspaper advertisements seeking information from former residents at the orphanage, dismisses the records as a cover-up by St. Colman's. In order to finally resolve the matter, it may be necessary to exhume Gilbert's remains and have them examined by independent forensic experts.

No matter what the outcome, however, the St. Colman's story is far from over. Ever since Gilbert's death became the focus of an inquiry, this page had received a steady stream of phone calls and letters from former residents claiming physical abuse at the hands of the nuns who cared for them. So have Colonie police. Some are graphic accounts of beatings with hoses. Others claim the discipline was much less severe but left permanent emotional scars nonetheless.

A common thread in all the claims is the disbelief that the young residents encountered whenever they attempted to express their fears to visiting relatives or local officials. No adult seemed ready to believe the word of children over that of the caretakers.

State lawmakers have an obligation to ensure that all New Yorkers, even the youngest and the orphaned, have a place to turn for help when they believe they need it. The Legislature should make it a priority this year to provide a hotline for youngsters who live in fear of the adults who oversee their care.

Granted, a young imagination can often see terror where there may be none, as shown in recent cases involving allegations of child abuse in day care settings. Still, that is no reason to deny that abuse can occur even in the most nurturing circumstances. Adult lawmakers should make sure someone will listen when it does.

Albany *Times Union* Article
Wednesday, January 24, 1996

AGENCY PROBES COMPLAINT ON ST. COLMAN'S
Marc Carey – Staff Writer

ALBANY – The state Department of Social Services has begun an inquiry into the allegations of a Colonie man who claims his children were physically abused at St. Colman's Home in the early 1970s.

The move comes at the request of Assemblyman Bob Prentiss, whose district comprises Clifton Park, Colonie, Malta and Stillwater.

A Social Services spokesman Tuesday also called for any former St. Colman's residents with complaints about their treatment there to contact the department.

"Anyone who has a legitimut complaint who want to contact us, we certainly would talk to them as part of our review," said Social Services spokesman Terrance McGrath.

The review of the allegations of Paul Koren, who had two daughters in St. Colman's for about nine months in 1970-71, is part of an overall "formal review" of St. Colman's that recently started.

The state Department of Social Services is the agency that licenses St. Colman's and allows it to operate. During a formal inquiry, agency officials interview staff and clients and examine records of the institution to determine if it has operated according to state guidelines.

"It's about time," Koren said. He said he became concerned about operations at the home last fall after one daughter, Tracey, now an adult, became withdrawn, and then finally said she was having problems coping with her memories of physical abuse at the home.

"It's a good thing," Koren said of the probe. "We ought to get to the bottom of this thing."

In a Jan. 16 letter to Prentiss from Acting Social Services Director Brian J. Wing, Wing said that the department "is vigorously investigating the allegations made by Mr. Paul Koren regarding St. Colman's Home."

"I'm pleased that the inquiry by the state Social Service Department is moving along," said Prentiss. "It's important for the community, especially now, to know what happened."

The results of the investigation will be shared with Koren, Wing said.

Last week, records released by the state on the 1953 death of a boy living at St. Colman's, indicated that he had not been beaten as his family claimed, rather he died of natural causes.

Albany *Times Union* Article
Thursday, February 1, 1996

COLONIE COPS TURN OVER ST. COLMAN'S PROBE TO DA CAPITAL REGION SECTION
Police End Their Investigation of Home After Four Weeks
Lara Jakes – Staff Writer

COLONIE – Town police have turned over their investigation of St. Colman's Home to the Albany County district attorney after exhausting its probe into an alleged 1953 beating death of a 10-year-old resident, officials said.

After more than four weeks of conducting interviews, surveying medical reports and researching the Colonie foster home, investigators this week relinquished its report to District Attorney Sol Greenberg for review, said Lt. Steve Heider. Unless new information is uncovered, Colonie police will not actively pursue the case, Heider said.

"We've taken it to the point that we can," he said. "The decision (to investigate further) will probably rest in their hands."

"When you get to the point where you feel you've derived all the information you can, you arrive at the decision to keep the case open or close the case," Heider said. "We've had no further information."

Heider would not say whether police found any evidence of foul play during its probe into the death of 10-year old Gilbert Bonneau.

The youngster's three brothers, all of whom live in the area, maintain that Gilbert was beaten over the head with a stick by a St. Colman's nun, causing a bacteria infection to end his life. St. Colman's officials continue to defend the home against any wrongdoing.

Assistant District Attorney Paul DerOhannesian would not comment on specifics of the case Wednesday, other than to say that his office still is investigating. Colonie police surrendered its records late Monday night, Heiger said.

Greenberg launches a grand jury investigation into the Bonneau case in early January, after dozens of former St. Colman's residents and workers claimed to also have been either victims or witnesses of physical abuse. Many people have also come forward to defend the home in the face of the allegations.

Because of a two-year statute of limitation on physical abuse and a five-year limitation on sexual abuse, criminal investigations legally cannot look into any claims of beatings other than Gilbert's. Under New York state law, there is no statute of limitation on murder charges.

The state Department of Social Services, which oversees and licenses St. Colman's, is conducting its own investigation into the residents claims. That query is still pending, spokesman Terrance McGrath said Wednesday.

Albany *Times Union* Article
Wednesday, February 7, 1996

ANOTHER DEATH IS ALLEGED AT ORPHANAGE CAPITAL REGION SECTION
Authorities look into claims a St. Colman's
resident died after kick to the stomach
Lara Jakes – Staff Writer

ALBANY – The Albany County District Attorney's office and the state Department of Social Services separately are investigating another alleged beating death at St. Colman's Home in Colonie, officials said Tuesday.

Assistant District Attorney Lawrence P. Wiest and DSS spokesman Dan Hogan confirmed that their offices are looking into the death of 10-year-old Mark Longale sometime around 1961.

St. Colman's attorney Alvin O. Sabo called the allegations surrounding Mark's death "pure nonsense."

The new investigations were sparked by phone calls from dozens of former residents of the one-time orphanage after questions surfaced publicly about the death of Gilbert Bonneau. Gilbert's three brothers allege that the 8-year-old died at the hands of a nun in 1953. But St. Colman's lawyers and medical experts say records show the boy died of pneumonia and bacteria in his blood.

Assemblyman Bob Prentiss, R-Colonie, said he received numerous calls from present and former constituents who claimed they witnessed Mark being kicked in the stomach by a nun. He died soon after, the constituents told Prentiss.

In a Feb. 5 letter to DSS Acting Commissioner Brian Wing, Prentiss requests results of any state agency review of Mark's death certificate and autopsy report.

Mark's father, Don Longale, 66, of Albany, said he was told his son died following a ruptured appendix. The boy lived at St. Colman's for two months and never complained of any abuse, Longale said in a telephone interview Tuesday.

"I don't believe somebody kicked my boy in the stomach," he said. "If it's true, how come I never heard about it? If he was, he would have told me, because I was up there and I saw him."

Colonie police and the district attorney's office met Tuesday and decided to continue pursuing all allegations of death by physical abuse at the foster home, Colonie Lt. Steve Heider said. He declined further comment.

District Attorney Sol Greenberg in December launched a grand jury probe into Gilbert's death. That step has not been considered in Mark's case, Wiest said.

"That's premature, and I do not know if it is necessary," Wiest said.

"Sabo, St. Colman's attorney, said he would release Mark Longale's records from the home if permitted by DSS, as was done with Gilbert's records.

Under a state confidentiality law, the agency has the final say on whether the records may be opened. DSS licenses St. Colman's, which is now a home for autistic and disabled people. It continues to be staffed by nuns within the Roman Catholic Diocese of Albany.

Meanwhile, two former St. Colman's residents charged Tuesday they were repeatedly raped by a school employee over a combined 18-year period, ending in 1988.

At a press conference, Nancy Barootjian, 32, and Judy Fowler, 34 claimed they never were informed that their alleged attacker had been exonerated, and accused Colonie police of not taking their case seriously.

Town police in 1989 investigated charges against the employee. The case was eventually dismissed in Colonie Town Court, Heider said. When a case is dismissed in favor of the accused, the records are sealed by a judge, preventing officials from commenting.

Colonie Town Court sealed the employee's case in December, 1990, Barootjian and Fowler said.

Albany *Times Union* Article
Friday, February 9, 1996

**BOY'S DEATH IN 1943 PROBED
CAPITAL REGION SECTION**
Allegations of abuse at St. Colman's Home continue to surface
Lara Jakes – Staff Writer

ALBANY – District Attorney Sol Greenberg said Thursday his office is looking into a third alleged beating death at St. Colman's Home in Colonie.

For now, the office is only conducting a preliminary investigation into the death of 6-year-old Andrew Rada, who lived at St. Colman's in 1943, Greenberg confirmed. Officials will examine Andrew's death certificate, autopsy report and other records and will interview people who claim to have knowledge of the case, he said.

"That name came up and it's preliminarily being looked at," Greenberg said. "A lot of these claims show nothing. We may never get closer."

"Records from St. Colman's files indicate that the boy died of pneumonia, said Alvin O. Sabo, a Colonie attorney who represents the home. Sabo, reached at his residence Thursday night, immediately denied any allegations of wrongdoing in the boy's death.

"We're already cooperating with the authorities in respect to that investigation," Sabo said, clearly exasperated with the latest round of allegations. "This is all coming from a group of people who want to close the home."

Andrew's death marks the third death that is alleged to have come at the hands of employees at St. Colman's. Currently, the district attorney's office is separately investigating the 1953 death of 8-year-old Gilbert Bonneau and the 1963 death of 10-year-old Mark Longale.

A grand jury probe is underway in Gilbert's case, whose three brothers maintain was beaten by a nun. Medical experts said Gilbert died of a bacteria infection.

Only sketchy information, thus far, has been available in the deaths of Mark and Andrew. Generally, officials will not open a grand jury investigation until reasonable, substantial proof is found that a crime was committed and that a certain individual committed the crime – in the case, murder. Sabo said records show that Andrew was taken to Samaritan

Hospital in Troy, where he died.

The allegations surrounding Andrew's case were sparked by telephone calls to Colonie police and the district attorney by unidentified people who claimed the boy was

Physically abused by St. Colman's staff. Colonie

police are aware of the charges but have not officially opened an investigation, Lt. Steve Heider said.

The state Department of Social Services, which licenses the home, is investigating not only the allegations of abuse, but is reviewing current standards of living at the home, now a residence for autistic and disabled people, said spokesman Terrance McGrath. He declined to speculate what could happen to St. Colman's if the allegations are found to be true.

LETTER TO THE EDITOR
Early March 1996
The *Troy Record*

Dear Editor:

I have just read with great interest the *Troy Record's* guest columnist piece from Attorney General Dennis Vacco. If he is indeed concerned about child abuse and violence, can he tell me why, when I made a report to the Colonie Police Department about seeing a child beaten at St. Colman's Orphanage and the child was dead about three days later that they were not interested in taking a statement from me. The detective actually told the child's family that I was mentally ill. There is not once ounce of truth to that! I run a state licensed adult care home for mentally and physically impaired adults. I have owned and operated this business for eight years.

In this piece, Mr. Vacco encourages people to help themselves. When I tried, I met with ridicule and disbelief because the abusers were Roman Catholic Nuns. It is probably not politically correct to challenge the Catholic Church or its clergy. But the truth is truth and the matter will not drop until this matter is investigated by someone without blinders on. When all the facts are actually seen, everyone will know what they did. Maybe just maybe I can stop crying every single night. When I can't sleep and I see this child screaming PLEASE, PLEASE and watching this NUN kick him on the floor yelling 'SHUTUP, SHUTUP, SHUTUP."

Susanne Robertson
Seattle Washington

Albany *Times Union* Article
Wednesday, March 27, 1996

SISTER SUES SIBLING OVER ST. COLMAN'S COMMENTS REGION SECTION
Lansingburgh women hit with a $500,000 slander suit
John Casher – Staff Writer

ALBANY – A Lansingburgh woman who called a radio talk show to comment on St. Colman's Home and allegations of brutality has been hit with a $500,000 slander suit –by her sister.

Gail Ruffer called a WQBK (1300) talk show February 8 during a discussion about the Colonie foster care home and challenged some allegations initiated by an out-of-state sister, according to court records. The sister, Susanne Robertson of Buckley, Wash., retaliated Monday with a federal lawsuit.

Robertson is among several former residents of St. Colman's who claim to have witnessed beatings at the Catholic home in the 1950s and 1960. She told officials that a young boy, Mark Longale, whose 1963 death was attributed to a ruptured appendix, had been kicked in the stomach by a nun. Authorities are investigating the circumstance surrounding Longale's death and other alleged incidents of abuse.

Shortly after Robertson leveled her allegations, Ruffer, who had also been a resident of St. Colman's, called the Paul Vandenburgh radio talk show and questioned her sibling's sanity and credibility.

Robertson's attorney, Martin D. Smalline of Albany, said Ruffer's on-the-air remarks harmed her sister's reputation, impugned her credibility with local authorities and jeopardized her occupation. Smalline said Robertson owns a facility for mentally and physically disabled adults in Pierce County, Wash.

"She relies on her reputation and good standing in obtaining state funding for this enterprise," Smalline said.

The lawsuit, filed in federal court because the sisters live in different states, seeks $250,000 in compensatory damages and the same in punitive damages. It is pending before Chief U.S. District Judge Thomas J. McAvoy and U.S. Magistrate Judge David N. Hurd.

Ruffer could not be reached for comment. Neither Vandenburgh nor

WQBK is named as a defendant.

Smalline said officials have so far declined to take a statement from Robertson in the Longale matter and speculate that authorities are unwilling to listen to her because of the sister's comments.

December 14, 1995

Bishop Howard Hubbard
Pastoral Center
40 N. Main Street
Albany, NY 12203

Re: St. Colman's

Dear Bishop Hubbard:

    This is just a short letter to advise you of my progress concerning child abuse at St. Colman's School.
    I put an ad in the Times Union concerning this matter and the response has been overwhelming and enlightening. I am sorry to say it is very sad as the nuns are portrayed as Nazis and should be wearing swastikas, not crosses.
    Over thirty calls have been received of child abuse, humiliation and giving drugs to children, force feeding to the point of illness and then made to eat their own vomit. These are the highlights. The lows are possible wrongful death of a child whose name and circumstances I will only divulge in person. Siblings were not allowed to see each other and even a case of a nun mandating a child to switch from being left handed.
    As you can see there is much more that just some frustrated nuns observing naked boys in the shower and then beating them as they leave.
    Please send a roster of present day personnel at St. Colman's as I feel that is more than a possibility that these four mentioned conditions still exist as some of the so-called nuns are still there.

Very truly yours,

Paul A. Koren, Sr.
(Address)
Albany, New York 12205
(Phone Number)

cc: Hon. Michael Hoblock, Albany County District Attorney's office, Wanda Austin-Peters

SUSANNE ROBERTSON

**(On Official Letterhead)
St. Colman's Home
Watervliet, N. Y. 12189**

January 31, 1995

Mr. Michael Ernest
(Address)
Menands, New York 12204

Dear Michael,

    We are enclosing copies of the information which we have in our records regarding your placement at St. Colman's. We hope this information will be helpful to you.
    May we take this opportunity to wish you a New Year filled with peace and joy.

Sincerely,

(Signature)
_____
Mother M. Carmel
Executive Director

THE THROW AWAY CHILD

(Official New York State Assembly Stationery)

January 2, 1996

Mr. Brian Wing
New York State Department
Of Social Services
40 North Pearl St.
Albany, New York 12243

Dear Brian,

    It has come to my attention that a constituent of mine, Mr. Paul Koren, has contacted your office with some widely publicized allegations involving St. Colman's School in Colonie.

    Since the State Social Services Department regulates institutions responsible for caring for orphans and neglected children, it is imperative that a determination be made as to whether there is any basis for these allegations that have been made, and if so, appropriate action be taken.

    Thank you for your attention to this matter. Please keep me informed of your findings.

Sincerely,

Robert G. Prentiss
Member of the Assembly

RGP/dm

cc: Sen. Hoblock, Mr. Paul Koren

Albany *Times Union* Article
Friday, January 5, 1996

Prentiss Seeks probe of Abuse Allegations at St. Colman's Home
By Marc Carey – Staff Writer

ALBANY – Assemblyman Bob Prentiss called Thursday for an investigation by the state attorney general into allegations of physical abuse at St. Colman's Home in Latham during the past four decades.

"I think it's vitally important we learn the truth either way," Prentiss a Colonie Republican said Thursday.

Prentiss initially called for the state to become involved in a December 28th letter to New York Attorney General Denis Vacco.

"Since the state Social Services Department regulates institutions responsible for orphans and neglected children, and in light of media reports, it is imperative that a public determination be made as to whether there is any basis to these serious allegations that have been made and if found true, appropriate action be taken," he wrote in the letter.

Prentiss said he had followed that letter up with a face-to-face conversation with Vacco.

A Vacco spokesman said Thursday that Prentiss' request was still being reviewed.

"If there is any role for us, we will be available to assist the Colonie Police Department," said spokesman Joe Mahoney.

Family members of 8-year-old Gilbert Bonneau, a resident at the home who died in 1953, have claimed that he may have received a beating that resulted in his death.

Last month Colonie police and a prominent pathologist said a 42-year-old autopsy report on the Bonneau's death gives them no reason to doubt that the child died of natural causes.

"Meanwhile, Colonie police said they have obtained a subpoena for St. Colman's records from the time of Bonneau's death.

"We've talked to dozens of people," said Lt. Steve Heider of the probe, on which a detective has been working full time. "We constantly, day-to-day, are interviewing people … this is a time-consuming thing."

Town police also have received other allegations about physical abuse of children at the home over 40 years.

However, due to the statute of limitations, Heider said, the only issue police can probe is a potential homicide.

Heider said pertinent findings of the investigation will be turned over to the appropriate state agency when the probe is completed.

Prentiss said be made the requests for the state inquiry on behalf of constituent Paul Koren, who had his three children in St. Colman's for nine months in 1970-71 and claims they were abused.

Koren said that as a result of a two-line newspaper ad he placed several weeks ago asking people to contact him about St. Colman's, he has received more than 130 responses, alleging both physical and sexual abuse at the home.

Paul Donohue, attorney for St. Colman's, could not be reached for comment Thursday evening.

SUSANNE ROBERTSON

(Official Attorney Letterhead)

February 8, 1996

Mr. Michael Bonneau
(Address)
Menands, New York 12204

Re: St. Colman's Home
Our File No ( )

Dear Mr. Bonneau:

    Please accept my apology for not sending you those portions of Gilbert's records which the State has allowed us to make public. I know that you had sent a letter to the Home requesting them, but then I saw you on television with a copy in your hand which I presumed had been given to you by the news media.
    In any case, here are the records. I am sorry I cannot give you the entire file, but the State will not allow me to do so.

Very truly yours,

DONOHUE, SABO, VARLEY & ARMSTRONG, P.C.

By: (signature)

AOS:fh
Encs.

Albany Times Union **Article**
Wednesday, December 20, 1995

Colonie Cops May Reopen 1953 Death Investigation
Lara Jakes, Staff Writer

COLONIE - An allegation of beatings at St. Colman's Home more than 40 years ago have police saying they are willing to reopen the case of an 8-year-old boy who died after being hit on the head with a stick by an orphanage nun, according to his relatives.

Although Colonie police said they have no evidence of foul play in the 1953 death of Gilbert Bonneau, investigators met Tuesday with Gilbert's older brother Michael Bonneau, 53, of Menands to review paperwork and hospital records.

"We're more or less covering the bases on this end," said Lt. Tom Breslin. "We might exhume the body, but we've got to find a reason to warrant it. Right now, we have nothing."

The investigation was spawned by stories published this week in The Record, in which Michael Bonneau and his brother William questioned whether Gilbert's death was due to meningitis, as his death certificate states. The certificate also had "death unknown" written on it, according to Michael Bonneau.

William Bonneau, 56, a postal worker who lives in Colonie, said a woman told him in 1978 that Gilbert had been hit with a stick by a nun, knocked unconscious and taken to Albany Medical Center Hospital.

The Bonneaus said they were told that Gilbert was buried in St. Patrick's Cemetery in Watervliet, but they cannot find the grave.

St. Colman's Home officials could not be reached Tuesday evening.

Albany Times Union Article
Thursday, December 21, 1995

Answers to A 42-Year Old Mystery May Have Eroded Away
By Dan Lynch

Gilbert Bonneau died 42 years ago last month, a ward of the state at St. Colman's Home for Boys and Girls in Colonie. At the time, the death of this 8-year-old welfare waif attracted little attention outside his own family.

But in 1978, a woman who identified herself as Marian Maynard phoned one of Gilbert's brothers. She told him that she'd seen the boy beaten to death by a nun, Sister Fidelia, 25 years earlier. The Bonneau family's subsequent quest for the truth about Gilbert's little-noticed death in 1953 has sparked a police investigation. It has also prompted a flood of calls to news outlets, the Colonie Police Department and the institution, complaining of decades of abuse at the century-old home.

Did Gilbert die after a beating by a nun? Was he a victim of a brutal institutional environment? Has the truth surrounding his death been covered up?

I've looked into these matters for the past several weeks now, ever since I saw a classified ad placed by Gilbert's surviving brothers and sister seeking any information that could clear up this mystery for them.

I've found myself caught up in a sad story of familial love and of mystery a murky quest for truth through the shroud of time. I've been able to determine only this much:

The woman who made the phone call to Gilbert's brother might well have been at St. Colman's Home at the time of Gilbert's death. She identified herself as Marian Maynard. There was a girl of about 12 at the institution at the time. Her last name was Maynard. She worked in the kitchen. I've been unable to locate her.

The nun that Marian Maynard said she saw beat Gilbert, Sister Fidelia, was in charge of the kitchen in the late 1940s. She was born Beatrice Dwyer. She suffered a nervous breakdown and left her order and St. Colman's Home in November 1950.

She could not possibly have administered a fatal beating to Gilbert Bonneau three years later.

Beatrice Dwyer spent more than 20 years in Buffalo, working in a clothing store. She married a man named Walter Zima. They later moved back to Troy, where Beatrice Zima was widowed in 1980.

She died four years ago in Wilkes-Barre, Pa., where her husband's family lived.

Medical records dealing with Gilbert Bonneau's death, while sloppy and flawed by modern standards, indicate strongly that he died of natural causes. The likelihood of determining that he died as a result of a beating is remote, even if his body is exhumed, which has been discussed by authorities.

That's because, in routine autopsies in the 1950's, internal organs were thrown away, leaving little material for pathologists of a later era.

The only evidence that could indicate death as a result of a beating would be skeletal indication of a skull injury, and that could have been inflicted during the autopsy itself.

So, it appears that the truth surrounding Gilbert Bonneau's death may never be known. Too much time has gone by. Too many people who might have firsthand knowledge of the circumstances surrounding his death are dead themselves.

But another question remains. Was St. Colman's Home a snake pit of abuse 50 years ago? Was it the scene of routine beatings with sticks bearing the names of nuns?

I'm assured by Mother Virginia a sweet, soft-spoken old woman who has spent more than half a century at St. Colman's that such accusations by former residents are baseless.

She dismisses them as the imaginings of troubled children who were placed unwillingly in the orphanage by the courts and have grown into troubled adults.

"We've given our lives for these children," Mother Virginia told me yesterday as snow swirled angrily about the ancient, red-brick institution on Boght Road. "Did we come here to abuse children?"

This story began in 1947, when things got pretty tough for the Bonneau family. There was a mother and a father and six kids. Then the mother got sick and ended up in a psychiatric hospital. The father had no job. Money was only a rumor, and he could not care for all the kids.

So three boys under 10 went to St. Colman's Home at the time an orphanage for destitute children and today a day care and residential teaching center for autistic children and young adults.

A baby sister went for a while into foster care. The two older boys stayed with their dad.

A few years went by. The kids at St. Colman's were in and out of the place. As they turned 10, an age when they might develop some interest in girls, they moved on to the LaSalle School in Albany.

Finally, Gilbert was the only member of the Bonneau clan left at St. Colman's. He missed his brothers. He cried a lot.

One day the family got a call. Gilbert had fallen ill at the home. He was at Albany Medical Center Hospital. Things did not look good for him.

"I still remember to this day," says brother, Bill Bonneau, a 56-year old postal worked who lives in Colonie. "He had tubes in his nose. He had tubes down his throat. And he had a bandage around his head. This was about 2 in the afternoon. They said he was just sick. He died around 5:30, 6 o'clock. We assumed he died a natural death."

The Bonneau kids grieved and grew up, got jobs, had families. Their parents died. Life went through its seasons. Then in 1978, Bill Bonneau got the phone call that changed his life forever.

The women said her name was Marian Maynard. She told him that in November 1953, she'd been a teenage girl at the home, and she'd seen Gilbert beaten with a stick by Sister Fidelia.

"She beat him to death," Bill Bonneau says he was told by this woman. "When my brother left the home, Gilbert was lonely, and he was just crying all the time. So, she told me that she'd witnessed the whole thing."

The woman said she'd been prompted to call so many years later because she'd recently bumped into the woman who'd administered the beating. Marian Maynard had seen her on a Troy Street, and things had come back to her.

Beatrice Zima was at that point in her life working at Russell Sage College as a caretaker, along with her husband, Walter Zima. Bill Bonneau asked the woman who'd called him to come forward, to speak publicly. No, she said.

"She was too scared, too panicky," Bill Bonneau recalls. "She said that when she was at the home at the time, they told her to keep quiet, that she'd be punished and all that."

The woman wouldn't leave a number. She said she'd call back. She never did. Bill Bonneau thinks she later decided not to get involved. Officials of St. Colman's Home suspect that her motives were more complicated, although they can't guess at them. They say only that she lied to Bill Bonneau about Sister Fidelia, who could not possibly have been involved in Gilbert's death.

Bill Bonneau recalls the bandage on Gilbert's head in the hospital. Gilbert's autopsy report makes mention of swelling of the brain. It also refers to pneumonia brought on by the aspiration of food into the lungs, to liver degeneration and of a bacteriological infection that possibly caused meningitis.

But the autopsy report also says the autopsy was performed some hours before the actual time of Gilbert's death, according to his death certificate and Bill Bonneau's recollection, so he doesn't know how much faith he should have in it.

The Bonneaus are not doctors. Nor are they lawyers. They once approached a lawyer to look into this matter, but the lawyer saw no money in the case and sent them away.

Years ago, Bill Bonneau approached Beatrice Dwyer Zima, Sister Fidela, to confront her about Gilbert's death. She denied any knowledge of it. The Bonneaus went to St. Colman's Home. But the director was not in, and a nun there said the home would speak only to their lawyer.

They asked the home's lawyer to provide them with Gilbert's records. The lawyer, Paul F. Donohue Sr. of Delmar, says the law forbids him to provide such documents without a court order, which he himself is now seeking. He contends that Gilbert's family has effectively waived privacy rights.

He's nearly 80, a retired trial lawyer of some stature. His son Michael spent 44 years at St. Colman's.

Michael Donohue was profoundly retarded and died 13 months ago at age 47. Paul Donohue says his son was cared for with immense love by gently, caring people. He's incensed at any hint that the aging nuns at St. Colman's were guilty of the brutality described by former residents.

I've talked to several former residents of the home. They tell horror stories. One woman, age 65, said she's unable to read aloud to this very day. As a child at St. Colman's, she said, every oral error was punished with a blow. Sister Regina, a warm, gracious woman who's been at St. Colman's for 45 years, told me yesterday that she'd never seen a child struck there.

"Look in my eyes," she said to me, clutching at my arm. "I'm telling the truth."

For the Bonneaus, every path they've followed has turned into a dead end. Gilbert was buried in a pauper's grave. They know the cemetery but they're unable to even locate his resting place.

And so the members of the Bonneau family grow older, and the facts surrounding the death of their little brother Gilbert sink deeper and deeper into the past every day, and they wonder and worry and wait.

And pray that someone will come forward with some positive proof about Gilbert's death while those who remember him and loved him so long ago are still alive to hear it.

Albany Times Union Article
Friday, December 19, 1995

Sisters at St. Colman's Caring and Compassionate
Maureen McGuinness Russo - Clifton Park

"I would like to thank you for Dan Lynch's well-balanced piece on St. Colman's Home. Some of the media used secondhand quotes that allege that abuse was rampant at the home. It has been my experience that when someone has a bad experience they are more apt to speak up, than those who had a positive experience.

The same sisters who reside at St. Colman's Home. It was a positive experience, and never did I see a hand laid upon any of the students.

I was also a volunteer at St. Colman's Home. What I saw there during my visits did bring tears to my eyes. Not because what was happening was so terrible, but because it was so wonderful. I will never forget the annual Christmas pageant at the home where severely autistic children would perform on stage, just as every other child does at this time of year. Quite frankly, the work these women have given their lives to is something most of us would never consider doing. Most of us do not have the patience or the strength to do what they do. Their work is thankless, draining, and they are on duty 24 hours a day, seven days a week, throughout the whole year. Despite this, I have yet to run into one of the sisters who did not have time to smile.

I agree with Mr. Lynch's conclusion that the truth surrounding Gilbert Bonneau's death may never be known. Was there ever an adult at the home who used physical force? Statistically this is possible. However, how many parents used this same force to discipline their children forty years ago?

This doesn't make it right, but if we are to string up the good sisters for what might have been done 40 years ago, we must also put into the spotlight every parent from this era whoever raised a hand to their child.

The words I associate with these sisters are care and compassion. As an elementary school student these were the women I wanted to emulate. I know there are many people out there, like me, who knew nothing but kindness from these remarkable women. I hope that whatever we find out about the death at the home 42 years ago, it does not taint our image of the women who live and work at St. Colman's Home today.

SUSANNE ROBERTSON

Letters to the Editor
The Troy Record
Saturday, January 20, 1996

Dedicated teachers – By Michael J. O'Reilly - Cohoes

Stories reported in *The Record* have portrayed the religious staff at the St. Colman's facility as little better than thugs in a habit, with a sense that no rod was spared so as not to spoil the child. These are reports that another newspaper initially refused to print, and that I find to be both outrageous and impossible to believe.

My family has been involved with St. Colman's for the past four years, as our daughter was in the Special Education-Early Childhood Development Program, our son attended the Day Care Center, and my wife has been a parent representative on panels that evaluate residential students' progress and recommended programs for the coming year.

Our experiences have been nothing but enthusiastically positive. The Sisters of the Presentation of the Blessed Virgin Mary, the order that operates St. Colman's, are outstanding teachers and individuals who have but one goal – to prepare every child to be successful in both academics and everyday life.

It is important to remember that the students at St. Colman's have special educational and emotional needs. They need special education, including speech, occupational therapy, vocational therapy, physical therapy, just to name a few.

There are also residential placements from many stations in life who have been placed by a social agency and/or the court system that is dealing with the children's parents. These children require adult supervision full time in a structured environment.

The staff at St. Colman's is uniquely qualified to provide this supervision and education, without the need to ever abuse a child. To know the sisters at St. Colman's is to know the most loving people of children I have ever encountered, and we have been very fortunate to have placed our children with them when their talents were needed.

One final point: Upon completion of our children's programs at St. Colman's, we chose to further their education at an elementary school operated by the same sisters, a further testament to our confidence in their abilities and dedication.

Caring about Kids – By Yaroslava Vorberts – Watervliet

I want to thank the director of St. Colman's Day Care Center in Watervliet, to which I applied in March 1984 with the petition Rev. John I. Kulish of Hudson about getting my daughter into the center.

Sister Regina filled love in their hearts and accepted my daughter in kindergarten.

We are very thankful to all the sisters and workers at St. Colman's Home for providing the best service to the children that can ever possibly be. They are very kind to every child that goes to the home. Furthermore, they are as caring about kids as they could care for themselves.

We will never forget nights that we spent with my daughter Christina during which children told stories and were happy that they were together around their good friends and teachers. They presented to the people nice dances, plays, and had a lot of fun.

Every person who works in St. Colman's Home is very kind, nice to the children and careful about everything. They are teaching kids how to become an educated professional in society today and this job is needed at the present time.

God bless them all.

CHAPTER 19

Gilbert Bonneau

1947 — Daniel, Michael, and Gilbert Bonneau were placed in St. Colman's Home. My brother Patrick was taken in by a family friend; I remained with my father. These untimely and tragic turns of events were precipitated by the sudden illness, hospitalization, and subsequent death of my mother (she was only 39 years old at the time of her death). Local authorities would not allow my father to keep us together; they did not believe my father would be able to care for all of us. Against my father's will, we were all separated – never again to be reunited in our youth as a family.

1950 — Daniel left St. Colman's and was transferred to another school. Sept. 1953 —Nov. 27, 1953 - My family was notified that Gilbert had taken ill and had been sent to the Homes infirmary.

The following day my father was informed that Gilbert's condition drastically worsened; he was removed from the infirmary and taken to Albany Hospital (n/k/a Albany Medical Center). My father, my brother Danny and I immediately went to the hospital.

Danny and I remember that day clearly as it was the last day that we would ever see our brother Gilbert alive. Gilbert was comatose; he had tubes down his throat and up his nose. His head was wrapped in a bandage. Both my brother and I recall spots of blood on the bandage. I was only fourteen years of age at the time of Gilbert's death and my brother Danny was thirteen. Our father, without question, readily accepted what the doctors told him concerning the cause of Gilbert's death. My father was heartbroken and was not able to talk to us about Gilbert's death after that point. My mother was never informed of Gilbert's death as it was thought that it might make matters worse for her.

Through the years after our little brother passed on, we all thought about him often and we missed him very much. It was very hard for us to know that Gilbert was the most helpless of us all and he was left in St. Colman's by himself and none of us (his family) were able to be there for him. Of course we all understand now that there was nothing we could do about it, as we ourselves were all very young and we also were placed in various living situations that were out of our control.

More than twenty years had passed since the death of Gilbert, when to our distress we received a most upsetting phone call from a woman claiming to have information surrounding the death of my brother. Her name was Marion Maynard, and she claimed to have resided at St. Colman's Home during the same period of time that my three brothers did. That would place her time of residency anywhere between the years of 1947 - 1953.

This mysterious call was made to us in 1978 and it has triggered a chain of events leaving our family with a great many questions that have yet to be clearly answered to our satisfaction. Our family feels strongly that the information given to us by this woman after so many years have transpired, must be true in light of the various discrepancies surrounding all the available paperwork and the suspicious nature and questions surrounding Gilbert's place of burial. Marion Maynard (caller) claims to have witnessed my brother Gilbert being struck several times over the head with a stick or a piece of wood by a nun. She gave us the nun's name and also stated that the nun threatened to punish them (other witnesses to the beating) if they repeated the incident to anyone. Marion also stated that Gilbert died the next day at Albany Hospital.

I hope you can now understand the impact that this call has had on our family and our deep desire to get to the truth of this grave matter. Our brother Gilbert was just a poor defenseless 8 year- old; in only nine days he would have been nine. His life is very dear and important to us and we feel strongly that those responsible for his well being, now, in light of the various discrepancies surrounding the extensive paperwork, need to thoroughly investigate and adequately answer all of our questions and address all of our concerns.

Many people suggest that we just let this go and forget all about it all. I ask you, if this child were your brother, or sister, or perhaps even your son or daughter, would you be able to let it go so easily? This issue has received extensive media coverage; we have all heard the experts making statements indicating that there was no foul play surrounding the death of my brother Gilbert, however, most of the paperwork we have strongly suggests a different story.

It is the intent of this article to allow the public to examine the facts as they have been presented to us in the relevant documents, and to allow those interested, to see for themselves the reasons why we are not giving up on our search for the truth and why we have so many unanswered questions that need to be properly addressed if our family is to have peace. All we have of our little brother is one picture and many troublesome questions.

The following is only one example of the many questions that we find disturbing to us due to the conflicting nature of the documentation presented to us alongside with a variety of other discrepancies surrounding the death and burial of our brother. My brother's life needs to be accounted for.

What was Gilbert's actual time of death?
 a) Was it 6:45 a.m. according to the Autopsy Report?
 b) Was it 4:00 p.m. according to the Death Certificate?
 c) Was it 6:05 p.m. according to the Medical Records at Albany Medical Library?"

By William Bonneau

Excerpts from an interview with Michael Bonneau on June 8, 1999 with Peggy Rockwell

For the Reader: anything in italics will be the interviewer's questions or comments, otherwise, all text will be the words of Ernest Michael Bonneau.

We are talking to Michael, Hi Michael.

Hi.

You told me that you were locked in a closet a lot?

Yeah, well, I don't know what happened. It is possible that I could not deal with the way they were trying to teach me things, or something, I'm not sure what happened, but I do remember stings with the sticks, and I do remember being in a place, like a cubby hole, I'm sure, you know, I just remember sad things in that place. Kids being hit with sticks, by nuns, and by I think they call them a layperson. She used to be an orphan in the home, she stayed in there all her life, but she was in charge of the boys, and she was pretty mean.

Well, you described for me yesterday in different terms.

Pretty mean. Oh yeah, well you did anything wrong, you got it from her. She would just stand there, smacking her gum watching you, and she would have that stick underneath her arm. She probably hit me, but I don't remember. You know, I did get hit many, many times because I can still feel the stings today. You know, that's what comes to my mind is stings. You know, I did see kids get beat up, I see them, put out in the solarium, well mostly all of us. We had to line out in the solarium out in the stairs, and watch these kids that wet their bed with sheets over their head. Of course, some of the kids screamed, and they hit them with sticks. Then they used to hang them down the laundry chute by their legs.

Who did this? The nuns?

The nuns and that lay person.

What was her name?

Katherine Fredette.

Hang them down the laundry chute by their legs?

Yeah. From the stair, they had the laundry chutes out in the stairwell in St. Colman's. I don't know, it was just a sad place. You know, there were good times. Very, very few good times in there, you know, like when they had the Knights of Columbus would probably put on a Christmas party for the kids, we would get out of there and go to a Christmas party. Summer time, we could not wait because they had field day, you know, like a field day outside. Um, and the movies, they, had movies every, I believe it was Friday or Saturday night. But as far as playing, if the weather was bad, they used to keep us inside in the playroom and we used to have to sit on benches all day long - for hours.

So, your experiences from St. Colman's are kind of confused because, I mean that's what...

Well, apparently they must have traumatized me. They had to traumatize me, because why can't I remember certain things? You know, I do remember the church, you know, we were always in church. But there are a lot of things I can't remember because, probably because we were scared. You know, they beat us. I don't know what happened. For all I know I might have wet the bed, I don't know, I don't know, I really, don't know. I remember getting hit, but I don't, it just doesn't connect. I mean, you see kids get hit, but, you know, when you get hit yourself, you know you got hit because you remember the stings. I don't know. Everything changed in that place for me.

In 1978 a woman named Mary Maynard made a phone call to your brother Bill?

That's correct.

And, can you talk about that. It seems to have changed your life.

Uh, yeah, well, as far as Gilbert when he died, we always thought he died from meningitis, you know a disease or something.

Why?

That's what we always, were told! I guess my parents were told that the nuns said that he died from a disease. And that was it. But, 1978, this woman, she was a resident when Gilbert was there at that time. She was older than Gilbert. She was probably a teenager. She called my brother Bill, and she explained to Bill that, you know, that Gilbert did not really die from meningitis, he died from a beating.

She also stated that she knew the name of the nun that did this to him, and at that time when Gilbert did get hit with a stick, they were told by that nun, these girls that witnessed Gilbert's beating that, they did not see anything. If they did, they'd get the same, or something. They probably had to keep hushed up about it. But, anyway the girl did see what happened, the reason why the girl did call my brother Bill in '78 was because, this girl that witnessed Gilbert's beating apparently ran into the nun, the ex-nun in Troy, NY, at the Vale house, over at Russell Sage College. From what the girl told me, I believe she meant this ex-nun was a hostess at the college or something, I'm not sure what. But she said, when she saw this woman's face, she, it brought back memories to what happened to Gilbert, and she just decided to call my brother Bill, and let us know what really happened to him. And we did try to, we were supposed to get contact with her, but she said she was moving or something, and that, you know, that she would get back to us, or whatever. I'm not positive of what happened. But, when we heard that we, I mean, myself and all my brothers, we went up to St. Colman's Home in 1978 and we rang the doorbell, and this nun comes out. I knew the nun by her face, I remembered her face when I was a kid up in that place, but I could not think of her name till later. We asked to see the Reverend Mother Bernadette. She says that she's not in right now, can I help you. We went in, and we explained to her what really happened, what we heard had happened to our little brother Gilbert, and she says, "Wait here, I'll be right back." Probably waited five minutes and she come back out with a pencil and paper, and she says, "Well, what's the name of your lawyer?" My older brother Bill said "Well, we don't want to say right now" and that was it. We haven't heard from anyone from St. Colman's home until this day as I'm talking to you right now about what really happened to Gilbert. Everything is silence since then. We tried to get in touch with this woman, you know, I ran ads in papers.

What woman?

Mary Maynard.

So, you never spoke to her again after that?

No, no. We did go see an attorney probably a few days after, or maybe the same day after we left St. Colman's.

Did that strike a chord in you, the question, "Who is your attorney?" Did that make you think?

Well in a way, yes, I mean, why would they want a lawyer? I mean, why would they want to know our lawyer? What, they must have done something wrong then, or something. But anyway, we did see an attorney. His name was Seymour Fox. And he said "If she witnessed this, well, where is she, you know, you'll have to contact her, she's got to come in and make a statement of some kind." He said, "Without that, you can do nothing." We could never get in touch with this women who witnessed Gilbert's beating, and we just let it ride, we just figured there was nothing that we could do.

Well, what did she say about Gilbert?

She says Gilbert died of a fractured skull. That's what happened to him. That's just the way she told us over the phone that he was beaten with a stick, and he probably died from a fracture.

How old was Gilbert when he died?

Gilbert was 8, he would have been going on 9 years old. He died when he was 8. He was 8 years old when he died.

When you received that phone call from Mary Maynard in 1978, it really did change your life. Am I right?

Oh, yes, it changed everything. It changed, I mean, you've got to remember that we believed he died from a disease.

Can you explain to me what happened? You went from thinking that your brother just died of a disease to thinking that he was beaten to death.

Well, like I said before, when that woman called us, we went to the home and went to see the attorney. The attorney said, "You have to have this witness come forward to sign this statement." And I said, we don't have any idea, she said that she would come back to us, she never left a phone number, or anything like that. She said she was moving, or something to the New York City area. But, we figured there was nothing we could do without that witness, so we let it go until, I'd say, we just let it go. Period. In 1995 I wanted to do a family tree. I wrote a letter to St. Colman's home to see if I could get my personal records, and I did not ask for medical record, I just asked for personal records. And they did send them to me. I also wrote another letter, not too long after that to see if I could get Gilbert's personal records, and I was denied. When they denied me Gilbert's, lets see, the only thing I would really know about Gilbert would be through his records. When they denied me, that's what made me go forward.

So, alarms went off in your head.

Yes. I started running ads in newspapers looking for Mary Maynard. I have done that for, well it was '95 in the summer, July, when I got my records, and then I tried to ask for Gilbert's. They denied me. So I ran the ads, roughly about a few months later looking for Mary Maynard to see if she could help us out. You know, I wanted to thank her for what she told us about Gilbert. How Gilbert's story broke was somebody from the *Troy Record* saw this article I had in their newspaper, and they were curious about what it was all about, so they sent a reporter to my house. That's how Gilbert's story broke.

You did finally get some records of Gilbert's, right? Regarding a prescription from a Doctor.

Well, when Gilbert's story broke, we had a hard time getting personal records. I had to hire an attorney to get his personal records. So finally, the courts allowed some of his personal records to be released. You know, we had to fight a long way to try to get these. It was not all his records. It was only, maybe a third of his records that the court ordered to be released, and New York State Social Services. But in the papers they did release, I found a prescription slip in there.

Can you tell me about the prescription? Why don't you talk about that. Who the Doctor was who wrote it.

Well, what it says on this one document found in Gilbert's file, it's a prescription slip, written from a Dr. Haverly from Green Island NY. He was the St. Colman's Home Doctor; like an industrial doctor, and from what I believe, the nuns took Gilbert down to see him at his office. He wrote out a prescription for the nuns to take Gilbert to the hospital for immediately hospitalization, diagnosis and for treatment. The date that was on this that I can see, and everybody else can see, is November 28, 1953. Upon studying this prescription slip, I did notice that the number eight was changed somehow. It was my belief that it was a one, twenty-one. That would be about seven days before he died. It's possibly a twenty-seven, and then somebody, the day he died, put an eight there.

Which is the day he died, November 28, 1953.

Correct, correct and...

What the script say? What were the instructions on the prescription?

To take, Gilbert Bonneau to be hospitalized immediately for diagnosis and treatment and it is my belief that it was a 21.

So, in other words, they never did anything.

No. If I were to believe the story and I do, because of the witnesses we have that saw Gilbert being beaten it is my belief that Gilbert was in such bad condition that the nuns did not know what to do, so they brought him down to Haverly. Dr. Haverly wrote out the slip, and the prescription slip for Gilbert to be hospitalized, and they out right denied Gilbert's rights. They let him lay in that infirmary for 7 days.

Do you think they were afraid to take him to the hospital?

Yes because of the beating. That's the only reason.

And it is significant that...

Well, if they brought him to the hospital, the place would have been closed down. Either that or they would have arrested somebody up there.

You would hope.

And I am sure that they covered everything up.

What do you think of Dr. Haverly?

No, I have faith in the guy because he wrote out the prescription slip.

So, the fact that the prescription slip was still in his file proves that it was never ... that he was never taken to the hospital. That they never followed the Doctor's orders.

Well, they might say that they made a copy of it, but I don't think they had copiers in '53. Why would you make a copy of a prescription slip in the first place? There is another slip for eyeglasses, that was never filled, but the main, the main prescription slip that could have saved his life was, was outright denied.

When you saw these documents, how did you feel?

Well, there was not much on them. A lot of the documents weren't signed by the nun, the head nun.

And you are still trying to get documents, aren't you?

Well, these were only certified copies. They were in camera review that the judge released. They did finally give us copies of his entire file, but the in camera review copies only. When I studied the prescription slip, I noticed the date being changed, and I hired a forensic document examiner and he told me that in order to really go through them, to see if there was wrong doing on these papers, you would have to have the originals. So, I had to hire an attorney to go back to the Supreme Court, County Court to get his original documents, and that's on hold right now. That's what we are waiting for.

Do you have any anger towards, like, I mean.

Towards St. Colman's?

Well, yeah.

People say forgive, but what really hurts me is that they kept silent about it. I don't understand why they are keeping silent. Why don't they talk to us? We haven't heard from anyone since 1978. That was the last time I ever talked to someone from St. Colman's. That was the nun we talked to when we explained about what happened to Gilbert. I have never heard from anyone to this very date. And for them to keep silent about Gilbert, I don't understand the religion. You know, it's got me upside down...

How did he feel about Gilbert's death? Do you remember that?

No, no, no. But from what my brother Bill said, he took it bad.

I asked you if you remembered the nuns who hit you and you said all you remembered were...

They all looked the same.

Yeah.

They all wore black. It was scary. The only thing, the only actual person that I can actually picture was that Fredette woman. I mean, because she was never dressed up as a nun, she was in civilian clothes. That's somebody you'd never forget. Today, when I look at World War II pictures about the concentration camps, and I remember seeing these women SS guards she comes right to the picture, this Fredette woman. She comes right clear to me.

And she had been brought up in St. Colman's.

Yes. I believe her and her siblings and there's a possibility that one of her siblings became a nun up there.

In 1995, when they did not release the records for Gilbert, that is when this media blitz really happened about Gilbert's death.

When they refused Gilberts' records, I felt that since I did not remember my brother that would be the only way I would know about Gilbert would be through his records. When they denied me his records then I was upset about it and I said well jeez, why do they need them, I'm the one who needs them. I need to know about my brother. But, what I started doing since I could not get anywhere there, was to put ads in the paper looking for the Mary Maynard Girl, or anybody else to see if they could let me know what they knew on what ever happened to Gilbert. That was going on for some time, a couple of months or so, and finally an editor from the "Troy Record" spotted my piece in the paper and he sent a reporter to my house. I explained to the reporter, I showed him, different articles about Gilbert and the home and that was when said that he would do a story for Gilbert.

What I found interesting about reading about Gilbert's death is that it opened up a wound in this community about orphanages, and a fight about people who were beaten and people who weren't. How do you feel?

Well, well, it's my belief that if Gilbert's story did not break that nothing would have came out about the abuse in that place, so...

Now, there are some notes that are in front of me that are "Bedside Notes" from St. Colman's, and they start on November 23, 1953, and they go to the 28th when he was supposedly taken to Albany Hospital.

Right, right.

But, there is no identifying nurse, no initials, no caregiver; it is all in the same handwriting. It looks like it was done in one day. Can we talk about this document a little bit?

Well, not really.

You don't want to talk about it?

Well, what can I tell you about it?

Well, I mean, who was the investigating ... What are these notes? You hired a forensic Doctor, did you not?

Yes a forensic pathologist.

You hired him to look at these notes.

Well, yeah. To look at Gilbert and his medical file and stuff.

He told you you had a case.

No, the only person who really told me I had a case was a forensic document examiner, who told me that I do have a case concerning the prescription slip, the dates.

And, why don't we talk about grave #. That was where he, they wanted to talk about exhuming the body, and they said that his grave was marked as grave# in Latham?

Right, at St. Patrick's Cemetery. But, according to their records, that's where he was buried, grave #. And, what happened, apparently, when we bought the stone for Gilbert back in the '60s, apparently the people we bought the stone from contacted St. Agnes Cemetery, and they gave them the information to where to place the stone. So, actually, the flat stone was not placed on grave #, it was placed next door to it. So we've been going there for roughly twenty some odd years, thinking it was Gilbert, which it was not, he was next door. The stone was in the wrong place.

So, you finally did have the grave exhumed, did not you?

Yes, in June (1998) last year.

You had to do that privately.

Yeah, we did that on our own expenses. Everything was done on our own expenses.

And, so, there was no ... Tell me about, you said there were twins. The Frawley Twins who were in the infirmary.

When Gilbert was there, yes.

Can you tell me, what happened? What did they tell you, one of the

Frawley twins tell you?

Well, I did speak to both of them. They talked to me on a radio show and told that she and her sister were in the infirmary when Gilbert was there. The one girl does remember Gilbert because she went to school with Gilbert, Gilbert was in her class. But, anyway, they were there, when Gilbert was in the infirmary, these two, the twins, they heard Gilbert crying for help. He kept saying, "Help, I need help." The one twin sister who was closest to the door got up and tried to get help for Gilbert, and they told her to get back in bed, and mind her own business. I'm not sure what night it was, but the other girl, the other twin stated that she, (long pause) that she saw two nuns and a priest come in finally. They weren't sure of the time, and they told her to turn around and mind her own business, you know, in her bed, go to sleep, or whatever. They were whispering something, or other and she said, they woke up in the morning, Gilbert was gone.

Gilbert was not there.

So, you had eyewitnesses. Did these people talk to the Colonie Police?

Yes. Both of them, and I guess they gave them a written statement.

So, the Police opened an investigation into Gilbert's death, and then they said they found no foul play. And how do you feel about this finding?

Right. Well, as far as I'm concerned they did not investigate at all, they, I mean…

You think they were part of a cover-up as well?

Well, definitely, what happened to Antoine Periard? He actually, he did see Gilbert get hit over the head in the infirmary?

Tell me about what he said? He was in the infirmary as well?

Well, this is another time. This is another day, when Gilbert was brought in. I mean, I don't know how many times he was brought in. Who knows, he was probably brought in so many times. But, Antoine says that when they brought Gilbert in, they were actually carrying him slumped over. They had that Fredette woman underneath his arms and Sister Regina had his legs. They brought him in and, from what Antoine stated, his head was swollen like a ball. His face was all red and blotched, and he stated that when they got him into the bed in the infirmary, they tied him down, his legs and his feet, and I guess he was twitching or something, I'm not sure. Antoine says that he sees this Sister Regina pull out a stick behind her veil and she whacked him once across the head. And, and I think that Sister Regina did say something to Antoine, I can't remember.

Isn't it true that that statement did not appear in the Police report?

Right. When the detectives from the Colonie P.D. decided to make their move to investigate, the deaths of the three kids, especially Gilbert, they asked that anyone who knew anything about Gilbert to give them a call. Antoine did call. Apparently he could not come down, so they sent two detectives out to his house with his sister and family present, and they took a statement from him. Antoine did state that he did see Sister Regina strike Gilbert with the stick in the head while he was tied down. A few days later we got a phone call from a detective, one of the detectives assigned to the case. We asked him how things were going, and he said that "we don't have anything yet." My brother Bill asked, "Well, what about Antoine Periard? You know, what he saw?" He told my brother Bill in front of me, my wife and his wife that Antoine did not see Gilbert get hit with a stick. And my brother Bill said, "What are you talking about? Antoine told you on his statement." Well, it's not in the statement. The detective said, "Well, if you want to go up and see Antoine and bring him down again, we'll take another statement." So, we went all the way out to Greenwich, NY and we picked him up. We went to the police station that night, to talk to Detective Reude, that was his name, Michael Reude. We asked the dispatcher if we could see Detective Michael Reude. The detective Michael Reude come out and he was militant, in a way, you know, he was sarcastic. My brother Bill said, "here's Antoine." Detective Reude said "Well, we're not taking any more statements." There was a sort of fracas going on there, in a way which seemed like he was pushing us, he was tempting us to do something. I don't know, but he was all wound up. Yeah! He was arrogant, arrogant and said, "No! They wouldn't put anymore statements in.

Did you have a lawyer at this point, or not?

No. I do have his statement too, his police statement. They sent it out to his house, the copy of it, and we have it and that statement's in there.

Is there any reason why you think the Colonie Police would want to cover it up? What are your suspicions?

Well, the Catholic Church is holding, they're just holding things back from us. I don't know. It's like running into a brick wall.

Now, you did finally have Gilbert's body exhumed, a year ago? And they did a DNA Test because there was some problem with the grave. They had to make sure the body was Gilbert's. The DNA came back.

Right, through Gilbert's teeth they took DNA. It did match my brother Bill. But, as far as we other brothers, they did not go any further testing. I don't understand why not. They just did Bill's. They took three samples of blood from Danny, Bill and Me. We had to hire somebody to take samples to send to the forensic investigator. Then he sent that to the pathologist. And then, I'm sorry, they sent it to the DNA people. And I still don't understand why they only took Bill's. I was closer to Gilbert. That's got me puzzled.

And, all of this was at your own expense?

Yes.

And, there was no fractured skull, which is what you expected.

Well, that's what they say.

OK, so you don't necessarily believe that that was Gilbert's body?

I will always have my doubts because the day Gilbert was exhumed the Colonie PD mentioned on the air that they believed that they weren't going to find anything wrong with Gilbert's body. When they made that statement, that's what made me wonder if it was Gilbert that they exhumed. Even though we had DNA testing done, and they say that it was Gilbert, I still have my doubts; I'll always have my doubts that that was truly Gilbert.

How has this affected your life? Now you are really committed to this right now.

How has this affected my life? Well, I'm definitely committed to it. Like I said before, when you're in St. Colman's there is no such thing as defending yourself. You had nothing to say, but later in years when I found out what really happened to Gilbert, I felt that I had to defend him. That's the way it is. You know, what are you going to do?

You were basically brought up in institutions your whole life.

Yeah. You could say that, yeah.

And how do you think that has shaped your life? I mean, you're retired now from the fire department.

The fire department, yeah. Well, let's put it this way.

And you raised six children of your own.

Correct. If I did not have money at the time, I don't think I would ever be doing what I'm doing today for Gilbert. I just had the money.

Now?

Not now, I did. I mean, it's cost me over $20,000 so far and that's a rough estimate. Over $20,000, I've spent already. The only thing that I want to happen is for Gilbert's story to be told, and I want the truth to come out. Why is it that the nuns have to keep being silent, I don't understand.

Is Sister Regina still alive, or any of these nuns?

Yes, she's still alive, but I don't remember her at all. Fidelia I might remember, I mean, I can remember Sister Alouisious. She picked me up by my ears one time. Certain nuns you can remember certain ones you can't.

Who was Sister Joan of Arc?

Oh, she was a nice nun to me. She was like somebody you could look up to. I might have been in some type of trouble, or they were beating me, I don't know what happened, but I do remember her, you know somebody to look up to. I don't know why.

Do you think that you have already told his story in 1995 and 1996 with all the controversy surrounding his death? When that unfolded, do you think that, or you don't think that you accomplished this?

Oh, no. I know I accomplished a lot. If it was not for the "Troy Record", I don't know where I'd be today, you know, with Gilbert's case.

So you feel like that really vindicated him to some degree. Well, you had a lot of support.

No.

No? Well, do you have anything that you would like to add?

Well, I just can't wait until we get the results to see his original documents to prove, that there was foul play, and that the nuns were responsible for his death. And I hope some day that they come out and tell the truth.

You said something about three children who had died?

Yeah, there was a boy by the name by the name of Mark Longale. I think he died around the '60s sometime. He was the boy who was supposedly kicked in the stomach by a by a nun according to the witness and he had a ruptured appendix. I think he was 12, I'm not sure. Then there was another boy by the name of, a younger boy, back in the '40s, I think. His name was Andrew Rada, I think.

OK. This is the conclusion of the interview with E. Michael Bonneau about Gilbert. Thanks.

Sure.

SUSANNE ROBERTSON

Albany Times Union Article
Friday, December 22, 1995

Town Stands Behind Autopsy Report in Boy's Death
Colonie police and hospital officials say there's no reason to doubt St. Colman's account of 1953 death

By Lara Jakes Staff Writer

COLONIE Town police and hospital officials say they have no reason to doubt that Gilbert Bonneau died of natural causes in 1953 not from being beaten on the head in a Watervliet orphanage, as his family alleges.

A 42-year old autopsy report, a copy of which was obtained by the *Times Union*, concludes that the 8-year old boy suffered from a myriad of illnesses, but not from head injury or trauma. It also states that Gilbert did not die of meningitis, despite what it says on his death certificate.

With the report, which police subpoenaed Thursday, Chief John Grebert said he does not believe at this time that Gilbert's death on Nov. 28, 1953, is suspicious. Records show the autopsy was performed 3 hours after the boy's death.

"Nothings stands out that would indicate that there's foul play here," Grebert said. "Right now, we've certainly made no decision to exhume the body. We would need something else, and right now, there's nothing."

Gilbert's three brothers believe that the youngster was beaten over the head with a stick by a nun at St. Colman's Home and that the injuries led to his death. Over the last 17 years, the family received two phone calls from different women who said they witnessed the assault.

The Bonneau brothers all of whom live in the area are wary of Gilbert's death certificate, which lists meningitis and a "cause undetermined" in the boy's death. They suspect that the autopsy doctors misrepresented Gilbert's death to protect the orphanage. "There's no doubt in my mind that there was a cover-up," said William Bonneau, 56, a postal worker, who lives in Colonie. "Those death certificates are not accurate, as far as I'm concerned."

But Dr. Barbara Wolf, who is advising Colonie police on the investigation's medical findings, said there is "nothing sinister" in the reports she's seen. Wolf is the director of anatomic pathology at Albany Medical Center Hospital.

"Everything is still being looked at, but the report indicates a natural death," Wolf said. "There is nothing to support a suspicion of a beating."

The autopsy shows that Gilbert died of pneumonia and bacteria in his blood, Wolf said. It also shows he suffered from complications of those infections such as swelling of the brain, collapsed lungs and an infected liver. While the autopsy was performed by an unidentifiable "Dr. Garcia" and "Dr. Bigelow," it was supervised by Dr. Arthur Wright, a former professor and chairman of pathology at Albany Med. The possibility that Wright would have lied about Gilbert's death is highly unlikely, Wolf said.

In continuing its investigation, Grebert said police also will subpoena records from St. Colman's and St. Patrick's Cemetery in Watervliet, where Gilbert supposedly is buried.

Grebert said that more than 20 people have called police this week to complain of similar abuses at St. Colman's, but none have provided any leads concerning Gilbert Bonneau's death.

Repeated telephone calls to Mother Superior Carmel, who supervises the home, and to Paul Donohue, the institutions attorney, were unanswered Thursday. As a result of the investigation and intense media coverage, dozens of former St. Colman's residents have come forward with allegations of abuse.

The Record
Final Edition
Thursday, December 21, 1995

Death Certificate Disputed
Baden: Boy at St. Colman's 'did not die of meningitis'
By Carmen Napolitano

COLONIE - One of the nation's preeminent pathologists said yesterday that the death certificate for the 8-year –old boy who died in the care of St. Colman's Home is wrong.

"The kid did not die of meningitis," Dr. Michael Baden said.

Baden, a former New York City chief medical examiner who frequently works with the State Police, said "there is no evidence to even suggest this and therefore there is need for further investigation. The findings are not accurate."

The death certificate lists "meningitis" in the cause-of-death box, but someone added, in another handwriting, "cause unknown."

Baden's statement, based on a review of a summary of the 1953 autopsy report, comes as officials consider exhuming the body of Gilbert Bonneau for a closer examination.

Gilbert's surviving brothers say they believe Gilbert was bludgeoned to death by a nun at the orphanage in November 1953.

The boy died Nov. 28, 1995. The family's belief is based on a 1978 phone call Gilbert's brother, William, now 56, of Colonie, received from a woman who claimed she and others had witnessed the beating.

The attorney for St. Colman's contends the child died of a contagious disease.

Colonie police launched an investigation after The Record reported this week on the family's charge and the murky circumstances of Gilbert's death.

Braden who recently returned from Bosnia, where he assisted the U.S. military in identifying scores of dead people, said the autopsy document the Bonneau's have found indicates that the boy was ill several days before he was taken to Albany Hospital, now called Albany Medical Center Hospital. He said it shows the boy suffered a form of pneumonia and in the days before his death experienced a loss of appetite.

The Record report has prompted dozens of other people who lived at the orphanage to call with their own tales of abuse during a span of more than 25 years.

Braden said the one-page document contains no evidence of blunt trauma to the head or related complications. He said that type of information, if such evidence existed, would have most likely been detailed in the rest of the pathologist's report.

Albany County Coroner Tim Cavanaugh said the full report is probably long gone. Cavanaugh said in the 1950s such documents were most likely stored in boxes in the basements of attending coroners or pathologists and that there was no coroner's office or central location were records were kept. Cavanaugh, whom police have assigned the case, said the original document was probably thrown out years before.

The autopsy was conducted by two doctors with common last names – Garcia and Bigelow – who did not give first names or even initials.

Officials at Albany Medical Center Hospital said they have no record of either doctor.

The report was approved July 7, 1954 by the hospital's chief pathologist, Arthur W. Wright, who died several years ago.

Because of the murky records and questions raised by the family, Colonie Police Chief John Grebert said detectives have discussed exhuming the boy's remains – if they can be found.

Written records given to the Bonneau's by St. Patrick's Cemetery in Albany show that Gilbert was buried there, but the section, lot number and grave number on a form provided by the cemetery are blank.

Rick Touchette, executive director of the cemetery, said he knows exactly where the boy is buried and has the records to prove it.

Michael Bonneau doesn't believe it.

He said he and a cemetery caretaker probed the grave site a year ago and struck the lid of a cement vault. Michael Bonneau said his brother was given a pauper's burial and that money would most likely not have been spent on a vault.

Detectives asked anyone with information relevant to the case to call them at 783-2754.

SUSANNE ROBERTSON

Albany Times Union Article
Thursday, January 11, 1996

St. Colman's Sues to Release Boy's Medical Papers
Institution seeks permission from Albany County to show
that nun did not kill 8-year-old at orphanage in 1953
By Lara Jakes Staff Writer

ALBANY – St. Colman's Home is suing Albany County to permit the public release of information that the home says will clear it of any wrongdoing in the 1953 death of an 8-year old resident.

Charging that the Colonie institution's reputation has been harmed beyond repair, attorneys maintain that the documents will show that Gilbert Bonneau, who was placed in foster care at the home in 1950, died of natural causes, and not at the hands of a nun, as his family alleges.

"The Bonneau family has charged that St. Colman's Home has engaged in a cover-up," according to the suit, filed Friday in state Supreme Court.

Unless the documents are released, the home "is incapable of defending itself against the aforementioned accusations of criminal conduct, causing irreparable harm to St. Colman's Home," the suit states.

Meanwhile, Bishop Howard Hubbard of the Albany Roman Catholic Diocese also called for the records' release.

"The more openness there is, the better people will be able to understand the issues and put it in perspective," Hubbard said in a telephone interview Wednesday. "The more forthcoming that we can be, the better off for the well-being of the institution."

Because of state confidentiality restrictions, St. Colman's argues in the lawsuit that it may jeopardize its child care license if it releases the records without county approval. Albany County's Department of Social Services licenses the home.

St. Colman's wants to release medical records and summaries of diagnosis and treatment at Albany Medical Center Hospital, where Gilbert was taken on Nov. 28, 1853. He died there that day, the suit says.

The lawsuit does not state the cause of death. But Dr. Barbara Wolf, director of anatomical pathology at the hospital, said last month that the autopsy report shows that Gilbert died of pneumonia and bacteria in his blood.

Gilbert's three brothers, who live in the Capital Region, believe that a nun beat the youngster over the head with a stick.

Colonie police began investigating last month after receiving dozens of calls from former St. Colman's residents.

Albany County District Attorney Sol Greenberg said Wednesday that he subpoenaed records from the home in December. He would not specify which records were taken and declined to say whether they would be presented to a grand jury.

"We're looking to see what the records show," Greenberg said. "Then we'll decide to see where we'll go from there. It may stop at that point."

The county will respond to the lawsuit within 20 days, said Albany County Attorney Michael Lynch. He declined further comment.

Albany attorney Alvin O. Sabo, who represents St. Colman's declined comment through a receptionist at his law firm. Repeated telephone calls to Mother Superior Carmel at St. Colman's were not returned.

Hubbard said the diocese oversees the home's religious aspects, but has no access to records dealing with St. Colman's former mission as a foster home or its current operation as a residence for autistic people.

The diocese has not investigated Gilbert's death because it was never asked to, Hubbard said. If a nun or any other employee at St. Colman's was proved to have acted inappropriately, "I would expect they would be disciplined and removed," he said.

In the 19 years Hubbard has headed the diocese, he fielded two complaints about St. Colman's both within the last six months, but before Gilbert Bonneau's story was reported in the media, he said. One dealt with distribution of medication to the autistic residents. The other concerned Gilbert's death, but Hubbard said the Bonneau brothers never showed up for a scheduled appointment to discuss their allegations.

Release of the records might not satisfy the three Bonneau brothers. "They might have some cover-up on them," said the eldest brother, Danny Bonneau, 55, of Albany.

***The Record* article**
December 22, 1995

MARION, COME FORWARD

Marion Maynard, please call us now.

You hold the keys to the riddle at St. Colman's orphanage.

Some readers say the tales we're hearing from former St. Colman's residents are made up – the products of troubled children who have turned into troubled adults.

We don't think that's so.

But we can't prove that the dire interpretations of what happened to a little boy there are true.

Only you can do that.

You probably feel that you don't want to get involved, that you did your bit in 1978, when you made the phone call that relieved your troubled conscience.

But you have to get involved. Here's why: If what you described in that phone call is accurate, you saw a terrible wrong committed. And it may have been part of a pattern. No one can bring back Gilbert Bonneau. There's no point in mindless seeking revenge on his behalf. But there's a chance that what you say you saw did not end decades ago. The Bonneau's anguished story prompted many people to call us with tales of abuse from the 60's, 70's, even 80's. Only the spotlight of publicity will show what has happened there and whether anything is amiss now. And you're the spotlight operator.

We believe you're out there. Mortality statistics suggest that you are still alive, and circumstances suggest that you're part of the local community.

So please, put aside your fear of getting involved and call us. Let us hear directly from you what you saw.

If you have called us – and we think that's very possible – call again. But identify yourself this time.

It's too late to stay uninvolved. The die was cast when you made that fateful phone call in 1978.

Sometimes, fate works in strange ways. The Bonneau's have been taking out classified ads for years, but it was only last month that an astute city editor here spotted one and turned it over to an inquisitive reporter, who started to probe beneath the surface.

In reality, you started that process and only you can end it definitively.
Call us.

For Gilbert
For his brothers
For his community
For you own sake
Call us now.

SUSANNE ROBERTSON

Albany *Times Union* Article
Saturday, January 13, 1996

ST. COLMAN'S GIVES FILES TO PROSECUTORS
Probe continues in the alleged beating death of a young boy in 1953
Lara Jakes - Staff Writer

ALBANY – A grand jury investigation into St. Colman's Home moved forward Friday, as a file of records concerning the 1953 death of an 8-year old resident was turned over to the Albany County district attorney's office.

Colonie attorney Alvin O. Sabo, one of the two lawyers representing the Colonie foster home, handed over the documents to Assistant District Attorney Paul DerOhannesian following a brief session before Albany County Judge Larry J. Rosen. Copies of the records were also sent to the state Department of Social Services and the Colonie Police Department.

Last month, District attorney Sol Greenberg subpoenaed St. Colman's for all documents concerning Gilbert Bonneau and other residents and staff who lived there at the time of the youngster's November 1953 death. Gilbert's three brothers, who live in the Capital Region believe that the youngster was beaten to death with a stick by a St. Colman's nun. After reviewing autopsy reports, Colonie police and an Albany Medical Center pathologist said they have found no evidence that Gilbert died of anything other than natural causes.

Greenberg's office got Bonneau's records Friday, but Sabo asked to withhold the background and medical history of the other residents, arguing that they were irrelevant to the investigation. His request was granted.

"We feel we can live without that," DerOhannesian said. "We're interested in the names of people who can assist us with the investigation."

With the list of names supplied by the home, the district attorney and police will attempt to locate anyone who lived at St. Colman's in November 1953 who may have any information related to Gilbert's death. DerOhannesian declined to comment when asked if he would use the names to look into allegations of physical abuse toward others at the home.

Sabo said Friday that the home has detailed, extensive records that show Gilbert died of meningitis and plans to present another medical expert to prove it. But based on the records that she's seen, Dr. Barbara Wolf has said that Gilbert died of pneumonia and bacteria in his blood. Wolf is the director of anatomical pathology Albany Medical Center Hospital and is assisting

Colonie police in the investigation.

The state Department of Social Services, which licenses and overseas St. Colman's, began examining its copies of Gilbert's records Friday, spokesman Terrance McGrath said. The agency's attorneys had not finished looking through the documents by the end of the day, but McGrath said the papers could be opened to the public Tuesday.

"We intent to allow the release of the bulk of the records, but before, we believe it's prudent to know what is in the records," McGrath said. "The only things we would not authorize would be personal information about some of the relatives surrounding the reasons why the child was in foster care; information that is not pertinent to any of the allegations."

St Colman's called for the public release of its documents in a lawsuit against Albany County last week, saying it had no other way to defend itself in Gilbert's death. Without the stat's permission, St. Colman's could lose it child care license if it disclosed the records.

"If there were some way that it can be worked out for the whole file of records to be released, fine. We have nothing to hide," Sabo said. "This has been horrible for the nuns."

Albany *Times Union* Article
Thursday, February 29, 1996

DESPITE LACK OF EVIDENCE, ST. COLMAN'S SAGA LIVES
State, county, and Colonie abuse inquiries find
nothing solid, but "survivors" press on
Capital Region Section
Lara Jakes – Staff Writer

COLONIE – It's been two months since police and other officials began investigating St. Colman's Home, and in that time, the story has taken on a life of its own.

Spawned by claims that three young boys were beaten to death by nuns at the Colonie foster care home, Albany County District Attorney Sol Greenberg in December launched an investigation into allegations dating back 33 years. But instead of being debated in a courtroom, the case is being fought in the media and over backyard fences.

It's a story that won't go away, largely because of a group of people who call themselves "St. Colman's survivors" refuse to let it.

But like it or not, officials said, there is no substantial evidence that St. Colman's was ever involved in the death of any of its residents. The investigation, Greenberg said, "may go nowhere. It's hard to come to any conclusions, and there are some people who may never let this go."

Yet more than a month after his office first began its probe into the 1953 death of 8-year-old Gilbert Bonneau, Greenberg confirmed in early February that two more alleged beating deaths at the home are being investigated. Now, Greenberg and Colonie police are looking into the case of 10-year-old Mark Longale, who died in 1963, and 6-year-old Andrew Rada, who died in 1943.

All three investigations are sparked by media reports and phone calls from former St. Colman's residents. They claim to have witnessed or heard of the alleged fatal beatings.

Since the first reports about Gilbert, dozens of people have called to report alleged abuse at the hands of the nuns at St. Colman's, and Colonie police Lt. Steve Heider. Some return later to change their original statements.

If Paul Koren of Colonie has his way, police will be busy for quite some time. Koren, 59, presides over the recently formed St. Colman's Survivors Support Group, an organization spearheaded by some of the home's former residents or relatives of residents. The group, which meets monthly, intends to lobby Assembly members to abolish the statute of limitations on sex crimes, said spokeswoman Nancy McGrath. The group also hopes to set up a toll-free number for people to call for support she said.

Koren makes it clear that the group will keep pushing for action on the claims of members. "Some of these people are credible, and you can really tell if they're telling the truth," Koren said. "Are (officials) going to call them all liars? They can't bury it like they've buried everything else."

In St. Colman's view, the story has been anything but buried. Instead, investigators and especially the media have been putty in the hands of the survivors group, said Alvin O. Sabo, an attorney in Colonie who represents the home.

Sabo said he doesn't mind a police investigation; in fact, he welcomes it. But the media probe is something else.

"The police have kind of an obligation to lean over backwards to investigate allegations," Sabo said. "But the media is getting used worse. Anybody can make an allegation, and the media (are) reporting as they're true. They're reporting on the allegations, not on the proof."

For every person alleging that they were wrongfully treated at St. Colman's, another claims that the foster home was a wonderful place to live. Two sides have opposed each other in several news conferences, most recently at WRGB (Channel 6) offices, where they debated the fairness of the station's news reports on the foster home.

As far as Greenberg is concerned, many of the allegations to come out of police interviews are based on hearsay or secondhand knowledge. The St. Colman's case may never be presented to a grand jury, Greenberg said. That's for him to decide.

Reacting to all the allegations and media reports, the state Department of Social Services is conducting its own investigation of the current standards of living at St. Colman's and spokesman Terrance McGrath, who has no relation to Nancy McGrath. The home is now primarily a residence for autistic and disabled people. The Albany Roman Catholic Diocese oversees the religious teachings of the home, which is staffed by nuns.

Social Services is looking into allegations of abuse at St. Colman's that go back so many years that neither police nor the district attorney can investigate, because the statutes of limitations has expired.

The records taken from St. Colman's show no indications of wrongdoing by the foster home, McGrath said. The state investigation is expected to be wrapped up soon, he said. "There's nothing we've been able to find so far," said McGrath, adding that fewer than 12 people have called the agency to report abuse.

Koren said he knows of at least two more boys who were beaten to death at St. Colman's, but refuses to identify them to police or the district attorney until the current investigations make some headway.

"They could be playing patty-cake over there, for all I know," Koren said of Greenberg's office. "We want to see how they're really going at it. If they're not taking these allegations seriously, I'm going to take it to the FBI."

Koren's zeal stems from the abuse he says his three children suffered while living at St. Colman's for about nine months in 1970-71. He said he doesn't have any proof that people were abused at the home other than the stories he's been told.

Without hard evidence, the case will eventually dissolve, said Heider of the Colonie police. "If there is no case I can investigate and pursue—I am sorry," he said. "Unfortunately, in cases such as these, victims are often not satisfied. Thee is never a case where the victim is happy."

**Albany *Times Union* Article
Thursday, September 12, 1996**

3 SEEK TO EXHUME BODY OF SIBLING
WHO DIED AT ST. COLMAN'S
They Also Want Personal Records of His Care
While at the Colonie Foster Home
Capital Region Section
Lara Jakes – Staff Writer

ALBANY – Three Colonie men who claim their brother was beaten to death 43 years ago is suing a Watervliet cemetery and the state in hopes of exhuming their sibling's body and obtaining his confidential foster care records, officials said Wednesday.

Charles T. O'Hern, an attorney for the three Bonneau brothers, filed two lawsuits in state Supreme Court Wednesday. The suits, aimed at the state Department of Social Services and St. Patrick's Cemetery in Watervliet, are the family's last chance to discover the circumstances of Gilbert Bonneau's death at the age of 8.

Gilbert died in 1953 while living at St. Colman's Home in Colonie. Autopsy records show the boy died of meningitis, and that his body was buried at St. Patrick's, which is near the foster home.

Gilbert's brothers maintain the boy died after being beaten on the head with a stick by a St. Colman's nun. The family had received an anonymous phone call in 1978 by a woman who claimed she saw the nun hitting Gilbert in the head. The boy died several days later. St. Colman's has denied the allegations.

Eight months after Albany County District Attorney Sol Greenberg launched an investigation into allegations of abuse at the home, the Bonneau brothers decided to pursue their own probe.

The Bonneau's are prepared to pay as much as $20,000 to have Gilbert's body exhumed and hire a pathologist to conduct a second autopsy, brother Bill Bonneau said Tuesday.

"It's up to us to make the moves," he said. "We feel we have to do this as a family to find what the truth is. We wouldn't be doing this if we feel there was not foul play."

Even if the body is exhumed the family is not sure whether the spot that is marked with Gilbert's headstone is really his. A preliminary probe of the grave this year revealed a cement vault liner – a luxury a pauper child like Gilbert could not have afforded, Bill Bonneau said.

St Patrick's Cemetery is "prepared to consent" with exhuming Gilbert's body as long as the disinterment follows guidelines set by the Albany Roman Catholic Diocese, according to a letter signed by Richard N. Touchette, cemetery executive director.

Because of a state confidentiality law, Social Services must have a court order to release the records that specifically deal with care Gilbert received while living at the foster home, spokesman Terrance McGrath said Wednesday. The agency did open the boy's medical records in January.

The Bonneau's filed a Freedom of Information request with Social Services in March for Gilbert's complete file, which was denied. Had the family then received a court order for the file, "they could have gotten the records in April," McGrath said. The pending lawsuit, which is scheduled to be heart Oct. 4th in front of Justice Joseph C. Teresi, "is unnecessary and I hope we can work this out," McGrath said.

When allegations of abuse at St. Colman's began circulating late last year, two agencies – Social Services and Greenberg's office – spearheaded investigations into care at the foster home. Social Services concluded its probe in March, clearing the home of any wrongdoing.

The criminal case is open in Greenberg's office.

Albany *Times Union* Article
Saturday, October 5, 1996

ST. COLMAN'S STUDENT'S RECORDS
TURNED OVER TO COURTS
Gilbert Bonneau's 1953 Death Is Still a Subject of Controversy
Capital Region
Lara Jakes – Staff Writer

ALBANY – The confidential records of an 8-year-old boy who died in foster care in 1953 were turned over Friday to a court justice by the state Department of Social Services.

In a 10-minute presentation in front of state Supreme Court Justice George B. Ceresia Jr., attorney's for DSS and the family of Gilbert Bonneau handed up all records pertaining to the boy's three-year stay at St. Colman's Home in Colonie more than 40 years ago. It is now up to Ceresia to decide whether the records – currently shielded by a state confidentiality law – will be made public.

That decision could come within the next few days, Ceresia said. If the records are opened to the public, Gilbert's three brothers believe the documents will shed new light on the events that lead to the boy's death.

"We don't know what's in there, but there's certainly enough evidence already to suggest that something bad happened to that little boy," said Albany attorney Charles T. O'Hern, who represents the family.

The Bonneau's maintain Gilbert was beaten over the head by a stick-wielding nun at St. Colman's, and that the orphanage personnel failed to stop a blood infection and then conspired to cover up the youngster's death. St. Colman's repeatedly has denied the allegations, and released 17 pages of Gilbert's medical records in January that show the boy died of pneumonia and meningitis.

DSS concluded an independent probe of St. Colman's in March, clearing the foster home of any wrongdoing.

Last month, the Bonneau's filed a lawsuit against DSS to get the records, which cannot be released unless under court order because of the confidentiality statute. The agency previously had turned down the family's requests, which were filed under the state Freedom of Information Law.

Both parties quickly agreed Friday to relinquish the records to Ceresia. "We're cooperating and trying to get any disclosure that the court deems appropriate," Assistant Attorney General Jeith E. Kammerer said after handing over the DSS records. The attorney general's office s standing in for DSS in court.

"The system looks like this insurmountable law, but it's not. But there are rules in effect today and we have to follow the rules," Kammerer said.

The records in question most likely include details of the boy's life at the Colonie foster home, such as attendance and disciplinary reports and general observations, Kammerer said. Whether those documents contain any clues to Gilbert's death is unknown, Kammerer said, adding that the stack of records is "not voluminous by any means."

"We are in favor of anything that will give that family peace of mind and if giving them the record does it, so be it," said Alvin O. Sabo, attorney for St. Colman's.

In January, Sabo filed a lawsuit against the Albany County Department of Social Services for permission to disclose Gilbert's records, which he said would exonerate the home. He later dismissed the suit, after the state DSS made Gilbert's medical records public.

The Bonneau family also is waiting to hear whether the Albany Roman Catholic Diocese will allow a grave marked with Gilbert's headstone at St. Patrick's Cemetery to be dug up, O'Hern said. The brothers are willing to pay $20,000 to have Gilbert's body excavated and re-examined, but are not even sure if the grave is his. A preliminary probe of the grave earlier this year revealed a cement vault – a luxury a pauper child Gilbert could not have afforded.

That case is pending, O'Hern said. A grand jury investigation led by Albany County District Attorney Sol Greenberg last December also is open.

Albany *Times Union* Article
Wednesday, June 18, 1997

OFFICIALS EXHUME BODY OF 8-YEAR OLD WHO DIED AT ST. COLMAN'S
Capital Region Section
Lara Jakes – Staff Writer

COLONIE – Forty-four years after the death of Gilbert Bonneau, officials Tuesday exhumed what they believe are the remains of the 8-year-old boy in an effort to finally determine whether the youngster was beaten to death by a nun at St. Colman's Home in 1953.

Following a series of accusations, police investigations and the threat of lawsuits over the last 18 months, Gilbert Bonneau's four surviving brothers hired forensics specialists to exhume the body from St. Patrick's Cemetery at their own cost.

The family has also hired Monroe County Chief Medical Examiner Nicholas Forbes to conduct an autopsy independent of what Albany Hospital – now Albany Medical Center Hospital – said killed Gilbert Bonneau while he was a resident of St. Colman's Home, a former foster home.

The family maintains that a nun with a stick beat the child on the head – an allegation that St. Colman's has flatly denied. Medical records show the boy died of either meningitis or a bacterial blood infection, but the Bonneau's charge that the paperwork is the product of a massive cover-up orchestrated by the hospital, police and the Albany Roman Catholic Diocese, which maintains the foster care home.

Even if the new autopsy does not turn up evidence that the youngster was bludgeoned to death, Bill Bonneau said he will not be satisfied. Using DNA, medical experts must first determine that the body dug up is Gilbert Bonneau's as the remains were found one plot over from where the boy was supposedly buried.

"I won't be completely positive it's him until we do DNA testing," said Bill Bonneau, 58, a postal worker who said his family spent their life savings to finance the exhumation and tests, which cost in the tens of thousands of dollars.

"If there's nothing that shows trauma or anything, that wouldn't convince me anyway. If it does show, then we'll know. It's up to Gilbert now – up to his body. He may speak."

Technically, the criminal investigation is still open in Albany County District Attorney Sol Greenberg's office, even if a lack of evidence has kept it dormant since early 1995.

Nuns at St. Colman's, which now houses autistic children, are looking for an end to the probe that has called into question the institutions credibility. Their attorney, Alvin O. Sabo, said Tuesday he also asked an independent pathologist to examine Gilbert Bonneau's medical records in early 1996 and is satisfied the boy died of natural causes.

"The sisters are looking for some kind of closure. If it turns out that the exhumation does that, they it'll be for the best," Sabo said. "The family wanted to do this, so fine. Let them do it."

Bill Bonneau said the results of the autopsy conducted by Forbes should be available within two weeks. Forbes, who lives in Rochester, did not return phone calls to his office Tuesday.

CHAPTER 20

The Children Speak

***The Troy Record* Article
Saturday, January 20, 1996**

Letter to the Editor of the *Troy Record*
By June E. Maloney

It is with a very sad heart that I pen this letter for in doing so it will cause many people great pain and distress especially my own family. It might cause people to examine their lives, questions their belief in themselves and the faith they have placed in others. I believe we are all too ready and willing to give up the rights and responsibility for our children's welfare to others thus having no accountability when tragedy strikes.

I know that children are gifts and should be loved, cherished, protected and natured to grow into what God wants them to be. They are like blank pages that are filled with what life brings to them, some of it good and some of it bad. Children need to know that they are wanted, loved, are valuable and will be safe from harm. They also need to know that if someone or something threatens that knowledge that an adult will make it right. I feel that these are the responsibilities of all adults; be they parents, grandparents, teachers, aunts, uncles or other caregivers.

I would ask this: "What is more precious than a child?" and respond not a thing. Who could hurt a child? What does the face of an abuser look like? I ask what happens to a child when those responsible for its life and well being fail? What happens when the child is neither loved, nor nurtured and is physically abused and emotionally and spiritually wounded? What happens when those responsible profess to love all God's children, profess to do God's work and are given sanction by the State and the Roman Catholic Church? What happens when the abusers are Roman Catholic Nuns? Do we take for granted that clergy would not hurt children? Are they vested with some special gifts from God that exempt them from human failures? What happens to this abused and frightened child? Who does this child go to for help? Who will believe this child? I answer, "NO ONE!"

As a successful, happy, Christian woman and mother I am charged by the laws of God and man to see to the welfare of all children. While in the care of the nuns at St. Colman's Home for Boys and Girls in the mid 1950's and 60's, I and many other children were mistreated. It was called punishment at the time but now is called abuse. I've been told that children are still being abused at St. Colman's Home. No longer can we accept abuse as a part of any child's life. It is wrong. You can't terrorize children and get away with it. Abused children become dysfunctional adults and history shows us that abused children frequently become abusers themselves. No one is exempt from the law, be it God's law or the laws our society has enacted for the good of all mankind. While I would love to see those responsible for the abusing of children held accountable before God and the law, I firmly believe that vengeance belongs to God when we leave this life, but feel that justice needs to be served today, now, to all the children who suffer abuse.

Unlike many others, mine is a happy story. I dealt with my early childhood a long time ago. I came to terms with the pain people can and do cause to each other. I put my faith in God and HE has never failed me. It is my faith that prompts me to write this letter. To hopefully right some wrongs of the past. Childhood abuse destroys families. I have seen my own family destroyed by events that took place so long ago than on one remembers what happened. My sister and father haven't talked to each other in over 30 years because of the abuse she suffered. She was not able to tell him for fear he would not and could not believe. She rebelled and he gave up on her."

Respectfully submitted for printing

June E. Maloney
Seattle, Washington

April 2002

After I wrote this letter to the editor of *The Troy Record*, my father never spoke to me again. I had humiliated him with my words. Imagine that, his children were abused in a Catholic orphanage for almost 10 years and he was publicly embarrassed! Some people don't ever get it ... I feel sorry for him...

Bill Maloney died a few years ago. My son and I went to his funeral. The only reason I went was because of my son. I believe that Bill actually loved his grandson. I think he tried to make up for his inability to be a father to me by being a grandfather to Andrew. We missed the wake because we were in transit from Seattle. I understand that there were hundreds of people in attendance. He did help a lot of people in his life ... just not his own children. I know that Carolyn, his second wife was surprised that we were there. She had neglected to put my name and my sister Susanne's name in the paper as surviving children ... imagine that. I suppose you have to do what you have to do to get you through the day.

June

Albany Times Union Article
Thursday, January 4, 1996

Ex-St. Colman's Resident Says She Witnessed Abuse
Mary Christine Yamin - Troy

I am writing in response to the recent articles regarding allegations of violence and abuse at St. Colman's Home.

It is deeply important for me to address the situation at St. Colman's in general and in particular, to address the reported statement of Mother Virginia and Sister Regina.

I resided at St. Colman's from 1960 through 1969. I was not a troubled kid and I am not a troubled adult.

I am a working professional with a master's degree in nursing. I am currently employed as a nurse practitioner.

I was not a victim of physical abuse at St. Colman's. In some ways it really was a home for me. So my motivation for writing has nothing to do with vindictiveness or the desire for revenge.

While I was there, I did witness both neglect and abuse.

What is most troubling to me about this situation is the response of the Sisters of the Presentation, which is a classic example of both denial and blaming the victim. The nuns said there were no problems and those who said there were should be dismissed as troublemakers and troubled kids. From my experience, that is simply not the case.

I am able to place St. Colman's of the '50 and '60 in a historical context. Catholic institutions across the board were rigid and discipline-oriented; nuns and priests got away with physical, verbal and emotional uses in pulpits, classrooms and confessionals; nuns and priests were next to God and their behavior was never seriously questioned in a public forum; scandals were hushed and never reported. The Second Vatican Council had yet to happen.

In this context, St. Colman's was in many ways like all Catholic institutions of the time.

The stories about abuse at St. Colman's are true.

Like all of us, the sisters will answer one day for what they did to so many little ones, if they do not answer already in the privacy of their consciences.

Albany Times Union Article
Thursday, January 4, 1996

Sisters Aren't Acknowledging years of Abusing Children
Barbara A. Easton – Clifton Park This letter via e-mail

In Dan Lynch's recent column, Mother Virginia of St. Colman's Home dismissed the claims of physical abuse by former residents as imaginings of troubled children who have grown into troubled adults.

The truth is that children were struck and sometimes quite violently in St. Colman's. I know. I saw it.

During the time I was there, November of 1957 to June of 1962, these kinds of occurrences were fairly regular. These are not delusions.

I wish they were. Shame on you, Sisters.

Not being honest about it now is a continuation of the abuse.

SUSANNE ROBERTSON

Albany Times Union Article
Sunday, January 7, 1996

Reader Says Abuse Claims at St. Colman's Are Wrong
John Vinson – Albany This letter via e-mail

Regarding you recent article about an alleged murder and abuse of a child at St. Colman's Home some 40 years ago:

I was a resident of this fine institution back in the early '60s and I have nothing but great things to say for the wonderful nuns who cared for me when my parents were going through some tough times. May I also say that I was never hurt by these caring and thoughtful nuns and I find it appalling that someone would doubt the sincerity of these special people!

St. Colman's has been a haven for the unwanted, unneeded or unloved child for many more years then when I was there and my six years under their care has given me a great insight to be loving and caring to others. May the Lord look upon these wonderful people their whole lives, for the service to the community would be worse off without their kindness and compassion?

***Albany Times Union* Article**
Friday, January 12, 1996

Don't Limit Investigation to Events at St. Colman's
Nancy McGrath – Albany

Regarding your Jan. 7 editorial urging the state Legislature to step in and demand an investigation of St. Colman's, I could not agree with you more. However, I believe the focus should not remain exclusive to the small group of mostly elderly nuns, but on the system that allows abuse to occur at institutions and agencies set up to protect and care for society's most vulnerable citizens.

I have formerly worked in human services as an advocate for Association for Retarded Citizens, and as a mental health counselor for Unity House.

I have heard the horror stories from clients about the physical, emotional, and sometimes sexual abuse they endured at the hands of the staff in the hospitals or homes they were forced to live in.

Fortunately as a result of this being made public many of these places have been shut down, or been forced to comply with stringent regulations for care and treatment.

This would not have occurred if enough people did not have the courage to speak out and demand these places be investigated.

I was personally a resident of St. Colman's Home from 1972 to 1980, at which point I left for Siena College. Although I was only beaten once, I witnessed examples of severe physical abuse of other children up until about 1976.

The social workers and psychiatrists we were assigned to by the county, who worked on the premises, did nothing to protect these children.

One of your readers even wrote claiming St. Colman's was a haven for the unwanted, unneeded or unloved child. I disagree.

I was placed there because my father had died and my mother was frequently hospitalized by a chronic illness. I was loved very much by my mother and was not willingly given up.

Most of the children there had similar situations; we were not "bad kids!" I was fortunate enough to have been loved and treated well before arriving at St. Colman's, therefore, I was able to recognize abuse when I saw it.

SUSANNE ROBERTSON

Albany Times Union **Article**
Tuesday, January 16, 1996

Thanks for the Memories, St. Colman's
Theresa Sutton – Special to the Times Union

I was placed in St. Colman's Home in May 1949 at age 6 and remained there until August 1957. I cried when I arrived because I was being taken away from my single mother, who had to work (I was placed there for reasons made evident in her divorce, not alcoholism or abuse), and I also cried very hard the day I left to go home with my mom and grandmother. St. Colman's was truly a wonderful place to grown up, and my memories of my nine years there are truly positive. My brother, who joined me there in 1951, agrees.

I remember tap and then ballet lessons on Friday Afternoons, music lessons at least once a week, recitals, plays, processions, dances with the boys from LaSalle, and more playmates than any child could ask for, 24 hours a day. I remember structure, organization and time enough for everything: Chores (which changed every six months and were called charges), school (an hour of homework each evening, starting in the fifth grade), and playtime, which was sufficiently unorganized to allow children to choose their own favorite thing to do.

There were always enough children for a baseball game, dodge ball, jump-rope, hide-and-seek or cowboys-and-indians. There must have been radios playing somewhere all the time, because we certainly knew all the latest songs and used to sing them at the top of our lungs while swinging on the highest swings I was ever on anywhere. During my two-year charge in the infirmary, I never saw a child admitted because of abuse or disciplinary action. Sister Peter had a motto: "good, better, best; never let them rest until the good is better and the better is best." That is how we were taught to clean, thoroughly, and when I do my housework I do it in a way that the nun's would still be proud of. It's much easier now that my four children are raised and the biggest mess is only cat hair. I also approach chores with a sense of play, which comes from nine years of performing charges with others who laughed, giggled, moaned and groaned, talked and sang while we went about it.

I think this is the reason my job reviews over the years have always portrayed and praised me as a really good team player.

I remember that Father Flynn taught me to play jacks and always chuckled at my made-up sins in the confessional (what does a 9-year old know of sin?) I remember crying on Sister Loretta's shoulder when I stopped my dad's visits, playing Mary Magdalene and Salome in passion plays, and finally being redeemed when they let me play Bernadette for the Rev. Mother's silver jubilee.

I remember envying the high school girls when they went to their formals and how excited the sisters were getting them ready, and how wonderful it was going to my first military ball at the Christian Brothers Academy with Paul and my second with Joey. These boys had been childhood friends since my early grades there.

I loved singing in the choir and knowing the sister's names before the entered the convent, because we sang at the professions.

Gregorian chant is making a comeback today, and I still can feel how wonderful it felt to sing it as a youngster. Chanting is used today as a meditation technique, and I knew the quiet state it could take you to as a child. A common method of discipline at St. Colman's (50 to 60 kids with one nun to monitor them could get out of hand) was to call a quiet time and have us sit or kneel with our hands placed on our heads for five minutes.

When I started practicing yoga 20 years ago (I now teach it), I remember that the combination of those quiet times and ballet lessons was my early training. The nuns knew what they were doing. Oh if one child got his hand cracked with a pointer or a stick resembling a ruler, it was enough to quiet the rest of us down. Occasionally I was that child; an angel I'm not. That was discipline, not abuse harsh by some standards, but I can tell you that from talking to friends about their childhoods, we had it easy.

As for Gilbert Bonneau being murdered, that is the biggest crock ever. I clearly remember the sad hush that came over the home when it was announced that a child had died. He was the first corpse I ever saw, and we were all quiet and solemn when we filed by his casket in one of the front parlors. (I never saw a nun with a 2-by-4 in her hand).

My memories are of field days with three-legged and wheelbarrow races. Christmas parties at Behr-Manning and the Rotary Club, Halloween parties and bobbing for apples, evenings listing to "The Lone Ranger" on the radio before we got television sets, running under the sprinklers before the pool was installed pillow fights and ghost stories. Every night was a pajama party.

I think it is time for all you alumni to remember how really good you had it with those sisters, to forgive them if you got a crack on the hand on occasion, and to remember how much fun it was to be part of such a loving community. And if you hated the creamed cod on Friday evenings, well so did I. Theresa "Terry" Jabob Sutton now works for the Regional Cancer Center in Nashua, N.H.

E-Mail Document
Thursday, January 24, 2002
Subject: These are the stories that I Karen and I posted
– Changed the names

I spent several years at St. Colman's Home. I am only 46 years old. I witnessed abuse of others and I was severely beaten many times and brought to the infirmary once. My sister who is 48 came up to the infirmary and she was not able to recognize me. My face was beaten beyond recognition. She only saw my face not my body which was also kicked, punched and dragged around a laundry room. The name of the nun was Sister Christopher.

I was probably only 6 or 7 at the time. I was told to leave the playground and go somewhere, this is murky. What was clear, was as I was walking down a hallway, someone grabbed me by the hair of my head and proceeded to throw me into a room with large silver laundry bins with wheels on them. I remember because they rolled around as I was being pushed into them. I was punched and slapped in my face many time. Then I was pushed to the ground and the nun proceeded to take her big black shoes and kick me all over my body and in my face, as I was struggling desperately to cover myself with my arms.

I can remember the large rosary beads that dangled from her waist and the large over-sized crucifix that was right at my eye level. It seemed that the beating was not going to stop. I knew that I shouldn't cry out as this tended to make things worse when you cried out. I don't remember much after that. I don't know if I lost consciousness or not, but I did wind up in the infirmary. After that, I spent a good deal of time in the infirmary, though, I don't know exactly how long, timeframe is murky. I never saw my face. I can only go by what my sister said. She said that my face was beyond recognition. My sister is a nurse with three grown children attending college and high school children. There were many other incidents of abuse and humiliation.

About a year before the Gilbert Bonneau story broke out in the Albany area, I went to St. Colman's. I wanted to confront them with what they did to me, and I wanted them to know what they did too many other children. I went with a friend. She went into the main office to kind of set the meeting up for me, as I was very nervous. While she was in there, I went for a walk on the grounds.

I walked into a large long room off the parking lot behind the building. There were large windows that looked out unto the lot. As I walked in, to my shock and horror I witnessed a man, (young – early 20's) abusing what appeared to be a young child of about 5 or 6. He pushed the young boy against the wall. With his head pushed tight against the wall, he took both of the child's arms and held them behind his head and then proceeded to push the child down to a kneeling position. Once the child was kneeling, the man put his knee firmly into the child's back.

Mind you, I was watching all this without his knowing. I was to say the least in shock, and words just wouldn't come out of my mouth, I felt paralyzed. Then suddenly, when the man seemed to be finished with his actions, the words flew out of me. I yelled. "What are you doing to that child?" The man turned and looked at me, rather surprised. He said: "This is what we need to do to children with behavioral problems."

Well I ran out so fast and barged into the office, yelling to my friend, who thought I lost my mind and I was being retraumatized by being in the place. I said, "It's happening again, they are abusing another child." Then I ran and told her to come with me. She followed me, but when we got there the child and the young man were no longer there. So, we proceeded to walk through the place looking for the man and the young child. Mind you the nun that was in the main office talking to my friend magically found her way there before we even got there.

Well, my friend and I found the child and the young man. My friend confronted the young man and asked if what I had said was true. The young man, said YES. My friend asked him to re-enact the incident. He did as I described. They claimed that this is the way that these children needed to be disciplined because they were autistic. Well, not know anything about autistic children, we left.

We went back to the office and proceeded to discuss my experience there as a child. They denied completely, though this nun, was not even involved. She denied, before even investigating the incidents. She said to have my lawyer call them. Well, I did not go with a lawyer I did not have a lawyer that was not what I went for. I wanted an apology. I wanted them to know that the abuses suffered there, affected my entire life in so many negative ways and only by the grace of God have I survived.

Well, after that, with no apology, the incident of the little boy bothered my friend and me. We called people who specialized in the treatment of autistic children and we explained what happened to this child. They were in terror and said that in no way is this treatment acceptable with these children under any conditions. Well, at that point we reported the incident to Child Abuse.

We have no idea what happened after that.

When the incident of Gilbert Bonneau came out in all the papers in the area, I told several of them of the incident of the little autistic child that was abused before our eyes. NOT ONE STORY OF that incident was put in the paper. NOT ONE??????? Just in case any of you care about this little autistic child, his name was Wally. That is all we know about this child. We have no idea what became of him. Was his parents informed about the incident? Somehow I don't think so, and once again, the children with no voice go unheard.

From the Desk of Susan Marie

To everything there is a season and a time to every purpose under the heavens. A time to keep silence and a time speak. Eccles. 3: 1 & 7

A sweet face dotted with reddish brown freckles, framed the bright blue eyes that held only trust. Reflecting the innocence of his thoughts, Wally smiled in spite of the situation. The docile mannerism of this little boy confused me at first; I could not understand why he stood so silently by in light of the troubling events that were being played out before him. I sadly discovered moments later that Wally was an autistic child and he had just been abused by a young man who apparently had some degree of authority at St. Colman's.

As some of you know, Barbara and I returned to the orphanage several years ago hoping to speak with the Sisters who were the primary caregivers during Barbara's childhood. At Barbara's request, I attempted to pave the way for what we perceived would be a sensitive conversation. While I waited for one of the Sisters to meet with me, Barbara decided to walk around the grounds of the orphanage.

Only moments into my conversation with the attending nun, I realized the futility of my mission; it was denial in summation with the standard "have your lawyers call our lawyers" response. I assured the nun that Barbara held no malice and was not seeking legal recourse. Before she could reply, Barbara burst into the office visibly shaken and she stated: "Susan you need to come with me now, a little boy is being abused" – I immediately followed her. After finding Wally and the young man in question, I insisted that he re-enact what Barbara had accidentally witnessed.

The young man consented, however, before he was able to do so, the nun I had been speaking with only moments earlier came running through the door. In spite of her presence, I was enlisted to serve in Wally's place and Barbara demonstrated what she had seen. The young man admitted that he had handled the child in the manner shown, but the nun interjected in defense of his actions stating – that it was standard procedure when dealing with autistic children whose behavior was out of line. Barbara and I were horrified!!

Wally had been pushed face first into a tiled wall; his arms were forced above his head, pressed up against the wall criminal style, and his wrists were tightly constrained. The young man proceeded to place his hand on the top of Wally's head and pushed down causing him to fall to his knees. He then jammed his knee into the back of Wally's neck holding that position until Barbara shouted, "Stop. What are you doing to that little boy?" Throughout the actual abuse, re-enactment, and subsequent conversation that followed, Wally never uttered a single word.

Barbara and I left the orphanage and called the Autistic Association recounting the incident to one of their counselors. She was shocked and assured is that this was not an acceptable form of discipline for any child, especially an autistic child. The counselor encouraged us to place a complaint with the Child Abuse Hotline, which we did. We also went to a local newspaper and relayed the account, hoping it would lead to some investigative reporting. The reporter assigned to the story seemed genuinely saddened to inform us that due to our lack of evidence, there was nothing he could do. Apparently, an eyewitness account of Wally's abuse was not sufficient. Several years have passed since this incident occurred and Barbara and I have never been able to let it rest in our hearts. We went to the orphanage that day seeking peace and resolve. We left with a deep sense of sorrow, anger, and defeat knowing that abuse was being perpetrated against autistic children. To this day we question whether our report of abuse was thoroughly investigated, and if so, what actions were taken on Wally's behalf to insure his safety?

As mothers, we often wonder if Wally's parents were ever informed as to the report we placed. We know that Wally would never be able to tell them; he was so docile and would without fight submit to any kind of treatment.

For many survivors of child abuse, time, circumstances, and a deep social slumber has served to silence the grief that is carried daily within the heart and mind of its victim. But now I believe the season is upon us; the time to speak has been born out of a purpose designed not of our own making, but a purpose designed by GOD. It is time for us to speak out on our own behalf and for all those who are not able, thus helping to bring about change in the way crimes against children are viewed and dealt with by society. A healthy society depends on healthy children. If yesterday's victims of child abuse demand that their voice be acknowledged today, the future will change for the better of our society. A child's life is in the power of our voices – Together, we can be the voice of the voiceless children; children like Wally.

So, to all I say, let us continue to speak of our memories born of injustice and let us do so in truth, pure motive, and love. If in speaking we find those who would ridicule or criticize us, attempting to dismiss our experiences as the imaginings of dysfunctional adults – let us understand that the light of love and understanding is sadly absent from their thoughts and spirits.

E-Mail to Susanne Robertson
From Carol McGlone
February 25, 2002

Dear Sue:

I don't know if you remember me, but I am a survivor from St. Colman's. My name is Carol. Karen and I worked on the survivor's Newsletter where we placed your poem "The Treasure Box". I know this is going back many years. Mike Bonneau tells me that you are writing a book. I think that is great. I am working on a website for Mike and he told me that he let you know about. I need to let you know that this site is not for public viewing. Please ... I beg you don't let anyone know of this site yet. It won't be long until it is up and Mike will advertise it in this area. I would also, like to ask you if you would want to place your poem and/or excerpts from your book on the site, or perhaps both. This is completely up to you, no pressure.

But please, let me know and get back to me. Also, let me know what you thing of the site if you have already reviewed it.

Thank you,
Carol McGlone

E-Mail from Tracy Koren
To Bob V.
March 22, 2002

My first memory of that jail they call a children's home was that on my first day I had to get a bare-assed spanking over the knee of a nun (probably a pedophile!) because all of the first graders were getting a spanking for jumping on the beds the day before. Although I was not there the day before, I had to get one anyway because I was a first grader. Before that, I don't think I was ever spanked so you can imagine to a six year old it's pretty traumatic. They said I took my punishment very well (I did not cry, I was too scared). It did not get any better from there.

I've been slapped hard across the face for dancing, smacked across the face for no apparent reason, spanked in front of the entire cafeteria over Sr. Regina's knee (she yanked me out of line as I was walking into the cafeteria to eat dinner), smacked in the middle of my arm right where it bends (they used to love doing that, doesn't really leave marks) for playing wrong on the playground, etc. I've seen them yank kids by their hair while dragging them across the floor. They definitely were not gentle creatures.

I was so afraid to tell them I was sick I kept it to myself and as I was walking into the cafeteria for breakfast I threw up all over the floor (sweet revenge!) They had their pets and you knew who they were. I was not one of them. They kept me from my brother and sister. On my seventh birthday, there was no mention whatsoever. Just another day! They used to give me medication without my parents permission to make me stop wetting the bed, some little red pill. Who knows what that could've been!

I made my first communion without my parents because they were never notified. I'm sure many of you have worse stories and I probably chose not to remember most of mine. I was there about a year. It was the worst year of my life. To think that this could still be happening and the authorities choose to do nothing makes them just as guilty of child abuse as those who are doing the abusing, Hubbard included. They all deserve to burn in hell which is where they will most likely end up.

To this day when I see a nun I have all I can do not to reach out and slap her across the face to see how she like it. I get so mad just thinking about the shit they got away with. It's ridiculous.

E-mail From Bob V.
To Tracey
March 21, 2002

Hi,

Oh yeah!!! He certainly has something to hide. The whole system that they are involved in is hiding even murder. I know that all of us were abused in one way or another. I remember Sister Cecilia hitting me over the head with a large stick. When the blood started gushing out, she got some snow and put it on my head. After the first handful of snow, she told me to do it myself. I still have that scar and where it hit, I am so thankful to just be here if you know what I mean.

I don't know about you Tracey, but I have never given up on God. I don't blame the Catholic Church I sure do lay the blame on many of the so called workers for God.

Late at night, when all of us were supposed to be sleeping, one of the priests went into the cubicle where the nuns slept and did their personal things. Do you remember those squares for them in the dormitories? That was one time. I think I have seen it about four times. I am not sure, but I am damn sure that I saw that happen that night. God never called anyone to celibacy. He mentioned to Adam and Eve to be fruitful and multiply. He also mentioned this. "Forbid not to marry". I did not see too much of God at St. Colman's. Those of us that were altar boys were not just randomly picked, if you know what I am talking about.

I pray that one day someone will not turn their back on this plea. I hope and pray that some of you that read this would help. I don't know how, but anyway will do. Maybe a lawyer or some one from the district attorney's office would just look below the cover of the book. Inside they would find out that little Gilbert Bonneau was smothered in front of one witness and the nun with the pillow. I'll tell you Tracey, you know, back in those years, you said nothing and if you did, you would get a beating like the one Gilbert got. He now has no more pain, but he was beaten to death and everyone besides the Bonneau and the rest of us who barely made it out of there.

Take care of yourself,

Bob

SUSANNE ROBERTSON

E-Mail to Bob V
From Tracey
March 18, 2002

I am curious. Has Hubbard every responded to you?

E-Mail From Bob V
To Group of People
March 18, 2002

My dear friends:

Folks, I am busting my ass to try to get someone to move. I have slammed Hubbard with mail, and everything I can do with a computer. Please tell me if you know of anyone else I need to get to and you folks know that I will do it. I have and am still working hard on this, but I need some more leads.

As God is my witness, I have to look Bishop Hubbard in the eye and I have to get into St. Colman's and just go eyeball to eyeball with the nuns and find someone who will talk to me. I am also a bible scholar. I never wanted to tell you all this. I am a former pastor here in Jacksonville and at one time was on sixty eight radio stations throughout the south. It can be easily proven so don't worry about that, but with the very word that they say they live by, I can show them what they will die by, and where they will end up. I never wanted to bring this out because I would have rather left this alone. But I want that justice for Gilbert so bad. You all know I am disabled and one day maybe I can get a decent car and come up there and then we can get around person to person. They could not dodge me if I was in Albany. I promise you that. Soon I am hoping that Medicaid will supply me with an electric wheelchair, and them, I don't mind asking for help to get a good car. These beating and killings in St. Colman's can't just disappear. Someone will hear us.

It just can't be forgotten. An organization like St. Colman's Home can just walk away from beating children to within an inch of their life, and in some instances as this one that I watched with my own two eyes, when Gilbert was smothered. Someone will listen I hope and pray.

Bob

CHAPTER 21

Year 2002 – The Quest Continues for the Truth

January 31, 2002

America's Most Wanted
Mr. John Walsh
P. O. Box Crime TV
Washington, DC 250016-9126

RE: Gilbert Bonneau
Date of Birth: 12-19-1944
Date of Death: 11-28-1953

Dear Mr. Walsh:

My brother, Gilbert Bonneau, died at the age of 8 while in the care of a catholic orphanage. There have been many questions that have come up over the last few years surrounding his death in 1953. My brothers and I were all in St. Colman's Home although we did not ever see each other. We all left at various times leaving Gilbert the only member of our family at the home in November 1953.

There are numerous people who claim they were abused while living at St. Colman's located in Watervliet, New York. There is a witness, Mr. Bob Vonzurlinde, who says that Gilbert was smothered the day before Gilbert was pronounced dead. This witness was recently found living in Florida. He was unaware that my brother's death was being investigated in New York. He was in the "infirmary" that same night with Gilbert as was a 12 years girl named Cathy, who incidentally grew up and became a Presentation Sister at the home. Her "job" was infirmary that day. Bob has lived with this nightmare memory since childhood and is relieved that it's now being told. There were two other allegations of the wrongful deaths of young resident children that surfaced in 1995 during my brother's investigation. However, I personally don't know the outcome. It's not newsworthy these days.

Our suspicions were planted by a woman who called my family in 1978 and claimed she saw our little brother get a beating the day before he died. We began to ask questions and found, after twenty years of searching, a witness who saw my brother being smothered by a nun, until he did not move or make a sound.

I will gladly provide you with any and all information you need that I have available. I am enclosing various correspondence and documents. You will notice that there are many suspicious inconsistencies and my brother's death is certainly questionable.

There are many others who are willing to come forward about the abuse they endured while living at this home. They are from various generations that spread over thirty years, maybe more. They have stories that you won't believe. The Catholic Diocese of Albany has allowed this abuse of children with their silence and their lack of cooperation in speaking about the abuse, past and present. The only thing they have spoken out loud about is their denial. The criminality of this case gets older by the day. We don't know if the person who did this is still alive but we'd like to know for sure, especially if she's still looking after children.

The facility still operates today as a resident home for autistic children. This facility still has resident children being raised by the PBVM. You will find also in these documents an e-mail from a woman who made a visit in recent years to confront what she endured and saw the horror all over again. She reported the incident to the Department of Social Services; however, there was no public mention of an investigation. This was around the same time my little brother's death was being highlighted in the local news regularly.

You will read in the autopsy report that my brother had what looked like dried blood in his nostrils and what looked like digested blood in his stomach. You won't read it anywhere else. It was never questioned.

Those of us still living, knowing that this place still exists today, are willing to speak out until this facility is thoroughly investigated. My family wants the murderer of my brother brought to justice. We all want the abuse to stop.

We are asking you, Mr. Walsh, to please look into these allegations. You will come across some that say they were treated well while living at the home, but I can assure you, they are the lucky ones. Our hands are tied here. The District Attorney's office doesn't want to butt heads with the Catholic Diocese. We all know by recent news that catholic priests aren't exempt from criminal acts and I can tell you that neither are nuns.

We would appreciate it if you could at least read everything and use your expertise in your analysis. Please do what it is you think right. We sincerely thank you for taking the time.

Sincerely,

The Family of Gilbert Bonneau

Please respond to:
Ernest Michael Bonneau
(Address)
Albany, New York 12204

E-Mail to letters@time.com
March 19, 2002
By Susanne M. Robertson

Your picture of the Cardinal on the front cover brought tears to my eyes. Please don't stop there. St. Colman's Home for children in Colonie, New York covered up their mess for years. I can not stay silent any longer. I saw Sister Regina beat the tar out of a little retarded boy in 1963. I was such a coward that I ran and hid in a girl's bathroom with my feet on the wall so that no one would see me in there. Mark was dead three days later. Sister Regina came up behind me and jabbed me in the ribs and told me Mark was dead and did I understand her when she said it might happen to any child there? It did not take a rocket scientist to figure out that threat. She had gotten away with killing him so what would protect me.

A man working as their maintenance person grabbed me in the summer of 1964. He pulled me into the boiler room and raped me. The nuns were told and they did not believe me. Did they take me to the Dr. or hospital? No. They took me to their infirmary and put a needle in my arm. I was drugged for a week. When I was insistent that I was going to tell my family, they sent me to a home for retarded children. I was locked in solitary confinement for almost 3 months. I was told if I did not take back my "LIES" that I would be incarcerated there for the rest of my life. They covered up what happened to me. Guess what? Sister Regina is still there only this time she is in charge of autistic and emotionally disturbed children. If she was brutalizing children who could talk what is she doing to kids that can't talk? Investigate this travesty. I have a long list of now grown up children who would like you to hear their stories of what happened to them in God's name.

You may contact me at (e-mail address)

Susanne Maloney Robertson
Seattle, Washington
(Phone number)

E-mail to: MSNBCInvestigates@msnbc.com
February 21, 2002
From Robert Vonzurlinde

To Whom this may concern:

My name is Robert Vonzurlinde and I have a story to tell that is more than news worthy. The Catholic Church has hidden some other abuses fairly well and it is not like what I am going to tell is something that has not been in the news before. I am 58 years old and lived through the hell that I am going to tell you about. Naturally, what you do with it is yours now. I live in Jacksonville, FL and have been here since 1968. I am a widower with five grown children, two of them are police officers and the other three are doing great. About 2-1/2 years ago, I got a computer for a gift and since I am home on disability, I have plenty of time to just search around and learn to use it. Now I'll get to the point.

I was an orphaned child living in St. Colman's Home for Boys and Girls in Watervliet, New York. We received many, many beatings while at St. Colman's and hundreds have testified to that fact. In November of 1953, I was in the infirmary at St. Colman's Home because I had just gotten beaten so bad with a stick that blood was all over me and I could not stand up straight. On November 28, 1953 while I was in the infirmary, in the fourth bed, there was another little boy named Gilbert Bonneau who had been beaten so bad about the neck and face and other parts of his body Gilbert could not stop screaming. I am telling you that I have never to this day seen a beating like the one Gilbert received. Like I said, he could not stop screaming. A nun kept coming in to tell him to shut up if he knew what was good for him and she told me to mind my own business, if I knew what was good for me. The next time the nun came in, Gilbert was still screaming in pain. She told me to turn around and I did but not to the degree that I could not see what she was doing. The screaming started to subside, so I took a closer look. That nun had a pillow over the head of Gilbert, and he was not screaming anymore and he was not moving. Now this had been all over the news in 1995 and I think 1996 in the Capital District Region of New York.

Now back to the computer and me moving to Florida. After I had been on the computer a couple of days, I placed on an orphan message board a message that said, if there is any family of the Bonneaus and they would like to know how their brother or friend died, to just contact me at my e-mail address. About four months ago, I got an e-mail from an Ernie Bonneau and he was crying up a storm is what he expressed when he found me. Something I must say here, I had no idea that there was an investigation going on, because I was in Florida. I did not even know if Gilbert had any relatives. I just saw a place where I could put that and never knew that I would every get any answers. How was I to know that Gilbert had three brothers? These brothers did not even know that they were related until after St. Colman's home. I say this because I don't want you to think I jumped on any kind of bandwagon. I am in Florida.

Sir or Madam, Gilbert Bonneau was not the only young boy to come out of St. Colman's Home on a slab. There have been three or four more questionable deaths of young boys from that place. Can you believe that the autopsy went from meningitis to natural causes! The body they exhumed in 1995 was not even the body under the grave marker. St. Colman's had a deal with the local grave yard. No eight year old dies from natural causes. He was beaten to death, literally. I do know that when that nun put that pillow over Gilberts head, he stopped moving and screaming.

Ernie Bonneau began sending me news clippings, and the poor excuse of the Colonie Police Department called me and the lieutenant that was talking with me and others is on an extended leave for a mysterious illness. I am going to put the Bonneau's e-mail address in the cc copy of this e-mail.

There were beatings beyond belief, being forced to stand in front of all the boys with excretion in your underwear, and having to wear it over your head for an hour. Knuckles on me broken by a 2 by 4 that was slung by a nun named Sister Cecelia; little girls getting their panties taken off and getting beatings right in front of the whole bunch of us gathered in the playroom.

Please listen to this. I have all the video tapes and the documents here. Ernie Bonneau sent them to me to look them over. I will gladly let your affiliate here in Jacksonville, FL take these and make copies. What you will see is as terrible as you will see and hear about what has been done to little boys and girls not only at St. Colman's. I know about the priests and the nuns joining together and then when a fetus is produced, it is done away with. I know what it is to have a priest or a brother make me go to my knees and have oral sex. I know what it is to be bent over a bed, and have a catholic brother screw me in the butt and then feel bad or so he claimed and make me stay on the bed while he rubbed Vaseline all over my bleeding rear end and then in a few minutes did not feel so remorseful and did it again. I do have my ducks in a row. I am not some sort of nut, maybe I wouldn't have gone this far had

THE THROW AWAY CHILD

Ernie Bonneau not contacted me through a message I put on a message board over two years ago.

I have the autopsy papers and the changes made. The bishop in Albany New York's name is Howard Hubbard. Just send a courier to my house and I will loan him/her the documents about Gilbert's death, and the real mess that really goes on. So many of those kids have not lived to be my age or are incarcerated somewhere. Bill Bonneau is a mail supervisor, Ernie Bonneau is a firemen and Danny, I am not sure but they all live in the Albany, NY area. They are finding something new everyday.

You folks see that priest that has just been convicted of molesting over 130 kids? Do you really think now's the time to let some murders and beatings and un-natural sex acts go by the wayside. Please remember that I am going to put the Bonneau's e-mail in the cc. Thank you for whatever you do or read.

Robert
Jacksonville, FL

SUSANNE ROBERTSON

March 10, 2002

TO WHOM IT MAY CONCERN:

I was placed in the institution called St. Colman's Home for children run by catholic nuns at the tender age of 6 years old. Being separated and abandoned by my parents was both painful and frightening. Suddenly finding myself in a brand new environment and in the company of strangers was scary, and my first night there was spent quietly sobbing myself to sleep. Unbeknownst to me there would be many tears to follow and new levels of pain and fear.

My first day there I was sitting with a large group of kids when an angry fat woman with a red face walked up to me and slapped me in the face. Her name was Kathryn Furdette. There was no reason for her to hit me. My first day was my initiation or baptism as it were into a world of violence hidden from the public. From that day forward I witnessed and was subject to many other such incidences of mindless savagery and cruelty.

The nuns at St. Colman's were an ominous sight to a small child as they walked about draped in black garb and headdress with large crosses hanging about their necks. Many children came with their brothers and sisters and the boys and girls were separated from each other.

This separation of blood relatives destroyed the bonding process that a normal home environment would have produced. Children have a remarkable facility to adapt and survive and with all earthly ties broken the child goes into automatic pilot learning to survive on a day to day basis. Who can say when that realization sets within a small child? But it does, because it has too. With all hope of being nurtured in a loving home behind me, and no hope of being nurtured before me, a child has to find a way to survive from that point forward on a daily basis. An institution can feed, clothe, and shelter, but it does not love, nurture or show affection to a child.

The atmosphere was electric with fear and trembling. The constant dread of being hit or beaten was a distinct possibility as I witnessed many such acts of violence inflicted upon tiny and helpless lives. My little brother, Salvatore Gerace was beaten with a baseball bat by a sister Eucharia. My little brother sustained head injuries that required medical attention and he was secretly whisked off to the infirmary where I am quite certain the medical records will not reflect the true reason for his being there as the catholic church knows well how to cover its ass. Many children were beaten to the point where medical attention was required later on and in each case the person or persons responsible had it covered up.

My little brother is dead now; he committed suicide and he was buried on June 17, 1979. He was never right and struggled through most of his life with mental illness a legacy I've long suspected had it roots in his treatment at St. Colman's.

St. Colman's was a place where absolute power in the name of God was exercised over the most helpless members of our society. These religious zealots handed out corporal punishment like Rockefeller used to throw dimes at peasants. There was no rhyme or reason to it. Many, many children were beaten unmercifully for the flimsiest of reasons. I can recall one such incident that will stay with me for the rest of my life. The nuns used to sit the kids on a large cold marble floor – sometimes for hours.

A large fat nun named Sister Mary Rose started to hit a small boy named Roger Buchanan. He was sitting with his left leg extended in an attempt to avoid getting hit when this big fat tub of lard put her right foot down on his leg and threw her full weight upon it (she probably weighed a good 200 plus pounds) whereupon a loud crack was heard that indicated to me something very serious had just happened. The little boy let out a blood curdling piercing scream that sent chills down my spine as I sat helplessly as she continued to apply foot pressure on the very place where she had just broken a bone and continued yelling at the child telling him to get up! Get Up! Regretfully I can't remember the outcome of the event – but it will be forever etched in my memory as long as I live.

The sense of terror our captors put us through was indescribable. I can sympathize with "Holocaust Survivors" who try to tell their stories only to be called liars by people who refuse to address the truth about human nature and its potential for depravity even when that nature is clothed in religious garb and symbolism or comes in the form of nazism or fascism – it is still evil and needs to be called what it is – CHILD ABUSE!

I remember nuns routinely slapping and beating up kids. In fact, each nun had her own special technique for hitting children. I used to think they took special courses to beat the devil out of us. And all too often these beating got out of hand and took a deadly turn for the worst.

In fact, a great deal of publicity came out in 1995 surrounding the questionable death of a little boy who was beaten to death named Gilbert Bonneau by a nun named Sister Fidelia. Unfortunately hard evidence is very difficult to obtain and yet so many people from all different walks of life telling this same horror story cannot be dismissed as a hallucination regardless of insubstantial evidence. The consistency of testimony from so many different sources is in itself "compelling evidence." Whether it can be proven or not, doesn't make it any less true. I know what I saw, and so do many others.

As I stated earlier in this letter, I was placed in St. Colman's at the age of 5 or 6 years old so that would be the years 1959 till 1966 a total of 8 years. Another incident that took place was when a Sister Mary Regina kicked my little sister in the side until she required hospitalization. Her name was Mary Ellen Gerace. These nuns had a free hand with the children who resided at the home and a great deal of trauma was perpetrated on these kids relatively unnoticed by the public for years.

I witnessed retarded children beaten on a regular basis. It seems someone was always getting hit at this place and it damaged the psyches of kids who had to grow up in an atmosphere of terror and fear. Unfortunately proof is difficult to find after so many years. I remember a retarded boy named Michael Donohue getting slapped routinely by nuns. I remember a specific incident involving a nun named Sister Mary Loretta where she started to slap Michael and he slapped her back (more as a reflex than self-defense) and her headdress came flying off the top of her head revealing a shaved head that apparently must have embarrassed her as all the kids started laughing and her face turned several shades of red. Then in a fit of rage she really took the gloves off and began to pummel this poor boy and all the children in the room could do was bear witness in abject horror and silence.

A sad footnote; In 1995 when people started coming forward to protest what went on in the home one of the people who staunchly defended St Colman's was this boys father. His comments can be read in the Times Union dated Thursday, December 21, 1995. His name was Paul F. Donohue, Sr. of Delmar (St. Colman's attorney). As I read his comments defending St. Colman's, I could only shake my head in dismay. I said to myself "Sir, you were not there, I was." I secretly suspect a lot of people go into denial over these things otherwise they would have to face part of the guilt for having put their children there in the first place.

The Catholic Church is a very wealthy institution and has many connections and will exhaust all it vast resources to counter any negative publicity. These nuns use to wear two masks. The one the children saw away from the public at-large and the one when parents come to visit their children. I remember how differently we were treated when my parents came to visit.

They were sweet as could be and full of affection and charm, but that side was reserved strictly for the visiting public. I can assure you that was not what the children saw on a day to day basis at the home.

So, I saw firsthand the hypocrisy and two-faced nature of this institution. The disparity between the well orchestrated public persona and the private hell we lived in can be contrasted like day and night. But now the public might be more receptive to such testimonies as mine in light of recent revelations about boys being molested in Boston by a catholic priest. It came out that even though the Catholic Church had prior knowledge of this priests conduct, yet they allowed him to remain and thereby endanger the lives of other young boys. If the Catholic's tried to cover this up – what else is being covered up and believe me after 18 years of being institutionalized at Roman Catholic homes this is only the tip of the iceberg. I could write a book chronicling events after event and incident after incident still fresh in my mind after all these years.

I remember outside organizations that use to throw parties for the kids at the home. The biggest one came every Christmas called the Behr-Manning Christmas party. I used to get excited about the cake and ice cream, the entertainment and the gifts the children got. But before we went, the nuns would line us all up and give us strict instructions with severe warnings for any child who misbehaved or failed to say thank you or for any other breach of etiquette that made the institution or the nuns look bad.

I'll never forget one year after the party was over the nuns lined a bunch of us up and began to call forward all the children who failed to measure up to these standards and beatings would take place, gifts were taken away from the children, the atmosphere of terror was resumed and all you could hear was weeping and crying and you sat there desperately hoping your name was not called out. These children were beaten for the flimsiest of reason's, you could be bloodied to the point of needing medical attention for simply forgetting to thank someone for giving you a cookie. Apparently public image is real important to Catholics' and if it means beating up little children to produce it, so be it. The nuns zealously safeguarded their public image even to the point of cruelty.

But behind the carefully constructed veil called "public image" was a terrifying and carefully kept dark secret known only to those of us who lived on the other side of that veil. But try convincing the public at large who have been successfully brainwashed by years of religious symbolism and lies perpetuated by this religious monster that poses as God's mouthpiece to the world. Rome is concerned with two things; power and wealth. Religion is just a tool to control people while secretly obtaining the latter.

Well I could go on but this letter is the truth and nothing but the truth so help me God. May whoever reads this letter be filled with a sense of outrage which leads to some form of justice and takes a stand for the helpless in our society? I end with a quote from the bible (The Living Bible Translation)

Jeremiah 5.26,29 – "Among my people are wicked men – (or women) who lurk for victims like a hunter hiding in a blind. They set their traps for men. Like a coop full of chickens their homes are full of evil plots. And the result? Now they are great and rich, and well fed and well groomed, and there is not limit to their wicked deeds.

They refuse justice to orphans and the rights of the poor. Should I sit back and act as though nothing is going on? The Lord God asks. Shouldn't I punish a nation such as this?" "End quote"

Psalm 68,5 says "For He giveth justice to the widows and orphans and the Fatherless. For He is a Holy God."

All we want is the truth to be knows and justice for the suffering of all these helpless children who could not speak for themselves.

Peter R. Gerace, Jr.
Rensselaer, NY

Remember this quote: "GOLIATH LOST."

March 26, 2002

TO WHOM IT MAY CONCERN:

I was the mother of three beautiful children and have only two of them left because while I was having medical and financial problem, I entrusted their care to what I thought and was always taught that the nuns at St. Colman's Home were the angels from God which I just recently learned they weren't angels at all, but the devil himself

Their cruelty was far beyond any sane persons. They'll have their day before God!! My beautiful little boy Salvatore born 11/10/1955 and died by hanging himself after several previous attempts on Sunday, June 17, 1979. I had the three children home on weekends and holidays and not once did they ever say anything bad was happening to them. Just recently I found out what really was going on in that torturous place. Stories I've been hearing and what happened to my son Salvatore, a little boy with only love in his heart; my daughter, Mary, very delicate and loving; and Peter very loving and studious.

For starters, one day while in the gymnasium, the big 6 footer 200 lb. Sister Ukerria decides to take a wooden baseball bat, beat up my son Salvatore about the head and face. He landed in the infirmary for about 2-1/2 months. I was not allowed to see him as I was told, too many other little sick ones, you may bring in germs. 'SOME BULL!"

Truth is: they did not want me to see the condition he was in and how Sister Ukerria beat the hell out of him while his sister had to stand by and watch and after the fact they threatened his sister not to tell anyone by saying "If she did, she'd never go home again". My daughter Mary had to have an operation on her right side for adhesions after High School because one certain nun always hit the girls in their right sides if their day was not sunny. I also heard this same story from other girls who were there. "HIT ON RIGHT SIDE"

Whenever I bought the kids new clothes, toys, books, jewelry or whatever I bought them they took back with them and you never saw them again. Big Businesses' should also learn how grabby the nuns are when they give big Christmas parties each year for the kids. What they don't know is that when kids got back to the home they were told to put the presents in a certain room all piled up and guess what?? All those beautiful expensive gifts meant for the kids end up on their yearly so called "Garage Sale" and they, the home and nuns, get to keep the money. Next time you Big Businessmen want to treat these kids, you can put the kids on a bus and treat them all to a nice family affair dinner or lunch at some nice restaurant but make sure the kids are from the Home! Otherwise the home will be selling tickets for $10 a piece to strangers saying the kids are from the home.

Another thing I learned just recently; my children were always threatened with "Don't you dare tell your mother what's happening here, SHE DOESN'T WANT YOU, NOBODY WANTS YOU AND YOU'LL GO TO A WORSE PLACE! WORSE THAN WHAT? What could have been worse for 6, 7 and 8 year olds?

The children all had chores to do! That's why that place sparkles all the time. The nuns would wake them at 5:00AM or earlier to do the chores before breakfast or school on their hands and knees scrubbing floors and whatever else that had to be done. Look at the money those kids saved them. Cleaning maids do not come cheap!!! "Some life for such small helpless ones"! They were never treated like children. They were treated like slaves, nobodies, cattle, sheep, anything but children.

I read once where a Catholic home for children up in Canada could get more money for children who were mental! So, what did they do!? They gave all the kids shock treatments to get more money. At this point in my life, the whole big question is this: If there is a God why does he anoint these nuns and priests who behave as they do? He supposedly sent them here as better examples for we lay people to follow. I truly believe our world is coming to an end, just like "Sodom and Gomorrah" just as in the bible. Lately all you hear and read on TV, newspapers, books, radios, and whatever form of media, nothing looks or sounds rosy Posey – just gloom and doom.

How right to a tee. Every since these crimes on my children came to light, I've put myself in a guilt trip and cry at the drop of a hat for putting them in St. Colman's. One last thought. I know that for every bad priest or nun, there are some good ones. Hopefully they are "not all cut out of the same cloth".

God! If you really do exist, please take care to see that all the children of the world have all the love and caring you know they deserve. They are our sinless angels who one day may rule the universe.

God bless everyone (yes) even the nuns at St. Colman's and the priests because sooner or later they all have to face the maker like all the rest of us.

God Bless us all
M. A. Zell

THE THROW AWAY CHILD

February 24, 2002

Mr. Paul Clyne
County Court House Room 218
Albany, New York 12207

Dear Sir:

I read the article in the Sunday *Times Union* dated 2/24/02 "Diocese Keep Problem Priests on the Job." The article describes the abuses children went through by Catholic Priests; cover ups and Settlements to keep everything quiet; and finally stories of abuse by Catholic Priest in Boston and Philadelphia area.

The story of my brother's death and the abuses at St. Colman's Home came out in 1995. The Albany County District Attorney's Office under the leadership of Sol Greenberg did nothing. Now with new information the Albany County District Attorney's Office under your leadership still chooses to do nothing.

In your statement in the *Tines Union* article you say that child sexual abuse is a despicable crime. What do you say when my little brother, Gilbert was **Murdered** by a Catholic Nun? Your answer Silence and do nothing. That tells me you are another politician elected to the office who chooses certain crimes to be prosecuted. When a witness comes forward and tells you he witnessed a Nun smothering my little brother, Gilbert and is willing to take a lie detector test to this, and you still ignore him ... that tells me that you and your Office are a disgrace to the Criminal Justice System.

I will tell you this. Eventually my brothers and I will get justice for our little brother Gilbert. It will cost us more money but in the end you and the county will pay the cost. We will file a Civil Lawsuit against you and the County for failure to do your duty and investigate and prosecute those responsible for our little brother's murder.

Sincerely yours,

William G. Bonneau

E-Mail to S. Robertson
From L. Sharpe
March 27, 2002

    A lot of innocent children were battered and some did not make it. All of the tortures that we endured at the hands of the Sisters of the Presentation were unnecessary. A lot of the battering was for no reason. Some of us had caseworkers who used to come and visit. Mine saw my battered face and bruised arms and she questioned me and I told her. I was given another beating. We were afraid to speak, afraid to smile and afraid to look the wrong way. I saw St. Colman's (at that time) as nothing more than a "House of Horrors." I think that now is the time that restitution is made for all that was done to our minds.

    One of the hardest parts for me was to be a witness to another child's beating. Our childhood was taken away from us as was our dignity, self esteem and trust. A lot of us who came out of St. Colman's came out very insecure. Some went for help while some committed suicide. What we witnessed as children is beyond compare. We were not just beaten with hands we were beaten with large boards. The food that was served to us was really nasty. A lot of us regurgitated in our dishes and we were made to eat it.

    We were put in a dumb waiter while the nun would stop it in the middle of floors and were left for long periods of time, hugging each other and screaming to be let down. I was taken out back of the orphanage with a group of girls. There was a casket with a little boy's body. Sister Loretta pushed my face into his and told that that "This is what is going to happen to you if you don't behave."

    I was beaten unconscious in the auditorium one night because I was talking during a movie. I woke up in the infirmary. My left hand was placed on a school desk and beaten until my knuckles bled. Sister went up to the blackboard and wrote "I am the devils child". She came back to my desk and put a pencil in my right hand. I refused and in essence got yet another beating.

    I was in the girl's dorm one day and told by one of the nuns to wax the floors. She said that she was going to the chapel and that the floors better be done when she got back. She then told me and this other girl Susan not to be afraid to use a little elbow grease. Sue and I went to the stockroom in search of elbow grease. When we did not finish our "special job", we were both beaten bloody.

    I was also sexually molested by one of the workers. Her name was

Catherine Fredette. A lot of children there were raped and or molested. I was there for 6 years and it was 6 years of hell. A lot of people are responding to the ad's I have placed in the paper. They have their own stories to tell. I can't believe that so many males responded as men are usually quiet. A lot of us are crippled or close to it. As I already have said someone needs to make restitution for what they did to our little bodies. It was nothing but cruel and inhumane treatment. So I ask you where was the County?

E-mail to S. Robertson
From David Icke
March 5, 2002

Hello, Susanne ... thank you for the information. Such horrors can only continue because the public do not know what is going on. So the answer to stopping it is public exposure and if this lady is going to be stopped you are going to have to shout very loudly at every opportunity – peaceful protests outside with people supporting you with banners and noise, and the media told what is going to happen, though not too far in advance, only on the day; letters to the authorities exposing the abuse; well-laid-out and nicely produced news releases to the media; get on local radio phone ins on the pretest of talking about whatever subject they are discussing and then calmly say what is going on before they cut you off. If you have friends who want to help you, get them to do the same on the radio. Call the newsrooms of the radio stations and local newspapers and them then what is happening. All this will let the institution know that they are, at the very least, in grave danger of public exposure and if I was them I would ditch the lady as soon as possible.

The equation is simple, Susanne. Secrecy means it can go on an on and so that's what they want. Exposure is their worst nightmare, so that is what we must give them.

Love,
David

THE THROW AWAY CHILD

**E-mail to T. Hewett
From: L. Lamountain
Forwarded to S. Robertson
March 16, 2002**

Hello Terry,

 I first heard of the stuff going on at St. Colman's from my sister a couple of years ago. She said there was something going on in the news papers. She is my half sister, we have the same mother. She passed away a few years ago. Then my brother David now living outside of Albany, where we were born sent me all this stuff on THE HOME! That was the way we always addressed St. Colman's! I have been reading some of the stories people are telling of beatings and even murder! Law enforcement has done nothing from at least 1947 till now!

 Almost 40 years ago we too, 6 of us were taken from our home during the divorce of our parents. We were already coming from an abusive family environment into another. But this one was in the name of God! At least the people running the place were to be representing His word. Most kids not all, who are placed into an orphanage, are coming already, as we were, from a stressful maybe even an abusive environment. St. Colman's was just another part of "that's just the way it is" of course it isn't just the way it is! From what I have read and all that has been written about and what has gone on and is still happening behind the "walls of hell", this place is above the law!

 I too, remember! A couple of years ago, my sister and her husband and my wife, my brother David and my 20 year old son, all went to visit St. Colman's. We did not go inside or make any attempt to contact any one there! We walked around looking the place over. David went in one direction and me, my wife and son in another. It was a lot smaller than I remembered at the time we were placed in their care around 1964 or so. We were or rather I was around 10 years old maybe a little less. Everything back then was bigger than I was.

 I too, as in many of the letters I have read, don't remember seeing any of my brothers or sisters while there; only when we had visitors like when my mother or father came to visit. At Christmas time we would put on a play for the visitors, mainly parents with a lot of dancing mainly tap and singing. Then we would walk with them through the place and show off the toys we had and then show other kids what we just received for Christmas from our parents!

I remember there were kids who did not see their parents or anyone else at this time of year and it was sad.

I am now 48 years old did I witness any abuse at St. Colman's? Well, I don't really know! I remember kneeling in an area, like a gym to pray. All of us lined up in rows, Kids! and a nun, not very tall but heavy set, sitting in front of us in a low chair calling names of kids who were not behaving as they should. I did not look up because I was to be praying! She called the name of David LaMontain my brother. He walked up to her and she said kneel down and put your head between my knees! I looked up at about the same time she came down with a lot of force with her fist and hit him right in the middle of his back! Very close to the spine. Him trying to stand and walk back to his place I wanted to stand and yell, but did not.

I think that was the day I realized what hate was because every part of me felt it! I too would receive the same treatment as David and many other kids that were there then. But the look on his face, the pain! What happened to me was not important. I learned to deal with it. I felt more pain for him and the pain in all the faces after. Does more need to be done to stop the injustice, the abuse, the cover up either by the state of New York, and maybe even law enforcement?

There is no statute of limitations on murder. Gilbert's remains should be exhumed and an autopsy performed period! Way too many witnesses not too. Justice is screaming for it much like he did in his last hours! Not paid for by his brothers or his sister but by the state. We the people of the state of New York demand it is how it should read.

I remember very little else of this place, but there are dreams that make no sense to me even to this day. Of long sticks, being hit in the ribs, of being pushed down to the floor, kicked in the side of the head by a nun. This too must only be a dream. This could not have really have taken place. After all these are memories of a child of long ago and we know how kids stretch the truth and maybe do not see things clearly as we adults do! There had to be a reason for the behavior these nuns were showing.

If I had a law degree, I would donate my time to this issue. If I was a news women or man, I would pursue this to the end or I wouldn't be much of a newsperson would I? There is one little boy in the ground, somewhere around St. Colman's with possibly his head smashed in. No one care's but us. We need to stop this from going any further. The cover up needs to end and just like in any murder or abuse case justice must be served. Even the Catholic Church is not above the law ... then or now!

THE THROW AWAY CHILD

I was not then or now a victim! I refuse to be! When you are willing to fight and not lie down, you can never become a victim. We as the kids of St. Colman's need to get together as one. This fight has only just begun and has to be won for we are the only ones who seem to care!

Thank you for your time.

Leo LaMontain

SUSANNE ROBERTSON

Post to a Message Board
4/3/2002
By Terry L. Hewett, Sr.

RE: Catholic child abuse and murder by Nuns !!!!!
In Reply to: Someone Who cares About the Truth on 3/14/2002

How can you possibly know the truth?

People that fight for truth usually are willing to attach their name to their cause. With that said you need to look at the bigger picture. You claim to care about the truth but you have no evidence to support your cause. You have made a fool of yourself!

Look at the responses to your post. Those must surely be the people that know the truth. Maybe I should explain!

Just from your post you had 5 responses (so far) from different survivors around the country that say the same things that all the other survivors say. The survivors are from different time lines, so it could not be some elaborate scheme. They are naming the same people.

The survivors have not wasted the service provider's time! They are the evidence that the service providers have failed children for quite some time now.

If the service providers are so concerned about the children of the present then they should listen to the children of the past. The children of the past know from personal experience whose abusing children. They know how their being abused. The service providers are scared to find the TRUTH! The truth is that the service providers (services) abuse children! The service providers would have to admit to abusing children to truly stop the abuse.

That is not going to happen. The service providers are in denial.

Neglect is abuse! Sorry guys, but I think this need's to be said. On the website in the gallery there is a picture that saddens my heart. EVIDENCE - that the children were neglected. Ripped heavily soiled clothes, filthy faces some very sad, others amused to get their picture taken including the nun. The odd thing is the nun's collar is pure white not soiled not ripped. Her face is clean and also not soiled. One might assume that the children have gotten dirty in the course of play. Lots of play would warrant the disgusting contrast of filth between the children and the nun.

What is more evident is the spots of dirt on the children's temples on both sides of the face indicate that the children did not have the proper guidance in personal hygiene that the nun herself had. Surely the facilities that cared for the nun's clothes could have handled the children's clothes as well. Or would it be that the nun's did not care as much about the children as they did themselves? Only God and the nun's know for sure. The rest is just some accusation huh!?

May God bless you in your endeavors for the TRUTH.

Irrational is not believing the truth laid before you!

Irrational is not believing eye witnesses.

Irrational is assuming that a child could not be abused and murdered in an uncaring loveless environment such as in St. Colman's.

Irrational is assuming that just because they claim to be God's servants that they could not succumb to anger and strike out against a small child.

Irrational is thinking that so called God's servants could not possibly sexually abuse a child.

What is rational is believing the truth and sorting the crap from facts.

Truth is that these children were abused in many heinous ways, and they are angered at St. Colman's and the service providers for blindly allowing abuse and murder to happen for many years. Furthermore, the abuse is still no doubt happening today at St. Colman's.

The abusers have devised many ways to cover their abuses. It is no wonder they have gotten away with it for so long.

Terry L. Hewitt, Sr.

Another Post on the Same Subject on the Same Day

To the person who posted the message about abused people who have come forth, I say to you, that I am not ignorant and the only thing that disturbs me is your lack of knowing what you are talking about. You speak of re-investigations that never happened. You speak of investigations that were controlled by the Catholic diocese of Albany County in New York. You posted by saying that you were someone who cared about the truth. I say you are a coward and you are hiding your identity because you can in no way call the death of an eight year old boy 'NATURAL CAUSES".

Bishop Howard Hubbard and many others, including the Albany County District Attorney have smothered this over for years. You sir are a coward. Were you ever at St. Colman's? Do you know of the other natural cause deaths that have come out of St. Colman's? I say again, you are an uninformed coward standing up for nothing you know about. Have you ever been beaten so bad that you had to be hidden from the rest of the population of kids at St. Colman's so that the bruises could not be seen? You are again a coward.

Have you ever had your head split wide open with a stick that was swung by a nun and blood running down your face and the nun giving you a snowball and telling you to hold it there until the bleeding stops? I can show you the scar you coward. You are faceless and nameless because you have no guts. You are a coward who blows with every wind. Did you ever wonder what happened to the nuns that got pregnant from the sperm of a priest who had taken a vow of celibacy? Did you ever wonder about what happened to that baby? Of course not, you are a coward and you have no idea of what you speak. You are still too busy praying to statues.

Do you know what it is like to be told to lean up against a wall with the palms of your hands facing the wall above your head and then getting whacked in the small of the back with a board? I know about this you coward. Finally did you know that there was another boy in the infirmary when Gilbert Bonneau was smothered with a pillow because he could not stop screaming from a beating that was witnessed in the play room? Did you know that after the third time little eight year old Gilbert Bonneau was told to stop screaming that the other boy in the infirmary saw the smothering of little Gilbert, until he could scream no more or move any longer? Do you know about that, you spineless coward.

Whether you are an official of the Catholic Church, a non caring Colonie Police person who could have cared less or best of all from the district attorney's office who shoveled this under the rug for years, you are a gutless coward and just maybe God will have mercy on you. But you see I am the boy who was in the infirmary in 1953 with Gilbert Bonneau. Now you investigate that and then come back with your paid for lies. I know you are not just another person. You are a person who is involved in this in some way and that way is lying as long as you can get away with it. I am the witness and had nothing to gain by coming forth. I did not even know that there was an investigation because I had moved to Florida and I live here today crippled by what happened to me in my childhood.

Do I sound like some disturbed ignorant person to you? I think not. I do pray that one day that potters field that the funeral home gave to St. Colman's home will be dug up and then see that there is a lot more than little Gilbert

Bonneau's body buried there.

    I swear by the God that I have come to love, and know that even though there were tough times, He never left me and it is by Him that I swear that what I have written is absolutely true, so help me God.

Robert Linde

April 2002

TO WHOM IT MANY CONCERN

I am compelled to try this one last time – St. Colman's. Are we all still in our comfort zones with the catholic clergy? Do we all still have the respect, hope, and trust in these catholic priests, brothers and nuns? Are we still filled with confidence in these clergy who are God's chosen ones to be of service to all of His children here on earth? These representatives in His service who will feed, clothe, protect, shelter and guide anyone who asks for help. Thank you to all of you servants who have taken vows of poverty, chastity and obedience. Do we have any qualms about any of these Heaven sent men and women who profess to do the Lord's work? Do we take any issue with the news headlines around the world of the Catholic Church in crisis? Do we have any questions or fears? In 1995 we did not. All was right with the world. We were all safe.

In December 1995, a story broke in the *Troy Record* of alleged child abuse in the mid 1950's and '60's at St. Colman's Home for Boys and Girls in Watervliet, New York. Stories also appeared in the Albany *Times Union* as well as other local newspapers.

These stories caused a firestorm of letters to the editor; witnesses to these abuses coming forward to tell their stories; contacts made to the Albany County DA as well as the Colonie Police Department and the Roman Catholic Church – Albany Archdiocese. These stories circulated for a while and sparked great debate in the print, television and radio talk show media. There were protests made at the orphanage on both sides of this issue with a great deal of television coverage. I have video tapes of these confrontations along with town meeting style gatherings. I have seen web pages devoted to these stories by family members who lost loved ones during this "orphanage of horror" time.

There was a story of the murder of an innocent child, Gilbert Bonneau, whose family (surviving brothers) want to know the truth. There was a statement made to the Colonie Police Department by my sister Susanne who witnessed the beating of another child, Mark Longale, which may have contributed to his young life being extinguished.

In this first instance, the family had the body exhumed. There was debate between the experts who could not come to the same conclusion on how this child died given the documentation they had to examine. Pertinent official records and documents no longer existed. The official "death certificate" is rife with inconsistencies. I personally would like to know of what natural cause does' an 8-year-old child die from! The family is still looking for answers. They believe this child was murdered, because of a phone call they received in 1978. The women who called them in 1978 told them of a beating she witnessed on Gilbert.

There is also a witness who lives in Florida who says that he was in the infirmary at the same time that Gilbert was there. He says that he was in the infirmary for the same reason. He had just received a beating. He says he saw a nun place a pillow over the head of Gilbert who was screaming and when she was finished Gilbert neither screamed nor kicked again. Shortly after, Gilbert was taken to the Albany Medical Center hospital where he died. This witness has lived in Florida since 1968 and only by chance came across a website and posted a message nearly two years ago.

When he received a response to his posted message, he was shocked, dismayed and angry beyond belief. He did not know that Gilbert had any family. He did not have to get involved but his conscience would not let him be silent any longer. He had to do something. He has tried to give an account of what he saw but no one is willing to take a statement or to hear his testimony. He has been in contact with Bishop Hubbard who refuses his calls and correspondence as does the Colonie Police Department and the Albany County DA.

In the second instance, the witness was tagged a nut case by a sibling and therefore was summarily dismissed. The sibling had gone on a public radio talk show to discredit any testimony that might come to light. The sibling had to write a letter of public apology to Susanne to appear in the local papers as part of a lawsuit settlement brought before a Federal Court.

I received a call from the NY State Office of Children's Welfare Division in Albany in the spring of 1996. I was asked what I knew and my thoughts on how this situation could be avoided in the future. I expressed my sentiments and was promptly blown off. As you can see, this story will just not go away. No one wants to hear the truth. No one wants to seek the truth and above all, no one wants to learn the truth.

This is my own take on St. Colman's as I was a resident there for almost 10 years.

The catholic nuns of the Presentation of the Blessed Virgin Mary would never hurt children. No, No, you former residents of St. Colman's from back in the 1950's and '60 you are all liars, dysfunctional adults or just plain troubled and not able to cope with the circumstances that placed you in the orphanage in our care and safekeeping. We won't hurt or abuse you. It doesn't matter that we are mostly young women and don't know a thing about taking care of 400 – 500 children. We have time for all of you and we will love, care and nurture every one of you. Most of you have no families that we have to be accountable to so we will raise you however we see fit.

No you can't be with your sister who is 2 years older. You are in kindergarten she is in the 2nd grade you must stay with girls you own age. We must maintain discipline. If one of you steps out of line you will all get punished. No, you can't play with your brother we do not allow the boys and girls to mix. As a matter of fact, when he is old enough we will ship him to an all boys home. We don't care if you are siblings and need to bond with each other to maintain a healthy relationship. As far as we are concerned you have no brothers or sisters unless your family is here to see you on visiting day or you are away from the home with them. You can be siblings then.

We don't care if this is your dress we have over 350 girls here, who knows what belongs to who. All clothes go in the laundry baskets and get washed together. You will wear the clothes that we give you, the clothes that we have hung on your locker. We don't care if it fits you, it is close enough. Who is going to see you except the other children! Yes when your families come to visit you will be dressed appropriately. They will see that you are well cared for and happy little people because you will smile and be polite and not bring disgrace to us. If you step out of line, we will single you out for some "Special Treatment" in the sewing room.

Yes you can go home with your Aunt and Uncle for the weekend. You must remember that what goes on here stays here. You must never tell anyone what is happening here or your will not be allowed to go with your relatives ever again. Our discipline methods are just fine with everyone. Yes, all children get spanked for no reason so bend over that bench. We must maintain discipline. Hold out your hands these "music sticks" and my paddle are hungry for the taste of flesh.

There are too many children here so you are going to have to help with the chores. This group will do laundry, this group will have KP duty, this group will clean the bathrooms, and this group will clean the dorms. We don't care how long it takes you and yes we know that you are only 7 years old. Come on children put some "elbow grease" into these chores. You can stand on a chair to set the tables. The best way to clean these hard wood floors is on your hands and knees. Johnson's Wax is really very good for the skin it will keep it nice and soft and washes off with soap and water. Roll it into a ball in the cloth just like we showed you. One of you can buff the floor and the other can sit on the buffer because you really are too small to be doing such a big job. No, don't be silly, the boys don't have to clean house.

Come on we don't have all day to fold this laundry. After you are done with the sheets and blankets we have to hand out clothes in the locker room. Besides it is very hot outside on the playground and you know how cold it gets out there in the winter time. You should be grateful that you are in here doing this chore. In just a few hours you will be done. This place will shine for our visitors. Everything must be in its place.

We don't care if you don't like this food, eat it anyway, we know that you have had the same thing several days running this is good food eat up. You will stay here until you finish. If you throw it up we will just feed it back to you. No, we do not eat the same food that you children do. Our sisters and the older girls have been out begging for food and this is what they were able to collect. The meals will improve when the State inspectors come. We will use the good china, you know the white ones with the black trim around them. We will use tablecloths and we will serve you ourselves. We will have meat loaf with green peas, mashed potatoes and gravy and even dessert.

See how well we are treating you. Yes we will have movies on Sunday nights but you must not talk or fool around. If you do you will be removed from the auditorium either under you own steam or with help from us. You will take dance and singing lessons. What do you mean you don't want to? All of you children will learn these routines. You must perform for the outside world at Christmas time or during our annual bazaar and for Reverend Mothers Anniversary. The public must see and be shown how well looked after you are and you must be appreciative of all of the kind people who want to feel good by providing for you poor orphans. We are one big happy family here.

After the Behr-Manning party you will place all of your Christmas presents in the laundry carts and we will send them to the truly deserving children in our foreign missions. Yes we know that you have been practicing these Christmas songs for hours standing in your lines in this playroom, you will continue to do so until you learn every word. Some of you embarrassed us at the last party by not wanting to perform and that must never happen again. These people have been good enough to give you this party and you will show them your gratitude and thanks. No, you can't go you are not on the party list. You still show some bruises from the last discipline session and we don't want anyone to see. You must never speak about the nuns to your family. What goes on here stays here. Why if your families truly wanted or loved you, you would not be here with us. So as you can see they truly don't care about you. And on and on it goes.

Yes I remember St. Colman's. I remember both good and bad times. Mostly I remember the terror and hopelessness of my childhood, especially when my Aunt Grace and Uncle Bill moved away and were no longer a part of our lives. I remember field day, my first communion, my confirmation, Cobb Memorial School for the Retarded children where my sister Sue was sent for an entire summer and where we went the day after confirmation because we were "Soldiers for Christ" and we were being rewarded. I remember being threatened with a beating in front of the entire population by Sister Loretta if I did not sing for the 6:00 Benediction service on Friday nights.

I remember the voice and dance lessons we were forced to take so we could perform for all those wonderful people who threw us parties during the Christmas holiday season. And perform we did. I am sure that if those good people knew what we had to endure to please them, that perhaps they might not be so generous to the poor orphans during this joyous season.

I remember being "chosen" to go to New Jersey over a Christmas holiday. The blood sister of Sister Regina was going to have a baby and she was having a hard time. This couple had a little girl my age and I was to act as her companion. Another older girl, I don't remember her name was also to go. She was to keep house and cook and watch over the niece and me. We were there for about 3 weeks. I have often wondered why I was chosen. I don't recall having a say in the matter, I just went. It was okay with my father if I went.

I have later learned that the reason I was chosen is because my sister Sue had received a terrible beating and was in the infirmary. It was so bad that the nuns could not take the chance of anyone seeing her. If I was at the orphanage I would tell my father when he came to visit. Since I was not there and my sister was very sick in the infirmary there was no reason for him to bring us home during the holiday season. The "special treatment" she had received would be hidden from everyone.

I was invisible. I never spoke up. I never questioned. I never caused trouble. Your must understand how small our world was. Nothing existed outside the walls of the orphanage or the gates and fences that surrounded it. We were beaten into submission psychologically and physically. Who was going to believe children over the catholic nuns who devoted their lives in service to orphans? We lived in terror of and absolute rule of these nuns. They were the ultimate authority and we were only children.

While I was typing and editing my sister's book I came across some articles published in *The Record* by staunch supports of the sisters. What great women these sisters are. How well they treat the "Special Needs" children that are now in their care. How grateful the parents are, how much faith is placed in these holy women. These sisters are angels. But the sad truth is that these are not the nuns of the 50's and 60's. There are now laypeople teaching school with the nuns. It is no longer a closed society. These nuns have to report to parents, state licensers, the archdioceses, children's welfare groups and others. The St. Colman's of today is not the orphanage of the past. At the end of the day, the day care center and school closes and the children go home. The residents today do not number in the hundreds. I rejoice that these children are receiving the love, support and guidance that all children deserve and need and not the "special attention" that the children of the past enjoyed. Yes 'the times they are a changing.'

The end result - Nothing happened. There was a wall of silence built around the abusers and it remains there today. There are still questions and answers to be asked and given. The irony of this whole story is the truth in all cases. Some children where never abused while others were severely abused. It all depended on the nun who had your group. She always had the ultimate power over your life. If she liked you and you did as you were told, never questioned her or her authority you were invisible and not subject to "discipline or special attention".

After reading this are you now ready to consider that these stories are true? Do these allegations have any merit? Are you going to stay in your comfort zones people? Will you continue to place your faith in the catholic clergy and ignore all the headlines we read about, see on TV or hear on the radio? Are the catholic clergy only doing God work and not abusing children? And have they never done so? Are all of the accusations of these abuses the words of dysfunctional adults?

June E. Maloney
Seattle, Washington

April 8, 2002

Dear Louise:

I really think that what you and Susanne are doing is great for all the survivors including yourselves of St. Colman's Home in Watervliet, New York. I've been blessed to have the opportunity to speak to you of my experiences at St. Colman's Boys and Girls Home.

I am 41 years old. I came to St Colman's Home when I was eight years old. I was born February 20, 1961. My mother put me in St. Colman's due to my mother's illness and my Fathers alcoholism. They both could not take care of me. I was very scared when the child worker brought me.

If I had clothes with me, I did not get to keep them. All my clothes they went for everyone to wear. I remember a lot of nuns from St. Colman's. Sr. Regina, Mother Virginia, Sister Carmel, Sister Adien, Sister Annunciata, Sister Bernadette, Mister Mary Richard, Sister Mary Claire, and Sister Joseph. When I was in St. Colman's I went through a lot. Nuns were slapping me in the face.

I wrote a letter one time to my mother and I got up in the middle of the night to go to the bathroom when a nun cornered me and said Judy, you know these things are not going on in here. I won't send this letter to your mother. I just went back to bed feeling hopeless.

I also remember a time when us girls were on the playground and it was winter time. We were happy to go out and play but the nuns only let us in when they were good and ready and I remember feeling like I was going to freeze to death and watching other girls cry because they were so cold.

Boys and girls were separated so if you had a brother or sister they could not play together. Boys and girls slept in dormitories. They were on separate floors.

In the summer time it would be so hot that your sneakers would stick to the blacktop. I was on the playground one time when Sister Mary Richard lifted me off the ground by her nails under my chin over her head. I don't know to this day what I could have done so wrong to deserve that.

We prayed before each meal and prayed when we got up and before we went to bed. Also if you were bad in the dormitories, you would knees all night with your arms out in the corridor. You would get you knuckles cracked by a ruler. The food would be terrible. Oatmeal would be thick and dry, the hot chocolate would have a film on it like skin. The rice would be scooped on your plate by an ice cream scope and loaded with pepper. You could not eat it.

When kids would play in the bathrooms and you had to go, I had to sit on the teeter-totter and hold my poop and pee in and if I should mess my pants, I would clean my underwear in the sink.

Also a plate of food with 10 to 12 pieces of toast with eggs and bacon would come into the playroom and there were about 15 girls and if you did not guess the right number you did not get something extra to eat.

I've seen the paddle and hair brush on my backside by Sister Regina. She was evil. She would say look into my eyes and her eyes were like glass looking right through you. You had a feeling she was not quite right.

Sister Ukerria was whipping the boys in the gym one time. I don't know why but you heard screaming and crying. Sister Carmel told me one time when I was playing my radio to turn it off or you'll be wiping your blood off the walls.

I believe kids that were in St. Colman's home have suffered some psychological damage somehow because I saw 2 girls when I grew up and they seemed messed up. Both girls lost their kids.

To all the survivors of St. Colman's pray that the Lord gives you closure and get on you're your life.

Love Judy Gregory
Survivor of St. Colman's Home

SUSANNE ROBERTSON

Wednesday, April 10, 2002

Dear Susanne:

My name is Peggy Zell, you spoke to my son Peter Gerace night before last and told him you witnessed my son, Salvatore Gerace being beaten by Sister Eukerria with a baseball bat in the gymnasium at St. Colman's.

Maybe you know his sister, Mary Ellen Gerace. She also witnessed it but won't speak about it at all. Since I've been in touch with Louise, "Louise Sharpe" I've been sick and feeling guilty for putting them there. As I am writing you, the tears just come falling down my face and asking one Question "God, where you when all this was going on? These were your little angels. Surely God if you are real as the so called Good Catholic Priests tell us, why did not you stop it???? At this point God, I wonder if you truly exist or are you also one of the Catholic's imaginary myths that they tell us to about to control us and know all our personal business to use us for their own purposes?"

I know my son Salvatore was even abused by the Brothers at "LaSalle School". I was told this by a boy who was there with him. He was abused also. I have visions of St. Colman's being the "house of horrors" and the nuns all dressed like the "devil" and devils they were! All my life I was taught to be a good Christian girl and follow in the footsteps of these wonderful nuns. S.O.B.'s! They were all along playing a part. Meanwhile, they abused physically and mentally all our young and helpless ones and when we the parent(s) showed up at their door, they were as sweet as honey! They all should be in Hollywood along with Frankenstein and Bella Lagosi in the "House of Horrors."

Salvatore had a head x-ray in the Veterans Hospital and it showed he was beaten by something or someone. It showed an old fractured to his skull from his childhood. I have his e-ray report and at the time could not say if he had an injury to the head because then I did not know about Sr. Eukerria's beating him.

I hope when your book comes out, the whole world will look differently upon the Catholic orders of priests and nuns and any other religions if they are doing the same cruel abuses on our children. They should all be locked-up for life because that's the kind of a sentence they placed on our children.

When I think back to the reasons I put them there, I might just as well have left them alone to mind each other. Those nuns scared them to death every weekend before I'd pick them up by saying to them "Now remember this, your parents don't want you – nobody wants you and if you repeat anything that goes on here, you'll go to a worse place"! Worse than St. Colman's!! Hell would have been better!!! Any place better than St. Colman's. I've called my son Peter and Mary Ellen crying asking for forgiveness. He says "Mom, you did not know and we were afraid to talk. Stop beating yourself up, their day will come when they meet their maker and they'll pay for it sooner or later."

Susanne, I hope I haven't bothered you. Maybe you can write me and let me know about the day you witnessed Salvatore being beaten. At least, I can prove it, you're his witness, and his sister witnessed it also but can't talk about it. I wish she would, it's got to come out sometime.

Let me know when your book comes out. I pray the whole world will read it so they can find out just how "HOLY, SWEET AND INNOCENT" the Catholic Church really is. I've heard that the Vatican has fortunes untold. Richest people on the continent and guess what and how they got it all? By bullshitting everyone world wide to fill their little baskets Sundays 2 or 3 times and laughing at us all the way to the bank!

On that note, I'd better close for now. Hope you can make this letter out because I'm so ticked off by now, goodness knows what I'll write. Thank you in advance for coming forward with your book to let the whole world know what "Son's of Bitches" the Catholic Church harbors. Please stay well and if there is a God bless you, keep you healthy and happy.

Your friend for life,

Peggy Zell Mother of Peter Gerace and
Mary Ellen Gerace and Salvatore
– Deceased, Suicide by Hanging

Epilogue

To all of the good and generous people of the Behr-Manning Co., I salute you. I want you to know that your kind deeds were not lost on me. My wonderful husband is an engineer at the Boeing Co. in Seattle, Washington and every year through Boeing we either adopt a family or a foster child for the holidays. We are given a list of the child's wants and needs and also their special wish, which is usually a big ticket item. In all the years that we have done this, we have never once failed to provide everything on the list including their special wish.

I would also take this opportunity to apologize for the deceit perpetrated on you by the Sisters of the Presentation of the Blessed Virgin Mary at St. Colman's Orphanage. I doubt that you would have been so generous had you known the truth about where your gifts would end up. A mighty shame on you sisters, shame on you!

Acknowledgments

I wish to acknowledge all of the now grown children and their parents who have chosen to share their souls with the world.

These individuals have brought the light of the truth out into the open after so many years of hiding their secrets in the darkness.

The fear and shame that numbed their being are now set free in the Glory of the Truth.

Author's Note

From 1957 until 1965, I resided in a Roman Catholic orphanage in upstate New York. I was not the only child to be tortured and abused beyond words. I am not sure where my courage and perseverance came from to survive, but I thank God for it.

It took many years for me to be able to think about my childhood. It took every ounce of my courage from the depths of my soul to write and reveal what happened to me there.

I share my experiences with my readers not as a hateful view, but rather, as more of a healing process for me and to come to terms with the pain that people can and do inflict on each other.

I share the marvel of the human spirit to adopt and survive in the face of moral depravity and mental, emotional and physical abuse beyond the limits of physical endurance.

Printed in the United States
16500LVS00004B/153